GHOST GIRL

GHOST
GIRL

PATTI M. WALSH

atmosphere press

Published by Atmosphere Press

ISBN 978-1-63988-573-2
Copyright registration number: TXu002332024

Cover design by Kevin Stone

atmospherepress.com

To my family—
the céilí
in my attic

table of contents

Study Guide

Characters

Anam (nickname; born Anamary Cara): Bonnie's aunt, Nog's wife, and Maura's best friend; Anam is a shortened version of *anam cara,* the Celtic concept of *soul friend*

Angus (a dog): Named after the ever-wandering Celtic god of youth, love, and poetry who can enter the Otherworld and resurrect the dead

Baylar: Bonnie's one-eyed antagonist who says that Bonnie is the reason her mother died

Benjy: Bonnie's half-brother

Bonnie Strongbow: 12-year-old main character, who has been sent to live with her aunt and uncle, Anam and Nog, after her mother's death

Dad (Ben): Bonnie's father

Deborrah (Deb-Horror): Bonnie's stepmother

Eileen: Runs the Fish House, a restaurant

Emmett: Nog's uncle who left him the inn

Erin: Bonnie's best friend

Glenda: Owns the Crystal Keep

Hermit: The village butcher

James: Joy's nephew; a lifeguard

Jenny: One of Bonnie's childhood friends

Joy: Owns Island of Joy, a home furnishings store

Kath: Runs the Voyager Café

Kitty: The hairdresser

Knobby: A descendant of Old Knob, chieftain of the Mac-Carthy clan, and Nana's husband; he must find a successor before he can pass over to the Otherworld

Maura: Bonnie's mother, Nog's sister, and Anam's best friend

Mo: A black cat

Nog (nickname; born Brendan): Bonnie's uncle, Anam's husband, and Maura's brother

Nuca: A statue that Nog likes to think is a Celtic princess

Sara: One of Bonnie's childhood friends

Smokey: Owns The Fiery Pig, a BBQ restaurant

Willy: A tabby cat

the invisibles

Aloysius: (al-uh-WISH-uhs) Gramp's son, who spelled his name on a computer screen; he was frayed around the edges, like a favorite book

Arthur: Knobby's son and Dobbin's twin, he was tall, thin, and lavender; first showed up at the old cemetery

Baron: Luna's father, who once lived in Companion Moon and liked to sit in the rocking chair in the parlor; he wore a dark blue sailor's outfit to paddle his boat and catch fish

Cookie Aunt Mary: A plump aunt who used crumbs to spell her name and smelled like vanilla

Dobbin: Knobby's son and Arthur's twin, he was the first Invisible to introduce himself by spelling his name on the bathroom mirror; his name means Robert, and Roberta was Bonnie's middle name

Edmund: An uncle who spelled his name on the foggy window of the parlor; he juggled red apples

Gramp: The great-great-great-great-grandfather who built fires and introduced himself by arranging twigs by the wood-pile; he glowed in the shape of an old tree with branches instead of arms, and felt warm

Jack: An uncle who balanced a glass on his forehead and spun dishes; he introduced himself by spinning red and blue dishes that appeared as a purple tornado, reminding everyone that change was constant

Jeanne: An aunt who loved to read; she introduced herself in the bookstore with colorful alphabet blocks

Kelty: An aunt and the family bard who told stories and sang songs; she stopped Bonnie from stealing a tiny bottle; she always wore pale blue, the same color as the vial Bonnie wanted

Luna: An aunt, whose name meant *moon*, wrote her name in the sky with clouds; her father was Baron, and her dog Angus looked a lot like Nog and Anam's dog

Maggie: Bonnie's grandmother who showed up as a burgundy and white snake in the shape of an *M*; her black enameled box, Bonnie's treasure box, had the image of a snake on it

Mamie: A descendant of Gramp's second cousin, once-removed, who started the Mountainside Dairy; she mooed her name, and smelled like fresh butter

Nana (born Mary Julianna): Knobby's wife

Paddy: An uncle who guarded Bonnie from Baylar; he looked like a chestnut brown horse and introduced himself with the neighing sound that horses make

Seamus: An uncle who wore an orange plaid hat (a tam) and smelled like cheddar cheese, which he loved to eat

Tess: A descendant of Gramp's second cousin, once-removed; she loved to knit and crochet, and introduced herself with crimson yarn

Tory: An ancestor who was an ironsmith and wore a teal-colored feathered hat; he wrote and recited poetry

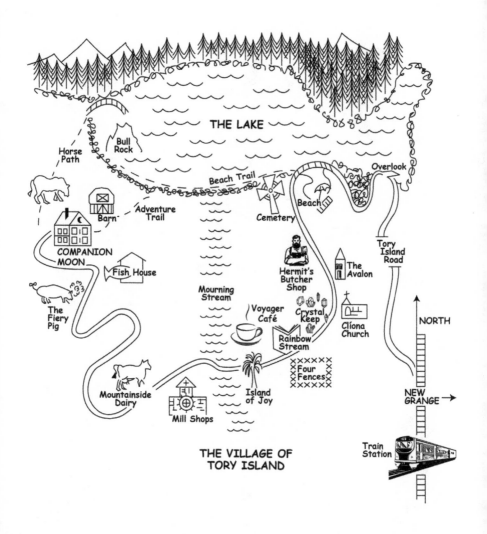

THE LAKE

Horse Path

Bull Rock

Beach Trail

Overlook

Barn

Adventure Trail

Beach

Cemetery

COMPANION MOON

Fish House

Tory Island Road

Hermit's Butcher Shop

The Avalon

The Fiery Pig

Mourning Stream

Voyager Café

Crystal Keep

Clíona Church

NORTH

Rainbow Stream

Mountainside Dairy

Island of Joy

Four Fences

NEW GRANGE →

Mill Shops

THE VILLAGE OF TORY ISLAND

Train Station

Illustration by William E. Green III

IMMRAM CHANT

By Caitlín Matthews

I do not know where I am bound.
I journey far across the foam.
I seek my soul, where is it found?
I watch the star to guide me home.

There is an island in the West
Under the sun, over the sea,
I travel far upon my quest.
I seek a guide to pilot me.

A branch of silver in my hand
With crystal bloom and golden fruit,
The mother tree grows on the strand;
It's there that I shall find my root.

There is an island in the sea,
Where waters flow and food gives life,
Where is no foe, where love is free.
I seek the place where is no strife.

I watch the star to guide me home,
I found my soul and spirit's rest,
I travelled far across the foam.
There is no ending to my quest.

"Immram Chant" from Caitlín Matthews' book, *The Celtic Book of the Dead* (Schiffer Publishing, ©2022), used with permission in all territories worldwide.

1

MIRROR
MIRROR

Puffs of forced air exploded in my face with each exhaled breath. I wanted everyone to think I was cold, not anxious, so I spewed a few more. Fingering the wristband that identified me as an unaccompanied minor, I waited and waited and waited in the bleak misery of a blustery train station on this unbelievably cold, early January morning. *Yeah. Happy freakin' New Year.*

After nearly an hour of signing papers and answering questions, it was finally time to leave on my first solo trip anywhere. I blew again and shook off my hoodie. Dad replaced it, then tugged at my open jacket.

"Zip up your parka, Bonnie." He lifted its hood up over my head. "We don't need to send you off with a cold." He pecked me on the forehead, knocking my glasses askew.

Scrunching my face to match my insides, I huffed a deliberately huge vapor cloud, as if it could erase my stepmother and half-brother behind my father. The effort shook free my hoodie yet again, and yet again, he replaced it with a Hollywood smile that could seal deals and steal hearts. That's my dad. To everyone else, he's Ben, marketing magnate and social superstar. Tickling the tip of my nose, he squeezed my shoulders. Despite myself, I yielded to a lopsided grin.

"Atta girl," he declared, his resonant voice muffled by a stiff northerly wind. "And zip up your parka. Where's your hat? You should be wearing a hat."

I hate hats.

Closing my eyes, I imagined it was just the two of us. And Mom, of course. She belonged at Dad's side. And I belonged with them. On the beach, I fancied, squinting into the sun, not squinching vapor clouds into a bleak January morning, or eyeballing the steel rails that prowled their way upstate.

Mom. Stuffing tears deep inside, where no one or nothing could reach them, I tried to conjure up her image. I didn't remember much, except her laugh, her eyes, and her hair. Thick auburn hair. It was the last thing I saw when a truck hit our car, killing her instantly. I was five. That was seven long years ago.

"You'll have to live with your father," everyone said. That wasn't a problem—I had seesawed between my parents since their divorce two years before the accident. Besides, Dad's condo was only a few blocks away from our little house, so I still had my school and friends. But the new arrangement wasn't for a weekend or holiday. It was forever, and I first became a speed bump and then a roadblock in Dad's methodical life. So, he found a nanny, which turned into a series of nannies. No one was good enough for me, he said. Not until he met and married Deborrah.

She pronounced her name *Deb-ORR-ah*. I called her Deb-Horror. With her, everything had to be so, so perfect. And I sure wasn't. Not only did she find fault with me from Day One, but she canceled my life and replaced it with If-ville. If Mom hadn't died, I wouldn't have to live with her. If she hadn't insisted on a new house, I wouldn't have had to go to a new school. And if I hadn't had problems at the new school, I wouldn't be stuck on this platform, banished to live in the mountains with an aunt and uncle I hardly knew. My godparents. Anam and Nog. Strange names. Strange people.

With cold resolve and even colder hands crammed into pockets, I glared at my stepmother, stabbing icicles into her soul as she snuggled my half-brother into a warmth that eluded me. It was as obvious as the skinny little nose on her copper-skinned face that she wouldn't miss me any more than I would miss her.

"Train 233 to Albany, Saratoga Springs, New Grange, and Montreal arriving on Track One." An invisible voice screeched my destiny like fingernails on a blackboard.

New Grange. Anam and Nog would meet me there and bring me to their place outside the village of Tory Island. Who lived somewhere called Tory Island? Worse than that, *outside* Tory Island? I called it the boonies. I would stay with them through Labor Day. September. Nearly nine months. That seemed like forever. Nog would homeschool me. What would that be like? More jitters, more clouds.

As the train rounded the curve from the south and whistled its approach, Deborrah stepped forward, Benjy tucked into her arms. For once, he wasn't crying. Without thinking, I reached out and stroked his cheek with the back of my index finger. It was soft like a cotton ball and warm like fleece. He smelled like the oatmeal bubbles that dribbled from his pink lips. Okay, I admitted, maybe I would miss him.

Wigwagging her hand, Deborrah stretched the word *byeee* into three syllables as thin as her personality. "You be good now. Mind your aunt and uncle." She chided me as if I had already done something wrong. I slipped a thumbnail to my mouth, a habit that she swatted away.

"*You* mind *your* aunt and uncle," I mumbled, jerking aside. With my back turned, I mimicked her tepid farewell and stuck out my tongue with a defiant head shake. The jiggling teased a corkscrew from the ponytail tucked inside my hoodie. Jeez. I whooshed it away as the train crept to a stop.

"Call me when you get there," Dad commanded. He never asked or suggested. Glancing at the train, his watch, and me—his speed bump—in that order, he noted that the train was two minutes late, and Dad did not tolerate late. "We'll be up, hopefully for your birthday." That was August. Pulling me into a quick but firm hug, he added, "Depends on my schedule." Of course, it did. Everything did.

"Yup." Short answers magnified my practiced apathy. It also was easier to agree with my father than challenge him. We'd been over this a hundred times. I was sure they wouldn't come.

"All aboard," a trainman bellowed, hopping onto the plat-form. He talked to Dad, scanned my wristband, and grabbed my backpack. I slung the matching tote over my shoulder, noting that the rest of the ensemble was being hauled toward the rear of the train as freight. Climbing onto a sleek car, I turned into the spotlight of a weak sunbeam. I felt like I was on stage, so I took a bow and bid my so-called family good riddance.

"Love you, Missy Mope." Dad winked at me. That's what he called me when I was stuck doing what I didn't want to do. Like now. *Make me*, my long face would dare. Beyond the reach of one final hug, I broke character and winked back. He blew a kiss.

"She's in good hands, sir," the conductor called over his shoulder, nudging me into a car, where a dozen or so people looked up from their timeworn blue seats encased in chrome. It smelled like old leather shoes and damp wool coats. The heat was cranked up so high that I broke out in a sweat. No need for a parka in here, I thought as I unzipped it. Hefting my backpack onto the overhead rack, the trainman introduced himself.

"Name's Porter." His body looked muscular beneath his uniform, probably from lifting all that luggage. He smelled like aftershave. With a thrust of his jaw, he directed me to an open seat on the left by the window. "I like that side. Nice views. And you can see your folks as we pull out." Yanking off my parka, I threw myself into the plush seat he suggested. "New Grange's the ninth stop, a little over four hours. I'll be by to see if you need anything, young lady."

He called me a young lady. No one had ever done that before.

Heaving a long *crrreeeeaaakkk*, the train pulsed away. My stomach flinched and my throat pinched shut thinking that I had already lost Mom, and now I was leaving Dad. But then everything relaxed knowing I was also leaving Deb-Horror and Benjy, the crybaby from hell. I shook my wild hair free of its ponytail, and giggled. Four hours. On my own! A broad grin accompanied my final wave as the train curved into a tunnel, instantly erasing both my family and my bravado, for in that second of immediate darkness, the window morphed into a mirror, reflecting a girl whose smile puckered into a scowl.

"Who are you?" I asked the 12-year-old girl who looked back at me. We simultaneously removed our glasses. With locked eyes and grimaced face, we sized each other up. The girl in the mirror bit her lip, which told me that she was scared. She gnawed on her thumb, which told me she was anxious. But she also reminded me she was a young lady.

She blinked away tears that told me she was alone—and nothing like the people who had just disappeared on the platform. For starters, they all had similar skin colors. Dad liked to joke about my lighter and freckled version of his rich caramel complexion. "I ordered *café au lait*, with extra cream and brown sugar sprinkles. And I got Bonnie."

I wasn't as dark as Dad, and not as light as Mom. She was pinkish, with freckles that marched across her button nose. I touched my own, which matched hers, freckles and all. Calling them fairy dust and me Bonnie Baby, she would tickle me with kisses. I would give anything for one last fleck of a fairy kiss.

My parents had been a striking couple—tall and athletic. Yet the girl in the mirror was short and skinny. Then there was the hair. Mine was a longer, tangled version of Dad's thick cinnamon brush cut. Mom's was windblown auburn. Dad's face was chiseled with a square jaw, tight mouth, and dimpled chin. Mom's was oval with a full mouth and soft chin. Mine was round and buckled with braces. But I had Mom's eyes. Green eyes that blinked back tears. I resembled both parents, but looked like neither.

"You don't belong," I told my perplexed self, covering my eyes with long elegant fingers—Mom's fingers—as if they could erase the last seven years as gently as they had wiped away tears before that. Shielding my eyes from myself, I thought about the avalanche of events that got me here.

When Dad married Deborrah, he said I needed a mother. I didn't need a mother—he did. Before long, she needed a house—the condo wasn't big enough, and the neighborhood wasn't good enough. Then she needed a baby. "I got me a built-in babysitter," she boasted to her friends, emphasizing each word with a shoulder thrust. Nobody bothered to ask what I needed.

As if I could erase those disasters, I closed my eyes and circled my fingertips from them to my brow and across to my temples. Resting my palms together below my chin and fanning my fingers across my cheeks, I opened my eyes. In that instant, the train cleared the tunnel. Watching my reflection dissolve into a rolling countryside, my hands sprung outward.

"I'm free," I said aloud. I liked how that sounded, so I repeated it. Then I bit my lip. Until I got to New Grange. Then what? Before I could kick that scenario around, the train slackened its pace across an intersection. A pack of teenagers in a pickup truck waved, and I waved back. To them, I was an adventurer. They didn't know I was a loser.

I wasn't always one. I sighed, remembering the world where I had had a real family and real friends, like Jenny, Sara, and Erin. Erin and I grew up next door to each other and stayed close even after Mom died. Although we didn't look alike—she had straight blond hair, brown eyes, and a big toothy grin—we called ourselves twins. We'd wear matching T-shirts and hair ribbons. We even dressed our dolls alike.

When we met Jenny and Sara on the first day of kindergarten, we instantly became the Cutie Club—that's what our moms called us—inseparable superheroes on escapades, or princesses on quests. Over the next five years, we traded Curious George for Harry Potter, Muppets for boy bands, and dolls for nail polish, pretending ourselves into the real-life women we might someday become. We were cool. We were Girls Who Code and budding filmmakers with the videography club.

But my stepmother shredded that life like cheese. My new school didn't have those clubs, and I didn't have friends.

I pulled out my phone to text Erin. My BFF. *Used to be*, I corrected myself. What happened to the *forever* part? I stared at my phone as if it were a crystal ball. It told me I couldn't remember the last time we'd been in touch.

After I moved away, Erin and I talked, texted, had a few sleepovers, played some games online, but that all got old. Or maybe we did. Did she ghost me? Did I ghost her? If she wasn't my best friend, was she still my friend? Friends were people who understood you, or at least tried. As each day, month, and year went by, no one seemed to understand me. While everything was the same for Erin, Jenny, and Sara, all I had was replacement feelings, a replacement family, and a replacement life. I missed my friends. It hurt to admit how much.

That's probably why I hated my new school. The only kids

who paid any attention to me were the other misfits. For them, breaking rules was chill, like skipping school to hang out at the mall. Of course, the one day I went along, we got caught. Dad gave me a pass, saying that he played hooky as a kid. He told me not to do it again. Although Deb-Horror kept repeating that she was "disappointed," she was forced to go along with Dad since she wasn't my real parent.

But she sure acted like she was, especially when it came to what I wore. She didn't let me dress like the other girls. They wore rad clothes, henna tattoos, goth makeup. In my attempt to imitate them I came off as a wannabe.

Deb-Horror pitched a fit one morning when I tried to sneak out wearing a borrowed lace-up vest and short skirt. I responded by kicking a hole in my bedroom wall with my platform boots. I didn't understand why *that* was such a big deal—I didn't hurt anyone. Besides, she and Dad had knocked a hole in my life. They made me see a social worker, who said I had something called an "antisocial personality disorder." That was harsh. I didn't have a disorder; it was my life that was disordered.

Next, there was the Juul incident. I didn't like vaping, but I liked hanging around with kids who did. When I got home one afternoon, Dad questioned the mango smell, made me empty my backpack, and threw away my pod. After a lame "father-daughter talk," we coasted for a few weeks. Then it was Game Over, big time, when my nosy stepmother checked my Instagram. She discovered the picture I had posted of a slap game we played on a new girl. It was just a prank—I didn't even take the picture—but Dad called it bullying.

In addition to taking away my phone and tablet, he grounded me, which I hated to admit was a good thing because I wasn't there when the other kids got caught shoplifting a few days later. Looking back, some of them may have had that disorder thing. Even if they weren't real friends, they were somebodies. Looking at my phone, I realized I missed having somebodies, anybodies.

That's how I ended up on a train, deported to a place I'd never been, to do who knew what, with people who were little more than strangers. Sure, Anam and Nog were my aunt and uncle, but I hadn't seen them in over three years. That's when they moved to Tory Island, where they were opening a bed and breakfast.

They called every few weeks. Anam was Mom's best friend. She sent cute cards that I was too old for. Nog was Mom's big brother, which is funny because he was way shorter. He would go on and on about his old house and his old dog. I never liked old stuff. Or old dogs. I did perk up, though, when he mentioned horses.

I laughed at the thought of Anam with horses. The only ones I could imagine her with were statues at the museum where she used to work. With her hair in a bun and her body swathed in too many clothes, she was as prim as Nog was gabby. Round and smiley, his hands and mouth moved constantly as he spewed his Nogisms. That's what everyone called his silly stories and daft expressions. Except Dad, who didn't abide silly and didn't like Nog.

When I told Nog about my troubles at school, he and Anam hatched a scheme. "Get her away from that crowd," he suggested to Dad. "Keep her too busy to get in trouble. She can take the train here—she'll love that. You can all come up this summer and we'll spend a week together." Deborrah frowned at that. So did I. But Nog persisted, referring to the inn as the family homestead where he and Mom—her name was Maura—spent their summers as kids. Finally, he sealed the deal.

"She can finish the school year with me. I *am* a teacher, you know." Dad and Deborrah agreed—maybe too quickly. Of course, no one bothered to ask me. Sure, I thought, just rent me out like a servant.

I thought about Erin again. I wanted to tell her everything. But where would I start? Admitting that I became a loser? Maybe I could invite her to visit, but I didn't know if *I* wanted to visit. What if I didn't like my aunt and uncle. What if they didn't like me. I didn't like me. Maybe this was all a big mistake. I realized I was still staring at my phone. At least Dad returned my screens as a condition of this arrangement.

I shook my head. With nothing to share, I shoved the phone back into my tote. It was part of a totally awesome ensemble that my stepmother bought for this trip. Of course, I pretended to not like it. That made me laugh. Instantly, my mood changed. That happened a lot.

Burrowing into my seat, I dug out the snack that Deb-Horror had made—something else she got right—a peanut butter sandwich and a box of chocolate milk. Placing the sandwich aside for later, I slugged some milk and pulled my tablet out of my tote and put in earbuds. But I didn't feel like reading, playing a game, listening to music, or watching a movie. Maybe I could post a picture to my Facebook page, or do a video blog on this trip. No, that only reminded me of how things had changed.

Bored, I put the tablet down and watched the misty scenery. I picked the tablet up to take a few pictures. But all I saw were blurred factories and trees. Ugly warehouses and trucks. Disjointed people and cars. I put it down. I was tired from not having slept much the night before. I had been too nervous.

The train's rocking lulled me into a half sleep. I tried to picture Mom, but I only recognized her absence. Momma. The rocking reminded me that's what I called her in my heart. Sometimes whole days went by when I didn't think of her. I felt guilty about that, like I didn't love her anymore, which wasn't true. After all these years, I was still wracked by the unfairness of it all. Why did she have to die? She was smiling and happy one minute, gone the next. I didn't understand it then, and I certainly did not understand it now. I never told anyone this, but I wanted to kill the truck driver who killed her.

Tears scraped my heart, burning it like a skinned knee. I stared out the window until the train stopped at a dingy station, where a handful of people got on. As we pulled away, Porter appeared at my side and startled me out of my funk.

"How's it going, young lady?" He looked like somebody's grandfather with his graying hair and ample smile. "There's a dining car in the back. Want me to take you there?"

"No, I'm fine, thank you." I put on my glasses and my grownup face. "I have snacks with me." I held up my uneaten sandwich. "I just, well, you see, I just never went anywhere all by myself before." Now why did I go and tell him that?

"Ah, I see. I remember my first trip alone. Out West. First day on the job. Left my family behind. I was older than you are now, but it don't make no difference. Whenever I got homesick, I pulled out a pocket watch my grandfather—my Pops—gave me when I was 12." With that, he fished in his pocket and pulled out a gold timepiece. "Still works. Reminds me that the past is history, the future's a mystery, and the present is, well, a present. Do you have something like that?"

I glanced at the bag that Porter had placed on the luggage rack. As if I had x-ray vision, I could see Mom's emerald ring tucked in my treasure box. I deliberately put it in my daypack and not my luggage, so that I could keep it close. Dad gave it to me the night before he married Deborrah.

"This was your mom's engagement ring," he had said. "Now it's yours. Because I love you." Of course, he had to spoil the moment by adding, "Don't lose it." I never wore it, except to try it on from time to time, pretending to be a beautiful woman. In that instant I longed to unpack it, slip it on, and press it to my heart. Maybe it would soothe the ache. I closed my eyes and pictured the green stone set within a gold Celtic knot. It did remind me of the past, the present, and the future. I found Porter's eyes.

"Yes, I do. Thank you."

"That's good, young lady. Always good to know who you are and where you're coming from, especially when you're going someplace new."

"It's my mother's ring. She died." I couldn't believe I told him that, too. But his kind eyes didn't even blink.

"Well, I'm sorry for your loss." He bowed his head before stepping uninvited into my soul. "Before he died, my Pops told me that in order to understand life, you gotta first understand death. See, where there is no death—where past, present, and future are one—you have freedom to live. That's a big lesson, but you'll figure it out." With that, he edged away and paced through the car checking tickets and answering questions.

Instead of pulling out the ring, I pulled up pictures on my tablet. Mom, Dad, and me, back when Dad lived with us, when we were a real family. Pictures of Mom and Nog when they were kids, and another of them laughing in a restaurant. Mom and Anam as young girls wearing funny hats and another as grown women on vacation. There was one of Anam holding me as a newborn. I studied her picture. She always looked like an old painting. We had nothing in common. I scrutinized those images for a sense of my family—past and future. And the present, well, the present was very confusing.

Outside, patches of scenery appeared and disappeared dreamlike in the mist and fog. Small towns and regal estates flickered by. Perhaps the inn would be like one of them. We zipped by railroad crossings. We stopped. We moved. People got off. People got on. Scenery appeared. Towns disappeared. We stopped. We moved. Stations loomed and tracks retreated. People got off. People got on. I lost track of the world as the train pulsed through the mist. Dad and Deborrah blended into

Nog and Anam. My baby pictures melted into Benjy. Momma combed her long auburn hair, her ring visible with each stroke. "Young lady," she called me. "Young lady." Not Bonnie Baby. I reached out to hold her.

"Young lady."

But it wasn't her voice. It was a man's and he smelled like aftershave. Jolted awake, I blinked. Where was I? I blinked again. Porter was leaning into my seat. It took a few seconds to realize where I was.

"Wake up, young lady," he repeated quietly. "This is your stop." To the entire car he boomed, "New Grange. Next station." Next station? How long had I been asleep?

I stuffed my tablet into my tote and wiggled into my coat as the train creaked to a stop.

2

TORY ISLAND

rabbing my bags, Porter leaped onto the empty platform before extending a hand to guide me down. I didn't have to force any breath clouds here—the freaking cold invaded my sneakers and shot through my whole body. Blinded by stinging drizzle and deafened by howling winds, I was surrounded by ice-frosted empty benches. Pulling my hoodie tight over my head, I zipped up my puffer jacket, pulled the fur-lined hood tight around my head, and jammed my fists into its pockets. I wished I had worn my hat, boots, and gloves, as Deborrah had told me to do, instead of packing them. I hated to admit she was right.

"Fine young woman you have here," Porter said to a couple of strangers who waved and called to me while they exchanged paperwork with him. How did they know my name?

Oh my God! It was Anam and Nog. I recognized their voices, but not their faces. Before I could respond, Porter extended his right hand to me. I reluctantly removed mine from the warmth of my pocket to accept his handshake.

"You'll figure it all out," Porter said. His handshake heated my entire body. Then he was gone.

Figure it all out? I had a lot to figure out. Like, who were these people?

"Bonnie! How was the trip? You look wonderful...getting so tall...so grown up...didn't recognize you...our first guest..." Their blubbering flew by much as the scenery had. I blinked, and blinked, and blinked. Instead of frumpy Anam, a chic woman in jeans, turtleneck, and down vest was talking at me. Her hair—long and wavy, glinting with silver—spilled beneath a fur-lined bomber hat. Uggs cradled her feet. My mouth hung open.

Nog caught me staring. "What do you think of my lovely wife? Looks 10 years younger, doesn't she?" With one arm around my shoulders, he wrapped the other around her waist and nuzzled her cheek. It looked soft, like Benjy's. "And what do you think of me?" Nog patted a lean midsection. He looked happier than ever, if that was even possible.

"You look good, Nog. You, too, Anam. I, um, honestly, I didn't recognize either of you. You both look so, so, young. Wait, I didn't mean that, not that you're supposed to look old ..."

"It's the inn that changed us, gave us a new life. It will do the same for you," Nog predicted. "First, though, let's get that band off your arm." He waved the papers he had exchanged with Porter. "You're no longer unaccompanied. You're with us." We went inside the station, where at least it was warm. I called my dad, but of course, my call went straight to voicemail. I left a message rather than call my stepmother.

While my aunt signed for me, my uncle retrieved my checked luggage and guided us toward the parking lot. Something was wrong. The only vehicle in the lot was a huge van, and we were heading for it.

Nog and Anam would never, never, have driven a van. They'd always had boring old sedans. Usually gray, or scuffy white. Nothing flashy, nothing new. But we were heading toward a shiny monstrosity that looked like a sunset red Amazon truck. Everything about it was wrong.

"Where's your Benz, Nog?"

"Right here!" He tapped the side panel three times. "A Sprinter. Great name, huh? Love that German engineering. Out here, I needed something more suitable for hauling things around. And to fetch visitors—like you," he winked, "at the station!" Great. I was now going to be driving around in a delivery truck. Like a package. He gestured toward the depot. "I call it my *station* wagon. Get it? Isn't it grand? Look. Seats 12 comfortably, 10 cup holders, integrated Wi-Fi hotspot." He sounded like the car salesman Dad bargained with when he bought his last car. As Nog opened the rear hatch to store my bags, he added, "It even parks itself."

Nog had a van? With integrated Wi-Fi? That parked itself? Anam stood there giggling in jeans and boots. Who were these people?

Before I could think about what might have come over them, my uncle opened the side passenger door. As I climbed in behind Anam, I looked around. It felt as if there were already people in the back, but the seats were clearly empty. Weird.

"That way is New Grange," Nog said, jerking his head to the right and sounding like Mr. Tour Guide.

"I thought *this* was New Grange." I pointed to the train station that we were pulling away from.

"I meant downtown New Grange. That's where we go to do business. Lawyer, bank, discount stores, dentist, and, of course," he said, winking at Anam, "the hairdresser. It's what I call the Big City." I looked everywhere and didn't see anything that looked like a city, let alone a big one. It must have been Nog's idea of a joke. There wasn't even another car on the road. But we sat at a red light anyway.

"So, where's the mall?" Crickets. As in no response. I shivered. Make that frozen crickets. Maybe they didn't hear me. "Is there a ma ...?"

"Well, no, not here." Anam quashed the question with forced cheeriness. "There is one down the road a bit, on the other side of New Grange." Guessing I wouldn't be going there any time soon, I dared not ask how far a *bit* might be. "But we do have shops. In Tory Island. That's where we're going first. It's a cute little village."

Shops. In a cute little village. I flashed on Amity Island in *Jaws*. Or Seabrook in *Zombies*. Madison in *Goosebumps*. Maybe if I was lucky, it would be like Portorosso in *Luca*, and I could escape to a warm sea. But, no, we were headed to Tory Island. In Freezerville. Save me, somebody, please.

Silently groaning, I slumped into myself to brood over my predicament. It could be worse. I could be the woman crossing the street in front of us. She plowed through the nasty weather under the forever-red light, hauling a couple of pillow-looking kids. I watched as they wadded themselves like spitballs on the corner, turned, and trudged past us. I followed them with my eyes, twisting my head over my right shoulder, bringing me face to face—once more—with a van surprisingly full of empty seats.

Sitting up straight, I took off my glasses, put them back on, and looked again. Some kind of shadowy cobweb billowed somewhere barely beyond my vision. Maybe I was tired. I rubbed the back of my neck first to confirm that I wasn't dreaming, then to relieve the prickle of hair standing on end. I felt that I was riding with—I don't know, something invisible. I dared not think ghosts, but yeah, maybe.

What else would I call a presence I couldn't see? I chewed my lip. This wasn't the make-believe kind of ghost, like the ones Jenny, Sara, and Erin and I pretended to be for Halloween. This felt real. My heart thumped. I took a deep breath and closed my eyes. In that second of darkness, I pictured myself not in the van, but in a small boat being tossed around a stormy sea with a ghost who told me that in order to be saved, I had to release my grudges. Then a whole crew of ghosts helped me weather the storm, a storm that washed upon the banks of a large moonlit palace, where I was ...

"... about 10 miles west of here." Nog's maneuver through the intersection jostled me awake. I was so tired that I had fallen into a quick dream.

"Huh?"

"I was saying that home—the inn, Companion Moon—is only about 10 miles west of here—as the crow flies, they say— but these mountain roads, this time of year, well, they add almost an hour. You know, with all the dips and curves. And ice." He waved his arms around to mimic the winding roads. "First, we're stopping in Tory Island to do a few things. We'll be there in about 20, 30 minutes. Then the inn is only a couple of miles beyond that." TMI, I thought, and way too much arithmetic for a stupid drive with, what? Ghosts? Dad always said that I had a vivid imagination, but this time, I really outdid myself. "You're awfully quiet, Bon. You okay?"

"Yeah, I'm taking it all in." I wasn't going to tell Nog and Anam what "it" was. Riding with ghosts? And being in a boat with them? After all the recent drama, they would probably think I was on drugs or else really crazy.

"You hungry?" Anam asked. My stomach growled a loud reply, reminding me that I had left my sandwich on the train. We all heard it and laughed. "Me, too. Let's eat before we run errands."

"You'll love the inn, Bonnie," Nog said. "I know you will." I wasn't so sure. My caretakers chattered away in the front seat, asking about my trip and my family. As the buildings thinned into wider spaces, their nonstop conversation settled down. Outside, cows grazed against snowy peaks and piney valleys. Finally, peace and quiet. I pulled out my phone. No signal.

"Sketchy reception out here," Nog said before I could ask, our eyes connecting in the mirror.

"What about Wi-Fi? You said ..."

"Wi-Fi? Eh, I haven't gotten around to connecting it." Seriously?

"Don't worry," Anam jumped in. "Digital communication is way overrated. Cellphones are dangerous, you know." As I stared at the phone in my hand, my eyes grew bigger than donuts. I'd heard of phone batteries exploding in high temperatures, but it was freezing outside. And unless I threw it at someone, my phone was hardly dangerous. I wondered if a flying cell phone would hurt a ghost.

After a few minutes of silence, Nog pulled into a scenic overlook. "The lake." He pointed to an icy swath. "It's why people come out here."

"He thinks it's his," Anam said.

"It *is* mine." He bonked the steering wheel for emphasis. "It's part of my whole life. Our property is out at the far western edge. You can't quite see it from here, but look over there." He punched a thick finger toward a hat-shaped rock surrounded by ice.

"Is that Tory Island?"

"No." He pointed down the mountain to a cluster of buildings that was barely visible through the trees. "That is."

"Doesn't look like an island to me."

"But it is. It's surrounded by water—the lake and a few small streams that used to be rivers. Besides, *island* has such a charming sound, don't you think? Remote. Mysterious. Some say it's named after the town where an evil, one-eyed giant lived. But I like the legend that Tory, an ancestor who was an ironsmith, was saved from drowning by men in a boat. He thanked them and predicted they would find what they were looking for by forgiving their enemies."

I shook my head in confusion. Didn't I just dream that? But before I could think any more of it, Nog pointed back to the hat-shaped rock.

"That's Bull Rock." I saw bull, all right. "Legend has it, that's where the souls of the dead gather. When the weather warms, I'll take you out there."

Spare me, I thought as we headed downhill. I already felt like I had the souls of the dead riding with me. Scattered houses and buildings squeezed themselves together, funneling the wide country road into a sleepy village.

Welcome to Tory Island, a sign read. *If you lived here, you'd be home now.*

No way.

3

myths, monsters,
and manes

s we drove over a little bridge, Nog continued to sound like Mr. Tour Guide, waving his arms right and left. I felt like we would never get to the inn. I would be stuck in this van forever with phantoms.

"There's the beach," he said. The sliver of sand surrounded by the woodsy hills was not what I would call a beach. "Not much going on there now, but you just wait." Well, yes, I could wait. And wait and wait.

"That's the Avalon," Anam declared as we passed an old Victorian mansion that was painted dusty pink and trimmed with yellow, turquoise, and lime. It was colorful, cool, and so out of place. I loved it. "It's called a Painted Lady," she said.

"Is that it? Is that the inn?"

"Oh, gracious no. We've got a way to go before we get home. The Avalon is the oldest hotel on Tory Island. Actually," Anam said, correcting herself, "It's the oldest *house* here. The owners turned it into a hotel about five years ago."

Three apples decorated the sign. Apples. My stomach growled again. Nobody heard it because Anam was explaining the architecture.

"Some say it's haunted," Nog said with deliberately wide eyes; Anam shut hers and shook her head. Haunted. That reminded me of the cobwebby things in the back of the van. I looked behind, and sure enough, I could almost make out a few flimsy presences. One seemed tall and skinny, another one seemed shorter, more delicate. I cringed to think I was describing ... what? Ghosts? I decided to call them the Invisibles. It sounded less creepy.

Anam, meanwhile, was pointing out other old houses masquerading as small hotels.

"That's the Singing Birds," she said. "And the Navigator. We like them because they'll send us their overflow guests. Without them, we might not be able to ... open." Her voice trailed off. Nog pointed to another building.

"That's the Clíona Church. Your great-great-great-great-grandfather built it in honor of the patron goddess of County Cork, Ireland." I knew I had grandparents, but never heard of any great-greats. Before I could ask about that, he continued. "That's where our ancestors came from. Have you ever heard of the Blarney Stone?"

"Is that like *Harry Potter? The Sorcerer's Stone?*"

"Ha!" Nog laughed. "I know as much about Harry Potter as you do about Celtic lore, though I suspect a lot of it overlaps. Clíona is said to have helped Lord MacCarthaigh—one of your ancestors—build Blarney Castle." Nog puffed his chest with pride. "The clan descends from the third-century King of Munster, you know."

"No way." I was descended from a *king*? Before I could take that in, Nog continued.

"And MacCarthy, our family name, comes from *Mac*, meaning son, or family, and *Carthach*, meaning love. Family of love. Isn't that grand?"

I was more impressed that I was related to a king and a lord who built a castle. I liked that, yet it didn't make sense.

"But my last name is Strongbow. Can I still be related to a king?"

"Better than that, my love," Anam broke in. "Your mother's name is MacCarthy. And she was royal in every sense of the word."

"And," Nog said, "your last name, your father's last name, comes from a clan of warriors. Archers. The Strongbows. More commonly known as Walsh."

This was too complicated, and the rest of Nog's story was weird. Clíona told MacCarthaigh that he had to kiss the first stone he found so that he could win a lawsuit. I thought that was gross, but Nog said MacCarthaigh kissed the stone, won the lawsuit, and then used the stone in his castle.

"It's now known as the Blarney Stone," Nog said. "And anyone who kisses it is blessed with the gift of gab."

"Bet you're not surprised that Nog had to kiss the fool thing when he went to Ireland," Anam said. "He didn't need to, though. He was full of the gab even before that. Now, Nog, enough of the stories. Park the van so we can go eat."

Nog didn't have to demonstrate the Sprinter's self-parking feature; there weren't any other cars or even people anywhere. When we got out, I followed my aunt and uncle down the street. Everything was closed—pizza place, donut shop, ice-cream parlor, drug store. With its stark trees, dead flowers, and narrow lanes, this island of shuttered doors looked like a ghost town—and I fit right in.

Walking down the cold empty street with the Invisibles was like walking through a parking lot at dusk with lots of overhead lights casting shadows in all directions. You think somebody is walking behind and then alongside you, and about to catch up with you, and you turn. But instead of someone overtaking you, that shadow dissolves as the one in front of you darkens, grabbing your attention. The cycle repeated itself for an entire block.

The aroma of freshly baked bread and a smoldering fire yanked me back to an ordinary street and the Voyager Café, clearly our destination. It smelled like butter, garlic, and sugar. Woody like a pizzeria, and yeasty like a bakery. Oh man, I was hungry.

"Hi, Kath!" Anam quickly hugged a middle-aged waitress who steered us past red-checkered tables and cushioned captain's chairs to a booth by the fireplace.

I unzipped my parka and settled in. Anam insisted we order tomato soup, which I thought was pretty boring until it arrived in crusty bread bowls, its bright orange thickness topped with dollops of sour cream. It screamed, *Eat me.* One bite was all I needed.

"This is to die for," I said between slurps, using one of Deb-Horror's expressions.

Tearing a hunk of her own soup-soaked bread, Anam sighed. "I believe that food this good is to *live* for." I thought about that for a second and realized she had just proved my stepmother wrong. I liked that.

"Kath makes all her own bread. I wish I could do that." Anam clasped her hands in front of her chest.

"I wish you could, too," Nog said as he ordered a plate of freshly baked cookies, coffee for them, and hot cocoa for me.

Finally toasty inside and out, I inhaled the steaming chocolate before taking a sip. This was not from a mix like Deb-Horror would fix when I got home from school. I savored a mouthful before swallowing. It was semi-sweet, slightly bitter, and creamy.

While Nog and I tucked into the cookies, Anam dabbed at her mouth and cleared a wide swath of table for the oversized notebook she hauled from her oversized bag. When she donned red-enameled reading glasses, my head snapped back.

"Whoa!" Fiddling with my boring wire frames, I couldn't help but remember the old Anam, the bookkeeper who had blended into her office at the museum, which was nothing but a cubbyhole full of old books. "Cool glasses." It wasn't just the ruby frames. It was the long hair and cool clothes. If she could change, maybe I could, too.

With a quick nod and a deep breath, Anam scrutinized a well-worn list, running her fingers over pages of items that were added and crossed out in multiple colors. Cradling cups of coffee, she and Nog huddled over the book, mumbling about plumbing repairs, electrical work, and fire inspections in between casual banter with Kath and the few other people in the restaurant. It seemed that once Nog and Anam decided to turn the house into an inn, they readily adopted this village as their own, much as this childless couple welcomed me. We were novelties. That reminded me of something.

"Hey, what about kids? Aren't there any kids around here?"

Nog and Anam puzzled at each other. This obviously wasn't on their list. Anam removed her glitzy glasses, pointed them toward Nog, and awaited his response.

"Well ..." He twisted his mouth to the side. Odd, I thought, that the teacher had forgotten about students. "There *is* an elementary school just north of the village, and the older kids go to school in New Grange, and well, today's Monday, a school day, and everyone's just back from Christmas break. So, eh, we'll find you some kids."

Sure, like find me some guppies. We sat silently until Anam sat up quickly, startling herself and us.

"Rainbow Stream!" she said. "The bookstore. Let's go over there. I wanted to order some local books for our guests. And there's Joy. She has a nephew or cousin—some kid—that works here in the summer." Oh Joy. Local books and some kid who works in the summer. I reached for the last cookie. "Don't ruin your appetite for dinner," Anam cautioned, nearly slapping my hand. I was just getting comfortable when she had to go and sound like Deb-Horror. "We have a nice dinner planned this evening at home."

As Anam returned to her notes, Nog leaned in, pointed to one item, and cleared his throat.

"First," he lifted his eyebrows as he looked up at me, "I need to see about our horses."

"They're not *our* horses." Anam's practicality failed to cool his enthusiasm. "They're hers." She jutted her chin across the street to a place called Four Fences, which looked like an overrun yard sale. A skinny woman limped around it with a broom. She had shadowy figures around her. Like the Invisibles in the van. Only darker. Much darker.

"That's Baylar," Nog said. "Distant cousin on my mother's side."

As if she could hear her name clear across the street, through the glass, and past the fireplace, the woman lifted her head toward us. One eye was clearly patched, like a pirate's. With the other, she glared at me, first scorching, then freezing my innards and turning my skin to goose flesh. Reaching for the warmth of my puffer jacket, I noticed that neither Nog nor Anam were affected. They were talking as if nothing had happened. First ghosts, now an old hag with an evil eye. I wanted nothing to do with her. Or this strange place, Tory Island.

"I call that business of hers a welter," Anam said. "A jumbled mess."

Hmmm, I thought, if a welter is a jumbled mess, then maybe it was a good word for my mess of a life. Nog startled me out of my welter of thoughts by pointing to the witchy merchant.

"A welter, perhaps, but she runs your aunt's favorite antique shop—and you know how much she loves to shop." Anam tightened her mouth. "We board her horses. She wanted to rent them out for day excursions and evening hayrides, but couldn't get the permits. Wouldn't pay for the permits, more accurately." Then he looked at Anam. "I'll also ask if she's seen Angus." To me, he added, "That's our dog. Always running away. Hasn't been home since last night."

"Good idea, and while you're at it," Anam circled an item on the list, "ask her what to do about the noises in the attic. I'll take Bonnie with me to pick up fabric from Joy and check out some of the other shops."

"You mean your islands of refuge." Nog got up, kissed his wife on the forehead, paid the bill, and trotted across the street.

We bundled up and headed to the Island of Joy. The sign featured a palm tree and the words *Fill Your Home with Joy.*

"Afternoon, Joy." Amidst plastic palm trees and wearing a paper lei sat a jowly, pasty woman who didn't look as if she had spent any time on any island.

"G'd afternoon, Miss Anamary Cara." I giggled to myself. Everyone called my aunt by her real name—except me. When I was a baby, it came out as Anam Cara, then just Anam. I grew up knowing that *anam cara* was Celtic for *soul friend*, but I never really knew what that meant.

"This is my niece, Bonnie. She's staying with us through the summer."

"Summer, huh? That's a long way off. Aha." Whether "aha" was a laugh or a cough, she was right. "Pleased to meet cha. I heard all 'bout cha, aha."

I don't like people, especially strangers, knowing a lot about me. She pulled a brown bag from under the counter. While Anam opened it, she and Joy chatted about fabric. I yawned and looked around. I noticed a woman and a girl behind the counter. The girl looked rumpled and clueless, and the woman looked like ... Anam! I gasped. It wasn't two other customers—it was a mirror. That girl was me! Yikes. I looked frumpier than Joy. Suddenly relieved that there really were no kids around, I tugged at my hair and straightened my glasses. I almost wanted to be like Anam. That thought scared me. Is that what *soul friend* meant? Anam paid for her purchase and was mercifully ushering me to the door before she stopped and abruptly turned.

"Don't you have a nephew, Joy, who works with you during the summer?"

"Ya mean James? Yah." She hitched her chin toward a photo of a totally rad guy in a soccer jersey on the counter behind her. How could they possibly be related? "Works real hard to look busy, but honestly," she raised her hand as if taking an oath. "Lazy as a dog's bone."

"Well, let me know when he comes around," Anam said. "Maybe we can introduce him to Bonnie."

"Eh. She won't like him. No ambition. Only comes up here to sit in the sun. Thinks he's a lifeguard. Here! Only knows how to guard his tan. Aha."

Anam steered me in the direction of the Rainbow Stream. From the street I could see bright beanbag chairs, colorful bookshelves, and a sizeable game section. As I grabbed the door handle, which was shaped like an open book, I noticed it was locked. "Mmmm," Anam said to herself. "Closed Mondays and Tuesdays. Well, we'll have to come back."

Disappointed, I followed her up the street where Crystal Keep, a bead shop, caught my interest, but it too was closed. I was so disappointed. Erin and I loved bead shops. I hadn't been to one since I moved. Along the back wall was a display case of crystal vials. Maybe I could fill one with some magic potion that would get me out of here. As I turned to leave, a shadow drifted near the display. Was it an Invisible from the van? Did it follow me here? I tried to blink it away, but it was still there. Everything about Tory Island was creepy and growing creepier.

"Let's get Nog," Anam interrupted my thoughts. "He can

spend hours with Baylar and I'd like to get home before the weather turns bad." Dark clouds overhead were piling upon themselves. As we crossed the street, I longed for beads and books, not dirty old junk with a one-eyed hag who looked like a broomstick.

"Come here, Bonnie, meet Baylar." Nog waved me over. As I approached, I noticed that the strange woman had thick shadows all around her, even though the sun wasn't shining. She stared at me with her one eye. Maybe it was the wind, but at that moment, I was gusted backwards. I yanked the hood of my parka over my head and fastened the top snaps. Before dropping my gaze to the sidewalk, I noticed her long nose, pointy chin, and big ears. Her skin was as gray as her stringy hair. Neither she nor I extended a hand in greeting. Nog placed a firm hand on my sagging shoulder as he introduced me. Then he continued his conversation with Baylar.

"Have you seen Ang ...?"

"Keep that dog of yours away from me," she snarled. "May the cat eat him, and the devil eat the cat." She followed the curse by spitting on the sidewalk. Nog gripped my shoulder even tighter. My wide eyes darted from the sidewalk to him and then to Anam. Gross! Even the misfits at school didn't spit.

"I'm looking for a coat rack," Anam said, breaking the awkward moment. "We need something for the back door." She bustled inside and I followed her into one dingy room after another. In one section was a display case with gold trinkets, in another, silver. I shuddered. I didn't want to touch—let alone take—anything from here. Until I found a shelf of grimy glass bottles in all shapes, colors, and sizes. Although nowhere near as enchanting as the crystal vials at the Keep, their pale tints and age-cracked surfaces in the dust-flecked light were fascinating. Engrossed in their details, I was unaware that Anam had come up behind me.

"Oooooh," she exhaled into my ear, sounding like a ghost.

I jumped, nearly knocking down the entire shelf. "Sorry, Bonnie. I didn't mean to scare you. Do you like them? We can clean them up and put flowers in them come spring. You know," she said after a few seconds, "They remind me of your mother. She and I used to pick dandelions and violets, put them in little jelly jars, and bring them home for our mothers." I could definitely imagine that. Mom and I used to pick flowers and scatter them in containers around the house. As Anam gathered the little bottles into a shopping basket, I felt someone—or something—behind me. But when I spun around, I saw real shadows and cobwebs, not an Invisible. Or was it?

"You listen here," I heard Baylar warn Nog as we walked out the door. Shady figures still surrounded her. "That attic stopped being my concern years ago." Seeing my aunt, she forced a smile, which only accentuated the hard lines and dark pallor of her face. "Come back in a few weeks, Anamary Cara. Might have what you need then. Got an estate down in New Grange I'm clearing out."

As Anam pulled out a few dollars to pay for the bottles, I told Nog that they reminded her of Mom. "She said they used to pick flowers and put them in little jars."

Unbidden, Baylar turned to me and hissed just above a whisper, "You're the reason your mother died. You ruined everything." With that, she and her shadows disappeared into the shop.

"What?" My glasses slipped down my nose as my mouth gaped. "What did she just say?"

"Hmmm?" Nog was uncharacteristically nonchalant.

"That I'm the reason my mother died."

"No, no, Bonnie." He cupped my chin and lifted my gaze to meet his. "She must have said you have your mother's eyes." Anam's buggy expression confirmed that Nog had lied to me. I knew what I heard. They heard it, too.

"We need to get going," Anam said as she looked skyward.

Holding out a mitten-covered hand, she caught a few snow-flakes, then whisked them off by brushing one hand against the other. It was almost as if she were wiping her hands of Baylar. "Don't listen to anything she says. Do you understand?" I dipped my chin in acknowledgment, but not submission. I was not letting go of this.

"We need to be on the lookout for Angus," Nog said as we headed to the van. "Baylar calls him a phantom dog, can you imagine that?" Anam glared at Nog, but he didn't seem to notice.

"You see, Bon, he's named after the ever-wandering Celtic god who can open a portal to the Otherworld and resurrect the dead. So, it's easy to see why Baylar calls him a spirit hound."

Anam elbowed him. Again, he didn't respond.

"Some say Knobby is his master."

"Who's Knobby?" I asked. "What's the Otherworld? And what do you mean, resurrect the dead?" This was getting way too confusing.

"Ah, Knobby's an ancestor. MacCarthy clan chieftain. Local legend. People say that when the Strawberry Moon rises, he summons his clan to find a new chieftain."

"Strawberry Moon? Chieftain?"

"Ah yes, Knobby will name a new clan leader during a Strawberry Moon."

By shifting the focus to Knobby, Nog may have shut down my question about Baylar, but Anam's face reddened and steam seemed to seep from her nose. Maybe her eyes and ears, too, but Nog didn't notice. "Baylar says she can see him."

"Sees Knobby? If he's an ancestor, isn't he dead? Is he a ghost?"

I wanted answers and all I got were more questions. "How can she see him? With one eye? What's up with that?"

"Don't know," Nog said, still ignoring Anam, whose mouth

kept opening and closing. "It's been that way for as long as I've known her, all the way back to my childhood. There are lots of stories, of course. Some say the patch covers her evil eye, that if she were to look at you without it, she would burn you to a crisp." Yeah, I could believe that. "Some even say she was attacked by bats ..."

"Enough!" Anam finally found her voice, and it was loud. We all stopped. She grabbed Nog's arm and glared her husband into obedience. "No evil eyes, no bats, no legends, no ghosts." She slashed each word with a swinging arm.

"Ghosts?" Maybe I wasn't so crazy. That might explain the invisible presence that was following me around. Or the shadows surrounding Baylar.

As we climbed into the van, there seemed to be a few more Invisibles in the back. Not that I'm saying I could *see* anything invisible. If my life were a welter before, it was becoming more of one now.

As we headed away from the village, the snow turned to an icy drizzle.

"Keep an eye open for Angus," Anam said. She described him as a large black hound with silvery flecks. Sounded like a wolf, I thought. That would be appropriate. It was barely four o'clock, but it was getting dark. "I know he always comes home, but I don't want him showing up all wet and dirty."

We crossed Mourning Stream, where Nog said nobody cried.

"Don't go into that pasture." My uncle pointed to cows grazing just beyond it, and wagged his finger. Right. Like I would be caught dead in a pasture. He caught me rolling my eyes. "Hear me out." He started into what the family calls a Nogism, and it was a doozy. "When you cross certain boundaries, you just might encounter strange circumstances and mythical beings, like swarms of giant ants, monsters that turn themselves inside out, headless horsemen, or invisible riders ..."

I looked around, thinking he might mean the Invisibles. "... on cannibal horses—kelpies, they're called. They look like horses, but if you hop on one, he'll run into the water, drown you, and take you home and eat you."

"Stop!" Anam shouted, holding both hands to her head before thrusting them forward like her head was exploding. "Stop. Stop the van. Stop. Stop." Nog pulled over. "Enough of this nonsense. Enough." After a long pause and with a forced calmness, she directed my attention to a hulking building with small dark signs scattered around its doors.

"Look, Bonnie, that's the Old Mill Shops. That's where I buy yarn."

"And," Nog added, pointing toward a large water wheel at its rear. "There, alongside the Mourning Stream. That's The Forge. That's where the ironsmith will make you weapons to fight off ..." Anam glared him into silence.

I wanted malls. Bright, warm, neon malls. With people, lots of people. No ghosts, monsters, weapons, or shops. My chest shivered with fatigue and anxiety.

As Nog eased back on the road, I thought this tour would never end. I felt rather than saw the smooth pavement gravel into a crushed stone roadway. Gray bushes parted in the hoary fog, revealing a hand-painted sign. *Companion Moon,* it read. I couldn't tell if it was a signpost of welcome or warning.

"This is it!" Nog said. "The island of our ancestors. Welcome home."

4

COMPANION MOON

A mansion, I envisioned, like the ones I had seen from the train. Graceful turrets and sweeping lawns. But we'd only get there if Nog moved. Instead, we just sat in front of the sign. "We've done so much work since the first time I brought my Anamary Cara here. Remember, my love?"

"How could I forget?" Anam touched her husband's arm as she turned to look at me. "I came home from work four years ago to find your uncle nearly bursting. He had a stupid grin on his face and was waving a letter around in the air, flailing his hands wildly, crying, *The house! My uncle left me the house!*" She playfully poked his now taut belly. "I wanted to see him more active, but his dancing around made me nervous."

"You need to understand," Nog said to me, "this house, on this lake, is where we came as kids, your mom and me. Every summer. With all our aunts, and uncles, and cousins. So did a generation before that, and generations before that. We would swim, hike, and eat all day and sing, dance, and drink all night—the grownups, anyway." He winked. "A *céilí*, it was, a big party with lots of food, music, and dance, with family and friends."

Since this was about Mom, I nodded. I always wanted to hear more about her. "Anyway, one night, a few weeks before I went off to college, in the midst of the *céilí,* your mom and I snuck off to watch the full moon rise over the lake. She knew I'd be leaving soon and she cried, said she was going to miss me. She was only six or seven at the time, so I told her a story. Imagine that, me telling a story!" Anam and I snickered.

"I told her that when we both looked at the full moon at the same time, no matter where in the world we each might be, that all she had to do was close her eyes and remember that moon, and even though I might be a thousand miles away, I'd be sitting right there with her." I closed my eyes and tried to picture Mom there with me, with us, but it wasn't working. Probably because Nog kept talking. "And for years and years, we did that. As we got older, we'd call each other when we were lonely, or happy—like when she told me she was expecting you." He paused, looked at me, and smiled. "Or for no reason at all. One of us would just say, *Companion Moon.* And we would just sit quietly together. It was sort of a password, a signal. It meant *Pay attention. I need you.* Then we would share what was going on." Nog pulled out a handkerchief and wiped his eyes.

We sat for what seemed like an eternity, but was probably 10 seconds, until Nog was ready to continue. "I did that just about every day for months after she died—couldn't call her, of course," he harrumphed. "Just conjured her face and voice. I felt that we were still children right here." I closed my eyes again. This time I could picture Mom, in perfect detail. *Pay attention,* I told her. *I need you.*

Nog shifted the van into low gear as he headed up a steep driveway that was pocked with icy patches. "That night was the last time I was here, until I got the letter. I didn't realize it at the time, but you hardly ever know when you do something for the last time. It's only after you look back on it."

He was right. I didn't know that the last time I saw Erin, Jenny, or Sara would be the last time. Or that the last time I saw Mom would be the last time.

Heaving a sigh, Nog continued. "Sure, the family still came, but it was never the same. The cousins went off to school, got married, moved away. The aunts and uncles all died or just got too old. Uncle Emmett, the last one to live here, had a stroke. He ended up in a nursing home, then died. We buried him in the cemetery on the other side of Tory Island. I'll take you there sometime." No way, I thought. No cemeteries. I already had these Invisibles hanging around. "I assumed Emmett had sold the place to pay for his care. Never gave it another thought until I got a letter from the law firm saying he left the house to me. It was mine!"

"It was his all right," Anam jumped in. "I kept asking what we were going to do with a house? On a lake? He wanted to turn it into a bed and breakfast. I wanted to sell it for our retirement."

"So, I told her we could sell it," Nog laughed.

"You fibbed," Anam interjected.

"I did. But I had to get you to see it. Selling it would be like selling my childhood." He pointed to a pile of stones that clumped around a curve in the roadway. "See those rocks? At one time those were my mountains." He shrugged like an elf. "I was their king. I know it sounds silly now, but ..." My mind drifted. I got it. Not so long ago, I pretended to be a princess.

It was easy to imagine how Nog plotted to get Anam here. He looked like a leprechaun. Tufts of hair softened his expansive jaw. His two eyebrows blended into one bushy one that lifted his whole face when he widened his eyes. He could even wiggle his ears. All he needed was a green hat and a pipe.

"There it is." He pointed up a short hill to the right. "The long-lost haven of my youth." I followed my uncle's finger in the gloom toward a sprawling lodge in the backwoods.

Bounded by sinister trees and an icy mist, the dimly lit and stone-cold house looked like it belonged in a bad horror movie.

"It was awful," Anam said. Still was, I thought. "Tiny windows tucked themselves under rickety gables. Bittersweet curtained the windows, field mice overran the cellar, and a flock of old birds claimed the attic."

Nog pointed to a silvery shimmer beyond the naked trees. "The lake," he said. "Isn't it pretty shining like that through the trees? There's a trail behind the house that goes down to it. I used to call it my adventure trail. I'll show you when the weather clears."

"Don't get me going on the trail," Anam said. "I had come to see a house, not a trail. And all I saw was a wall of prickers and poison ivy that sheltered wild animals and maybe a murderer or two."

"Yes, you looked like a banshee, with your hair streaming, vultures circling overhead ..."

"There were no vultures," Anam said. She was always trying to cool Nog's enthusiasm with logic.

"But you did look like a banshee," Nog said, also turning to me. "That's a female spirit who announces death by crying and wailing."

"Your death, maybe," she countered before continuing with her version of the story. "He started running wildly toward the woods. Things got out of control." Even with her new look, my aunt definitely did not tolerate things getting out of control. "I kept shouting at him to come back."

"She called me *Brendan*." Brendan was his real name, but no one called him that, except Dad. We all knew that Grandma Maggie nicknamed him her Little Noggin because he was a bald baby. The name stuck, even after hair finally appeared, then eventually disappeared, except for a fluffy fringe around his ears. "That's when I knew the trail would have to wait." With that, he finally, *finally* guided the van gracefully over the last stretch of a dirt road.

Our approach triggered a sensor, and a burst of lights brightened the yard and de-spooked the house. Its two-story stone façade was trimmed with dark wood and gabled windows. Orangey, rough-cut tiles defined the steep roof. A large red door stood at the center of a front porch that ran the length of the house. It wasn't a painted lady, but it had its own colorful quality.

I scrambled out of the back seat, but halted. Something dark and wolflike hulked on the front porch. Its movement triggered a flutter of little birds.

"Ah, there he is! The Wandering Angus. The pup with a peripatetic propensity." Nog roughhoused the dog. "Even the birds—the chickadees—love him."

"No," Anam teased, "they love you." To me, she added, "He feeds them suet and peanut butter." Peanut butter. That reminded me that I was hungry. Again.

Wagging his tail, Angus unfurled his rangy blackness into a strangely stately stance. Like he owned the place. Then he cocked his head to one side as if to ask me about my journey. I patted his head. He looked so gentle that I wondered why Baylar thought he was evil. Once more, Nog answered my unasked question.

"No one knows how old Angus is and where exactly he came from. He was sitting here the day we arrived. Birds and all. As I said, he's named after the Celtic god of youth who can raise the dead."

My aunt ignored that comment and wrestled the dog's ruff. "Whew. You stink." She scrunched her nose. "On that first visit, Bonnie, Angus nudged me into petting him. Can you imagine? Me, petting a strange dog!" No, I couldn't, especially a dirty one, except I did see it. I couldn't wait to tell Dad.

"He kept me company while Nog traipsed through the house, smudging make-believe flowers into imaginary window boxes, and babbling about beds and breakfasts. When I realized he meant turning *this place* into *our bed and break-fast*, I cried." Her head shook slowly from side to side. "I thought we were saving for retirement. Unlocking the front door of this house was like opening Pandora's box," she said. I remembered Pandora. She was a Greek goddess who opened a box full of great troubles and unleashed them on the world. I looked around at the house. Yeah, I could see that this place was full of trouble.

"The heck with retirement," Nog said. "This was a chance to start a new life together." They ogled each other, like they were escaping into another world. But Nog suddenly bounced back to cold reality.

"Come on, Bon." He wrapped his arm around my quaking shoulders and opened the door. Its bell jangled a warm and friendly greeting. "Let's get you inside."

5

ELSEWHERE

"Here." Nog gallantly waved me over to a comfy bench by an enormous fireplace and draped a nubby blue shawl over my shoulders. Into its softness I snuggled. "Have a seat. This is Gramp's hearth, the same great-great-great-great-grandfather who built the church. You'll be warm in no time. I'll get your bags." In and out the door he went, up and down the stairs he trudged.

Meanwhile, without a word, Anam pulled on huge work gloves, grabbed a shovel, and crawled into the firepit, leaving nothing in sight but her rear end. What if she got stuck? Speechless, I watched her scuttle about on hands and knees, knocking around a lump of ashes, and blowing on them. Reaching behind to her left without even looking, she grabbed some newspaper and scraps of wood, feeding them in succession to the glowing and growing embers until ... *poof* ... a flame danced to life. My mouth hung open.

"How did you do that?"

My aunt backed out. I looked at the smudges on her face. Another story to tell Dad. He would smirk at the thought of Anam building a fire. *Inside* a fireplace. With a dirty face.

"It takes practice, but it's really quite simple. Hand me some kindling." She pointed to a wire basket nearby full of twigs and sticks. "At night, we do the reverse. Bank all the hot coals into a pile and cover them with cold ashes. This way we never have to start a fire from scratch. In an old house like this, you need a good fire quickly, especially in the winter, even though we have central heat. You'll learn." I nodded in fascinated agreement as she fed a few small branches, then larger ones, and finally a few logs.

Scrambling clear, she straightened herself and poured a kettle of water into a black pot that hung nearby. It hissed. I lurched, startled.

"Got to keep the house hydrated. Wood fires will dry everything out."

I looked around. The fireplace—Nog had called it a hearth— divided the kitchen from a living room—Nog called it a parlor. Both rooms shared a wide-planked floor. Where the parlor was dark and upholstered, however, the kitchen was bright, uncluttered, and modern with stainless steel appliances, lots of cabinets and workspaces, overhead lights, and a nook by the window.

Off to the other side was a small dining room with a sideboard set up with a coffee urn. Tucked into the corner by the front door was an alcove that looked like an office with a computer. A small library graced one wall. I saw a few games there—*Scrabble, Jenga,* checkers—as well as a few decks of cards. I figured that's where Anam wanted to put her local books. Maybe I could find a few more interesting games. Like *Game of Thrones Monopoly* or *Harry Potter Clue.* Something I might play. Especially if Deb-Horror wasn't looking.

I closed my eyes and rested the heels of my hands along my jawline, splaying my fingers across my cheeks. At once, I was assaulted by the stench of a swamp or sewer. Angus. Yuck.

"Ana My Cara," Nog called as he clumped down the stairs.

"Why don't you help Bonnie unpack? I took her bags upstairs. In the meantime, I'll give Angus a quick bath with that water-less shampoo you bought."

Unlike my spacious room at Dad's, this room above the kitchen was so tiny that it reminded me of my old dollhouse. Wow, I hadn't thought of that in years. Dad built it for me back when he and Mom were still together, before Mom found out about his girlfriends. I must have been two or three years old. Erin lived next door and every day we would bounce our dolls from room to room, their dialogue lifted from our everyday lives. *What's for dinner? You look pretty. Why are you late?* I wondered what happened to that dollhouse. Not that I would have any use for it now, but it was a piece of my past. A piece of me.

"Isn't this cozy?" Anam broke my train of thought as she bubbled around the room, straightening pictures and fluffing pillows. My stepmother didn't like *cozy,* saying that's what you call small when you want it to sound big. Or better. That's how she finagled Dad into buying a McMansion.

"Yeah, it's cozy." With its single bed, dresser, and vanity with matching chair, it reminded me of a prison cell—except for ruffled pillows and a pink window cushion, on which I plopped. Clutching a satin pillow to my chest with one hand, I parted the simple linen curtains with the other. In the flood-light, I saw Nog toweling Angus. They both seemed to be smil-ing, despite the snow and ice that accumulated around them.

"Look." Anam picked up the edge of the bedspread and repeatedly flipped it over and back. One side was black with intricate white leaves; the other was white with big, bright flowers. "It's like an old-fashioned thaumatrope," she demon-strated, flicking it back and forth. "You spin it to make two images seem like one. Do you remember Nog made you one?"

"I do remember!" Mom had already died, but Deborrah hadn't yet come into the picture. I was probably seven, but the memory came back in sharp detail. Nog drew a picture of a bird on a round piece of paper and a tree branch on the other. He glued the two sides together with a piece of string between them. When we twirled it, the two pictures became one picture of a bird in a tree. "He called it magic. He said that's what you call it when things that can't be possible really are happening."

"Well, I don't know about magic. Don't believe in it. But believe this." She glowed like a teenager, still playing with the coverlet. "I made it."

"*You* made it?"

Anam didn't make things. She bought things. Dad always said the only thing she made was dinner reservations.

"Oh, Bonnie, we're going to have so much fun. We'll go back to the Crystal Keep and Rainbow Stream. Make some jewelry. Read some books together."

As much as I wanted to go back to the bead shop and bookstore, I was afraid of the Invisibles and increasingly uncomfortable with my aunt. I wanted the old Anam back. Fat Anam. Frumpy Anam. It was like aliens had abducted her and left a defective clone.

"I love the pillows." I choked back tears and I stroked the embossed surface of the one I was holding, then tossed it into the air. Anam caught it and giggled.

"I made them, too. Got the fabric from Joy. And the furniture from Four Fences." I shuddered to think I'd be sleeping in a room that had any connection to Baylar and those shadows around her. What were they? Ghosts? And why did she say that Mom's death was my fault? Before I could give it any more thought, Anam plunked my backpack onto the window seat and lifted my two large suitcases onto the bed. I didn't realize she was so strong. "Let's get you unpacked."

Nodding, I emptied the items in the backpack onto the window seat. I carefully unwrapped my treasure chest, which I had swathed in a soft scarf. It was an elegant black cloisonné box inlaid with a graceful snake that had yellow, black, and burgundy stripes and a white mark by the eye. Grandma Maggie had given it to Mom, and Dad gave it to me. In it I kept not only Mom's ring but other jewelry, pictures, and stuff that had meaning only to me. "Oooh!" Anam blurted when she espied it. "Let's put that here." She placed it on the vanity. "Can I look?"

"No." It took a second for that to settle in.

She blinked away her surprise—or was it hurt? But then acted like nothing had happened. "Okay, well, how about your suitcases?" We spent an hour figuring out where to put things. Underwear, socks, and pajamas went into the dresser. We hung jeans, shirts, sweats, sweaters, jackets, and a couple of dresses in a minuscule closet. In the back, there were shelves where we put bathing suits, tank tops, and shorts. Deborrah had taken me shopping for the summer stuff. I doubted I would ever need them in this frigid wasteland. Below the shelves was a shoe rack. Everything fit perfectly. When everything was unpacked, Anam kissed my forehead.

"Bonnie. I'm so glad you're here." I wasn't. She just stood there smiling, hands clasped in front of her heart, like she had done earlier. A loud *tap tap creeaakkkkk* broke the silence. I jumped.

"What's that?"

"Oh, it's an old house. That's just the attic. At first, I thought it was just the birds up there. Then I thought maybe bats, or mice." First ghosts and bats. Now mice. "Don't go up there. I'm not sure the floor's not going to collapse." I looked down at my feet and then at her. "Oh no, the floors here are fine. I think." She pointed to the ceiling. "But I'm not sure about the floors up there. So just in case, don't go up there."

I was pretty sure I wasn't going to go anywhere with mice and bats and collapsing floors. Or fields of cattle and monsters. Anam toured me through the rest of the house. On the other side of the bathroom, sitting atop the parlor and dining room, was what she called the master suite. In contrast to the rooms in the rest of the house, it was huge.

"This is our retreat, separate from the inn. It's important that we have our own space." Back in the hallway, on one side of the stairway, was a door that she quickly dismissed. "That's the door to the attic." She twitched her head and hands, signaling it was taboo.

The other side opened into the guest wing, which was once what she called a carriage house. "We renovated it to give the guests a separate entry. Downstairs is a two-bedroom suite, good for families or people who can't get up and down the stairs. And two other single rooms. Up here, four single rooms." They were all bigger versions of mine, but were basically empty. "I have furniture in the barn that needs to be cleaned up—you can help me with that. I'm still working on a few afghans to make everything nice and homey, you know."

"Dinner's almost ready," Nog called up the stairs. Saved by Nog. I needed to get away from Anam, who was heading downstairs.

"Let me wash up, Anam. I'll be down in a few minutes." I didn't realize a couple of hours had passed. I needed alone time to absorb all this. In the bathroom, I ran hot water and coaxed a smile out of the sad girl in the mirror. She and I shook our heads. How had my life come to this? Living in a cozy jail cell. I pulled out my phone to call Dad, but there was barely a signal. I texted him instead, just to tell him I was at the inn and all was okay. After washing my face and brushing my hair into a ponytail, I pulled on a sweatshirt and headed downstairs. Dinner smelled good. Spaghetti and meatballs.

But before I could twirl a forkful, Anam insisted on saying grace.

"Thank you, God, for this food and for bringing Bonnie here safely."

"Amen," Nog hailed and dug in. I followed his lead. The meal was even better than it smelled—thick, earthy, chunky. Garlic bread that was crunchy on the outside but soft and buttery inside. The salad, crispy and herby. It was so good, I had a second helping.

As we ate, we talked some more about my family, the train ride, and the house. After dinner, we cleared the table, with Anam directing me on kitchen logistics—composter, recyclables, dishwasher, leftover containers. Nog stoked the fire and Anam shooed us into the parlor.

"I'm fixing tea and cupcakes. You all relax." The parlor side was, well, cozy, with a love seat, two armchairs, a rocker, an overstuffed chair, and an ottoman arranged around a coffee table that sat on a tufted rug. A side table with two straight-back chairs was set for a game of chess. In the corner was a piano. Outside, a howling wind pinged ice pellets against the windows; inside, Nog relaxed into his favorite chair and a sweet-smelling Angus curled up by the hearth.

As I plopped down next to the dog, a black whoosh shot up. "Aaakk!" Fearing a ghost, I jumped up, nearly falling over Angus. He instantly stood between me and the fire to prevent me from pitching toward it. "Oh!" I gasped with relief. "A cat!"

"Mo," Nog said as he picked up *Farmers' Almanac* and used it as a pointer. "And over there in the corner is Willy."

"I can't believe you have cats, too."

"No, they have us. When we first got here, Anam was convinced that the house was infested with mice."

"Yeah, she told me," I cringed.

"See, Mo and Willy were hanging around the yard, so we invited them in. No one has ever seen either one with a mouse, but then again, no one has ever seen a mouse. So, either they earned their keep, or just wheedled a way in." Mo slinked back over to me, tentatively offering her nose for a scratch and making it clear she wanted her seat back. Willy, a gray tabby, purred his way over, as if the mere mention of his name was the invitation he needed. Angus sat undisturbed, letting Willy swat his flicking tail.

It was so serene as to be cliché. Even the *tap tap creak* seemed normal. I was about to ask about the big-screen TV that blended into the dark paneled walls when Anam strolled in with a dessert tray and a steaming pot of tea. Then she froze mid-step, nearly dropping everything.

"Oh my, my ..." Her gasp shot through the room like lightning. The cats bolted in unison. With her face drained of color, she resembled her old self, but now I didn't like it. "I, I, you, this ..."

Nog puzzled up from his reading. "Ana My Cara, what is it?" She gaped. I sat stock-still silent. "What, Ana? What?"

Even the house seemed concerned. *Tap tap creeaakkkkk?* It seemed to ask. *Tap tap creeaakkkkk?*

"Déjà, déjà vu," she finally said. My stomach churned. I'd heard of déjà vu, but never experienced that sense of having been somewhere before. I didn't understand what was happening. My aunt's eyes darted from Nog to me, back to Nog, then Angus, me again, then Nog. The cats slinked back in from the hallway, stretching their curious necks in unison around the corner, as did the Invisible—or was it more than one?—who appeared around the hearth. We all stared, first at Anam, then at each other, then back at her.

"I, I saw this, this, this same scene, before, when, when ..." She was flustered, and Anamary Cara did not fluster. The old one, anyway. The whole scene was quite unsettling to me. I was already forlorn and confused. "... when Maura ...," she glanced at Nog. "When your mother ...," she glanced at me. Placing the tray on the coffee table, she sank into the ottoman, settling her trembling hands into her lap.

Nog and I peered at each other. As one, we looked back at her.

"Oh dear. How can I say this? When she, your mother," she directed her eyes to me, "your sister," then to Nog, "came to our apartment and told me she was, she was ... was pregnant ... with you," she looked back at me. "I, I saw a young girl ... in what I can only call a vision." She glanced at Nog, then back to me. "I forgot about it," she looked at me. "But as clearly as I see you now, you were sitting by a fire—this fire—with, with your thick hair in a ponytail." I touched my hair. "With a dog. A black dog. Angus. Your Mom said it was the most wonderful day of her life. Oh my ..."

My belly tugged. The wind howled. I had no idea what any of this meant, but I, too, felt for a second that I was in Anam's old kitchen, the one in the city, like Anam had transported herself and me somewhere else. It was very disconcerting. For both of us.

"I saw you here," she whispered, barely recovering her composure, "even before you were born. Even before we came here. Even before Angus. I saw you here." She paused, then added, "Here, but not here." She held my bewildered gaze for a second longer and then said, "Elsewhere."

"Elsewhere," I repeated. It felt familiar yet far away.

She looked at Nog again, then me. "I think," she managed to utter after stuttering, "I think, it must mean that, that you, that you belong here."

The Invisibles nodded like one massive shadow, brightened by the fire.

Nog cleared his throat and the moment. "Of course, she belongs here. Now, where's that tea?"

6

BRIGHT
AND SHINING

Ice pelted the windows for days. Snow swept beyond forever. The house was a dead zone—and I don't just mean
the ghosts who kept showing up.

Internet service was sucky, cell service was at best one bar,
and worst of all, no Wi-Fi. No Wi-Fi! Dad would hit the roof
when he saw the data charges on my phone, but it would serve
him right for sentencing me here. In fact, when I called Dad, I
had to use the landline. With a dial tone. And zero privacy.
Whenever I complained, Anam simply said that digital communication was dangerous.

I was frozen, like the movie, trapped in an endless winter
with ghosts, a landline, and vinegar.

Yes, vinegar. Mom and I used vinegar to dye Easter eggs.
But for Anam, vinegar was for cleaning. Despite the weather,
she and I trudged out to the barn every morning to work on
her collection of old furniture. While Nog tended to Baylar's
horses, my aunt and I wiped down every surface of every piece
with soap, water, and vinegar. I would rather have taken care
of the horses. Instead, I had to use an old toothbrush to get
into the crevices of old chairs, tables, and bureaus. Then

everything went to Nog for repairs and refinishing before he lugged them upstairs. Sometimes I helped with that, too.

"Why spend all this time on these old pieces of junk?" I asked, thinking of creepy, old Baylar. "Why not buy new stuff?"

"It has charm," Anam said with a sniff and her chin tilted toward the ceiling.

"Each piece tells a bit of history," Nog said. "Furniture reflects people's needs and preferences. And restoring it requires careful calculations. That's how we'll study arithmetic."

Nog was homeschooling me, getting me through seventh grade without further drama. Except, of course, the kind he added. His workshop in the cellar, which he called the crypt, became one of my classrooms. Unlike the barn, which smelled of hay and vinegar, Nog's crypt smelled like a bowling alley. He said that was because of the wood shavings that littered the floor and the lingering odor of the paint, turpentine, and oils he used to restore the furniture.

He put me to work, and while we worked, he taught me. Like when Nog was painting an old box that Anam was going to use as a side table, we studied the Puritans. He said they were straight and severe, like their furniture. They used basic furniture for different things. A storage box could also be a chair or a table. He laughed when I said it reminded me of IKEA stuff and the tiny house trend. He said that after the American Revolution, people were fascinated with Greek and Roman styles, so everything they built—from courthouses to chairs—reflected that. And when he refinished what he called a *neoclassical* piece, he emphasized its straight lines and tapered legs.

We measured surfaces to estimate paint, or to let Anam know how much fabric to buy for cushions. I learned how to measure the length, width, and area of squares, rectangles, and circles. I converted inches to feet and feet to meters. Once we needed new hinges for a cabinet and took the measurements to the ironsmith at the Old Mill. He made them exactly to fit. It was so much more fun than studying geometry from a book.

But I'm getting ahead of myself. My first week at Companion Moon seemed to be forever in a frozen prison. After a few days, the ice storm transitioned into slow, intermittent snow. That lasted a few more days. Blustery winds gave way to a soft breeze that sifted snow from the trees. Finally, soft sunlight crept through the kitchen, shining a hazy halo into the breakfast nook where Anam and I ate oatmeal with raisins. Oatmeal reminded me of Benjy, and the soft snow reminded me of his baby cheek. As I stared out the window, I stroked my own skin, trying to remember the texture of his.

In the bright and shining morning, ice sparkled like diamonds on tree branches. I spotted a glimmer of the lake past the barn. The brightening sky lifted my mood and inspired a scheme. While Anam pored over her notebook, Nog stomped snow from his boots in the hallway he called the portal. That's where the doors to the inside and outside, back stairs to the attic—which he called the belfry—and the crypt intersected.

"Hey, Nog." I hailed him before Anam could sniff out my plan. "Would today be good to show me your adventure trail?" He paused mid-step, craned his neck around toward the window over the sink, and nodded.

"Splendid idea." He arched his bushy brow, scratched his head, and pulled his ear. "In fact, it's a perfect day for clearing brush from it." I wanted a fun walk in the snow, not more work. But anything, *anything,* was better than cleaning old furniture. "What do you say, Ana My Cara? Can you spare Bonnie for the day?"

Anam looked up from a page with lots of bright red numbers.

"Eh?" She grunted through twisted lips. "Sure. I need to work on the budget. Speaking of which, Nog, if we don't get more guests, we won't break even." Her voice trailed off as it did in the village when she mentioned the other hotels. She glanced at him but looked at me. "Bonnie, let me get you something warmer and sturdier."

Just call me Lumberjack, I thought as I assessed myself in Anam's padded overalls, flannel jacket, and old work boots. I wouldn't be caught dead wearing this dork outfit anywhere else. For the second time since I got here, I was relieved that there were no kids around.

"Let's hit the trail," Nog said.

In my lungs was piney air; beneath my feet, crusty snow. Foot by foot, we breathed in the former and tramped down the latter. In between, I puffed cold-air clouds. I dragged fallen branches into piles of kindling while Nog hacked off broken limbs that clung helplessly to trees and heaped them into the wheelbarrow. Before long, we were shuttling wood between the trail and the woodpile outside the kitchen. This was hard work, so each time we got to the kitchen, we stopped for water and cookies.

"Wood heats you thrice," Nog said, unzipping his jacket and mopping perspiration from his brow. "Once when you gather it, then when you cut it, and finally when you burn it. And pleasant company," he added, "warms the heart."

Sweat by sweat and section by section, the tangled path stretched into a six-foot-wide trail. All the while, Nog told stories about the relatives, insisting that I memorize their names and personalities.

"Why?" I insisted.

"Because knowing your history grounds you. Helps you know who you are and where you're coming from. Gives you a sense of belonging in the present and a framework for building the future. You're the last descendent, Bonnie. Our family line ends with you. If no one knows our history, it's lost forever."

"That sounds like the guy on the train, Porter. He said that the past is history, the future's a mystery, and the present is a present. And something about where past, present, and future are one—you have freedom to live."

"Smart man, that Porter."

"So are you, Nog."

While we worked, he told stories about when he and Mom were kids.

As soon as they arrived, Nog would burst from the car, run down this trail, strip off his clothes, and plunge into the lake. Even though I had worked up a sweat, I shivered just thinking of jumping into cold water.

Back then, he said, the house belonged to Luna and before that, to her father, Baron.

"How am I supposed to remember these names, Nog?"

Their stories, he said, would make it easy. Luna meant *moon*. And Baron ruled the lake, paddling his boat day and night to catch fish. Luna also had a dog named Angus, who looked a lot like the current one. Nog said that some locals believed that it was the same dog—a spirit hound. That's what Baylar had called him. I shivered every time I thought of Baylar.

Aunt Jeanne was an accountant who loved to read. She was also strong and athletic, and taught everyone to swim. Uncles Art and Dob were twins. They led races to a raft they built.

"They were named after Knobby's twin boys, Arthur and Dobbin," Nog said. "Arthur means *bear* or *king*. Think of King Arthur. Dobbin is an old Scottish name for Robert. We have so many Roberts and Robertas in the family that if you ever need to call someone by name, *Bobby* is a good guess."

"Roberta—that's my middle name, and Mom's."

"I know that. But I bet you didn't know that it means

bright and shining." I didn't, but I felt warm inside. Although I didn't know anyone on my mother's side of the family except Nog, the name gave me a sense of belonging.

With a faraway look in his eyes, he talked about the ancestors. Although Grandma Maggie had died before I was born, I knew her from pictures. I didn't know my Grandpa John, Nog's father. But I'd seen pictures of him, too. He died in some war before my mother was born. Nog said he was strong and brave. Aunt Kelty sang songs. Edmund juggled apples. Jack balanced a glass on his forehead and spun plates into colorful whirlwinds.

"He reminded everyone that change was constant," Nog said.

I loved the name Cookie Aunt Mary. She, of course, made cookies. Seamus loved cheese. Great-great-great-great-grandfather Gramp loved barbecuing. While he grilled dinner, his son, my great-great-great-grandfather Aloysius, grilled the children on their ancestors. Just like Nog was doing with me. Aloysius insisted that everyone know the definitions of cousins once-, twice-, and three-times removed. Tess and Mamie, for example, were descendants of Gramp's second cousin once-removed. They loved to knit. Mamie also would sneak sips from not-so-very-well-hidden flasks of whiskey. I wanted to know these relatives. They sounded fun.

"When I walk down here and think of the ancestors, it reminds me of a labyrinth," he said, tracing an intricate pattern in the air with his index finger. "That's like the puzzle where you trace a path through a maze from the beginning to the end."

"I know, like a corn maze. Do you remember Erin? My best friend?" Nog nodded. "Her parents took us one year to a fall festival with pumpkin-carving contests and a maze through a cornfield."

"Yes," he nodded. "A labyrinth is a maze, but it also refers to the journey through life. A pilgrimage, so to speak, to a sacred place. You start by looking into yourself. Thinking about the ancestors gives me perspective, soothes me. Life seemed so simple then."

Although it was a lot of work, the trail wasn't really that long. After a lunch break and shortly before sunset, we had cleared it all the way to the lake, which Nog talked about with passion. Anam was right—he did think it was his. We paused on the icy expanse long enough for Nog to explain that glaciers carved it after the last ice age.

"*Ice Age?* Like the movies?" I had seen each of them like a hundred times with Erin, but I wasn't sure what they had to do with this lake. Nog suggested that we do a geography project on ice ages, glaciers, and lakes, but my thoughts were fixated on Manny, the woolly mammoth who only wanted to head someplace warmer. I wanted to take a long hot shower.

As we headed back, Nog talked about planting flowers and building benches in the spring. Spring? Spring couldn't come fast enough.

I headed to the bathroom. I cranked up the hot water to shower the day's sweat off my chilled body. As the water ran over me, I lathered myself with lavender soap and thought about Nog's adventure trail, his labyrinth. Although I didn't really get what he meant, I couldn't help but think about the journey that I'd been on for less than a week. Already there was too much to take in. Baylar. Angus. Invisibles. Ancestors. My head was swimming with the various worlds I seemed to be living in. I found myself thinking about Nog's family. My family. That my middle name meant bright and shining.

After dressing in soft sweats, I returned to the bathroom to towel-dry my hair. Nog said the journey through life began by looking into yourself with discipline and quietude, so I looked in the mirror.

That's when a billowy shadow moved from the periphery

of my vision to the corner of my eye. When I swung my head in its direction, it didn't move. It was an Invisible for sure, tall and thin, floating about a foot off the floor. Although it had no facial features, I was sure it was the one that originally rode with me in the van.

"Who are you?" I demanded, shocked at my own bravery. "If you are going to follow me around, tell me your name." But the shape disappeared.

I shook my head and turned toward the mirror. Written in the condensation was one word. *D-O-B-B-I-N*.

7

OTHERWORLD

og had told me I needed to learn the names of his—of my—ancestors. Dobbin was an ancestor. Did that make me related to a ghost? Were the other Invisibles my family, too? I shuddered. While everybody in the world had actual families, I had ghosts.

Since Anam had called Baylar's jumbled mess a welter, and that word described my life, I decided that's what I would call the Invisibles. My welter of ghosts lurked like secrets in the shadows of closets, under beds, or in corners of the barn.

The one named Aloysius showed up one evening as I worked on a family tree for a history project. I was going to show how my ancestors were related to events around Tory Island and New Grange, starting with Knobby, who escaped a famine in Ireland to settle here. His sons, Dobbin and Arthur, were undertakers at the cemetery where Uncle Emmett was buried. Gramp helped build the train station, and Mamie started the Mountainside Dairy.

Anyway, the computer was old and prone to crashing, which it did while I was working on this project. As I grunted with frustration, the letters A-L-O-Y-S-I-U-S flashed one by

one across the blue screen of death. Aloysius. The ancestor
who insisted that the children know the names of their
ancestors. Sure enough, I looked over my shoulder to see an
Invisible fluttering in the corner. Unlike Dobbin, who was tall
and thin, Aloysius was a bit frayed around the edges, like a
favorite book that's been read many, many times.

Cookie, another Invisible, used crumbs to spell her name
one morning. We had just finished a breakfast of sausage, bran
muffins, and homemade applesauce when I noticed C-O-O-K-
I-E written across the table. I stared at it, then at Anam, who
scolded me for leaving a mess. Before I could say anything—as
if I could say anything—she used one hand to sweep the cookie
crumbs into the other. When she tossed them into the trash, a
plump Invisible wafted up from it, smelling like vanilla. Her
eyes looked like chocolate chips. She wiggled like an aroma,
then disappeared into the shadows of Nog's portal.

Tory flew in one day while we were at the ironsmith's shop
at the Old Mill. He wore a feathered hat and recited a poem
about budgie birds that hold no grudges.

Gramp, who built the train depot, also liked to build fires,
so he arranged twigs to spell his name. He glowed in the shape
of a sturdy oak tree, with branches instead of arms. He felt
warm.

By the time I broke a dish after supper and the fragments
spelled J-A-C-K, I was no longer surprised. Jack could balance
a glass on his forehead and juggle dishes. He especially liked
to spin red and blue ones until they turned purple. I started to
laugh, but Anam told me it wasn't funny.

One night, Edmund spelled his name on the foggy window
of the parlor, in the same way that Dobbin had done in the
mirror. Of course, neither Nog nor Anam noticed it, but Angus
did. "Look," I said without thinking, pointing toward the
window. All they saw was Angus making little yipping noises
while prancing back and forth beneath it.

"What do you see, Angus?" Nog talked to the dog as if he were a person. "You see a ghost?"

If they only knew! Anam would freak out. Nog might understand, but what would I say? That Angus was indeed seeing a ghost? That I knew because *I* was seeing ghosts? That they were our ancestors? Even I found this hard to believe. Would he think I was doing drugs? Would he tell Dad? Would they think I was crazy? Was I crazy?

I kept my mouth shut with my aunt and uncle, but not with the Invisibles. I kept asking them their names. It was like a game of hide-and-seek that I called Ghosted. It was fun. Until Luna showed up. Then it got spooky. The day started as mundane as Cheerios.

Anam had rushed into the kitchen that morning while I ate a bowl of cereal. She was all dressed up with makeup, bomber jacket, knee-high boots—I still couldn't get over her appearance. She used to look 40 going on 80. Now she looked 40 going on 20.

"Joy called. The fabric I ordered came in. I'm heading into the village and then to New Grange for groceries. Would you like to come with me?" *Boring*, I thought. "Or stay here?"

To avoid answering, I shoveled more cereal into my mouth and pointed to my exaggerated chewing process then to the table to indicate, *Here*.

"Well, okay then." I watched her walk out to the barn where Nog was working. She handed him a list. They talked, pointed to the list, looked toward me, and waved. Nog folded his list into his shirt pocket and headed toward the kitchen, full of smiles.

"We're going to paint a few chairs outside, Bon. It's too nice a day to be stuck indoors." He was right. Although it was February, it was brilliantly sunny and an early thaw was melting the ice and snow. "Come meet me by the barn when you finish eating. Dress like a lumberjack."

I took my time pulling my unmanageable hair into a manageable ponytail and changing into old clothes. From the window in my room, I saw Nog set up a sunny work area right outside the barn, where he hauled tarps, paint, and four sturdy wooden armchairs that Anam had found at Four Fences. Nog had already sanded and primed them.

With Anam gone, I finally saw my chance to get some answers. I marched outside as Nog pried the lid off a can of sky-blue paint. Behind it were quarts of hot pink, lime green, and sun-kissed orange.

I wasted no time.

"Nog." I planted my fists on my hips. "Why did Baylar say I was the reason Mom died? That I ruined everything?" Nog's brow lifted. His ears shifted back. He went from a fun-loving leprechaun to a gloomy gnome in the blink of an eye—one whose eyes darted around looking for diversion. Although his mouth was pinched shut, mine was moving. "I know what I heard, and I know you heard it, too. And who's Knobby? And why won't Anam let you talk about him?"

Nog stirred the paint for longer than necessary, then looked upward. "What do you think, Bon?" I followed his gaze. Puffs scudding across the sky spelled L-U-N-A, right above the house that once belonged to her. Brushing aside my questions about Mom and Baylar, I had the perfect opening to talk about the welter.

"Nog?" I pointed skyward. He followed my finger. Together, we fixated on the visible heavens for about a minute. He broke the spell.

"You're right. We should mix in some clouds, some white."

Was this some kind of delay tactic? Or did he not see Luna's name? I figured he didn't, because if he had, he would have launched into a story. Instead, he rambled on about paint and chairs. Ignoring his banter, I watched the skywriting dissipate much the way the paint's odor did.

"Bonnie, are you paying attention here?" Snapping back, I bobbled my chin while he rambled on. "The chairs are called Adirondacks, named for these mountains."

"Am I going to be tested on that?" Crossing my arms in front of my chest, I glared at him. I wanted answers, not a furniture lesson. Since he didn't see Luna's name, I pivoted back to my initial questions. "I want to know why Baylar ..."

Shaking his head ever so slightly, Nog held up his hand to silence me. Addressing the chair, not me, he said, "See how deep the seat is slanted? That's so you can sit upright if you're on a steep hill." He edged the corners with a paintbrush before handing me a small roller to paint an armrest. "Use long, deliberate, horizontal strokes."

Scowling, I refused to paint anything. Nog scratched his bald head, pulled his ear, and finally eyeballed me.

"Let's start with Knobby."

"No." I plopped on an unpainted chair. "Let's start with Baylar."

"Actually, Bonnie," his voice dangled much as the brush did from his right hand, "we need to put everything into context, so I have to start with Knobby. Once you understand him, you can begin to understand what Baylar said."

Aha, he did hear what Baylar said. I knew it.

"Knobby is the family patriarch, the male head of our entire family. He was my great-great-great-great-great-great-grandfather." He counted the generations on his paint-smudged fingers. Here he went again with the great-greats. "That makes him your great-great-great-great-great-great-*great*-grandfather. Old Knob, an ancient clan chieftain, was *his* great-great-great-great-great-great-grandfather. Which would make Old Knob too many greats to even count. I call him the Grand Ancestor."

"So why doesn't Anam want you to talk about him?"

"She doesn't mind that I talk about *him*, it's the *legend* that she doesn't like, that Knobby is still among us, that he's waiting ..."

"Stop. He's still here?" My widened eyes scanned my surroundings. I noticed Dobbin, Aloysius, Edmund, Gramp, Jack, and Cookie settling in for a good story. Luna loomed overhead and other distinctive shapes and glimmers were sneaking in, too. "Is Knobby undead? Like a zombie?"

That would be a deal breaker. Phantom dogs, okay. Ghosts, maybe. Zombies, no way. Anam would definitely object to the undead walking around her house, and on that, I would agree one hundred percent. Did the undead cause the incessant *tap tap creaks* coming from the attic? Is that why Anam told me not to go up there?

"No, no." Nog looked amused. "Zombies aren't real."

"But you just said Knobby's like hundreds of years old, and he's still hanging around. So, he's undead."

"Well ...." Nog rubbed his square jaw from corner to corner with his left hand before wiping it across his entire scrunched face. "In a way that's true, but not really. He gave up his body, so he's dead. But since he hasn't crossed over yet, he's a specter."

"A what?"

"A specter."

"Hasn't crossed over what?"

"To the Otherworld."

"What other world? Heaven?

"Not quite the same as what people think of as Heaven."

"Is Mom in the Otherworld?"

"I believe so."

"So, it is Heaven. Everyone said she was in Heaven."

"It's more like a mirror reflection of this world. Think of the lake." He pointed toward it with his brush. "The surface reflects the sky, clouds, trees, even you, if you look into it. But if you look beneath the surface, you see there's a totally different world down there. And if you swim under water, you can look up and see the sky, clouds, and trees. But not yourself!" He chuckled at his own analogy. "It's the opposite of this world. Here, when you get old, you get, well, old. Like me. But in the Otherworld, you never get old."

"But Knobby is old, right? Why doesn't he cross over and get young?"

"He has unfinished business."

I didn't like the idea of zombies, specters, or whatever wandering around with unfinished business. I looked at the welter. Were they specters, too? Did they have unfinished business? Their heads—if I can say that ghosts had heads— swayed left and right, seeming to say *No*.

"Knobby's waiting for the right time to convene a *céilí* to name a successor. Then he can cross over. But before he can do that, before he can become a great-great-ancestor, like Old Knob, he needs to assemble the clan to name a new leader."

Trying to take this all in, I looked to the sky. Maybe there would be a sign from Luna, but I saw only blue. Nog continued.

"Knobby was a rather interesting guy. You see, he was sort of a slave who believed ..."

"Wait. A slave? My great-great-great-great-great ..." I counted my fingers as Nog did, but I lost track. "*Great-great-great-great* ...? Grandfather? A slave? Was he African?" I thought my darker skin came from Dad. This would be an interesting splash in my gene pool.

"No. Knobby was Irish, what we call indentured ..."

"Dentures?" Dad's father wore dentures. I did not know what teeth had to do with slaves or ghosts. I wanted answers, not more questions. Anger built inside me.

"No," he shook his head. "Indentured. Different word. Come to think of it, both words mean *teeth*. Indentured means *held*—sort of like a dog gnawing on a bone, not letting go. Indentured servants worked for food and shelter—but no money. So, in a way, they were treated like slaves." *Here we go again*, I thought. Language and history. Not the lesson I wanted. "Slaves, by the way, come in all colors, from all countries, ever since the beginning of history. Indentured servants worked for the people who had paid their way here, usually for five or seven years. But didn't get paid. Then they were set free. Knobby came over here as an indentured servant, about 300 years ago, fleeing a famine."

"What are you talking about? An Irish zombie—or whatever—escaped starvation to come *here*?" I stood up and spread my arms to demonstrate the absurdity of anyone wanting to live in this vast emptiness. "And he wants to cross over *there*?" I pointed to the lake. "And how do you know what happened 300 years ago?" I stretched myself as tall as I could, which isn't much for five feet. Then I shook the paint roller at him. "And, what does this have to do with what Baylar said about Mom? And *me*?"

"It has everything to do with Baylar," he heaved. "But I digressed." Nog always got lost wandering off somewhere in his stories. He paused with his paintbrush in the air before hopping back on his train of thought. "Okay, somewhere around 1750, during the American colonial period, Knobby escaped his servitude. Probably fought in the Revolution against the Brits. After the war, he landed in New Grange as a laborer in the trade markets. But he didn't like being a menial worker, told everyone he was from a long line of warriors, that he needed to establish a clan, and that he was the descendent of royalty." Nog twinkled. "That would make you a princess."

"Right!" My mood changed instantly. "We're descended from the king of Munster." I gloried in that while Nog babbled about the original house and the frontier. By the time he finished his monologue, he had transformed a lowly chair into an azure throne. One that—once dry—would accommodate me, the princess.

"Not bad," he nodded. "But it needs a second coat, so we'll let it dry while we start another. What color next?"

"Pink." I checked the sky. No Luna. We cleaned the brushes and poured paint into a second roller tray.

"Knobby married Mary Julianna. We call her Nana. Some say she was the true leader of the family, the matriarch. I don't know much about her, except that she was Irish, too. I think her ancestors emigrated a hundred years earlier than Knobby. Other than that ..." His voice trailed off and he shook his head. "She was very mysterious. They say she was the source of life itself—beautiful, self-assured, and powerful. Sort of like your mom." While painting long deliberate strokes of pink paint, I daydreamed myself into a princess. I didn't notice that Nog had resumed his story until he said, "I like to think that Knobby was on an *immram*."

"A what?"

"*Immram*, an old Irish word for a mystical journey. A pilgrimage to find the meaning of life."

"Didn't you say that's what a labyrinth is?"

"Why, yes. I hadn't thought about that. Now you've taught me something, Bonnie. An *immram* is like a labyrinth, except it's in a boat. On the open seas. There are lots of versions, but I like the one about Saint Brendan. You know, I'm named for him. Some even say he discovered America, a thousand years before Columbus. Anyway, his story is based on an even older one. That of Máel Dúin, who went on a long voyage, seeking revenge for his father's murder."

Revenge? I knew a few things about revenge. I wanted revenge against everyone who upended my life. That reminded me of Baylar. Before I could bring that up, Nog continued.

"Instead, Brendan found forgiveness. His father's death gave meaning to his life. That's what God told Brendan, too. Be brave. Go on living no matter how great the loss. Teach others to forgive. He was free to live." That reminded me of what Porter, the guy on the train, said. "Finding a meaning to life. That's the purpose of an *immram*. Mine led me here, where I finally found meaning. Same thing with Knobby."

"How do you know that Knobby found meaning? Have you talked to this undead patriarch, or whatever he is? You're making this up."

Nog threw up both hands in self-defense, splattering paint as he did. "I tell tales, not lies. You know, I read everything. Books left in the house. Records down in the courthouse. And I listen to everything, and everyone. Several of the folks who came to Uncle Emmett's funeral told me stories about the family. So, no, I don't talk to Knobby. Nobody does. But some people, Baylar in particular, say they can see him."

We were finally getting around to Baylar, but this made no sense.

"What do you mean she can see him? With one eye?"

"Ah. You don't need eyes to have the Sight," Nog said. "That's what you need to see the Otherworld. That's what allows you to see people who have died. Your Aunt Luna, you know, she had the Sight."

Did I have the Sight? Is that how I could see the Invisibles? Is that how they introduced themselves to me? I looked skyward. Sure enough, Luna's name reappeared. Now was my chance.

"Look, Nog." He followed my gaze but didn't react to it. "Do you see it, Nog? The clouds spell out *Luna*. See?" I traced the letters L-U-N-A. He squinted and cantered his head one way and then the other.

"Can't say I do, but you certainly have a wonderful imagination." This was not imagination. This was as tangible as Cookie's crumbs. But even that sounded crazy. "Poor Luna," he sighed. "As she got older, most of the family thought she was, well, demented, when she started talking to people who weren't there. I knew she was crossing over to where everyone she had ever known really did exist."

I knew what demented meant because Dad's mother had Alzheimer's. Now I definitely did not want to tell Nog I could see the Invisibles. Everyone would think *I* was demented. I changed the subject.

"Do *you* have the Sight?"

Nog looked around, then lowered his voice to just above a whisper. "I don't. But sometimes I can almost see Knobby on a darkened porch up under the attic roof. Up there." He pointed toward the single eave under the roof. My eyes followed. "The porch is gone now. You can't see it."

But I did see it! Not only did I see the porch but also a man sitting there in front of a window. It was fuzzy, like a heat mirage rising from asphalt on a hot summer day. I adjusted my glasses and blinked the man into focus.

Nog lapsed into a faraway look and shook his head. "I swear, he sits up there, in ever-gathering darkness, his face round as the moon. I can almost see his bulbous nose, watery eyes, and oversized ears."

Holy crap! I *could* see what he was describing. A dizziness, like Jack's tornado of spinning plates, consumed my head and a weird tug seized my stomach. Folding my legs beneath me, I sank to the drop cloth. I was crazy. Demented. I had to change the subject.

"I think we're done with pink," I pointed to the chair we had just painted. "Time for orange?"

While Nog washed our brushes and opened a new can of paint, I stared at the tiny flecks of paint on my gloves, then glanced to the eave and the sky. The nonexistent man on the nonexistent porch had disappeared, like Luna's name.

"They say he sits alone." Nog didn't even look at me, wrapped up as he was in his story. He was right. Knobby sat alone. "All pale and shadowy, almost transparent, a pipe in his left hand, a half pint of tepid ale in his right, an abandoned bottle of whiskey at his feet." Right again. "And a bat on his shoulder."

"A *bat*? Was he a vampire?"

"No, no, no. Bats are messengers from the Otherworld." Okay, at least I didn't see a bat. "He's waiting for the right time to convene a *céili*."

Was I a kindred spirit that Knobby was calling to a *céili*? Were the Invisibles Knobby's clan? I looked to the welter, and it nodded as if it were one entity. I'd had enough. I stood up and jabbed my forefinger toward my uncle.

"Let me get this straight. This ghostlike Knobby is undead, but he's not a zombie. He hangs out with bats, but he's not a vampire. He drinks warm beer and waits forever for a party, so that he can cross over to an upside-down lake called the Otherworld."

"That's about it," Nog seemed quite pleased with himself. "In Irish, the Otherworld is called *Tír na nÓg.*"

"*Tear not, Nog?*"

"Close. *Tír na nÓg,* but I do like your pronunciation. It means the land of eternal youth. Sickness and death don't exist there. It's beyond this world, a parallel universe, you might say. A shimmering realm full of life, where people, music, and life come together. Where no one is hungry or thirsty, and happiness lasts forever."

"I think I'd like that, the happiness forever part." I settled down. We finished the orange chair in silence and started on the green. "The Otherworld, is that where Mom is? How do you get there? Only when you die?"

"They say you can visit, if you ride the magic horse Enbar without letting your feet touch the ground."

"Enbar? Isn't that one of the horses?" The others were Epona and Rowan. I liked grooming them, but Enbar was my favorite. He was the smallest of the three. He had a white coat and amber eyes. I loved to nuzzle his damp velvet muzzle. I swallowed hard. I knew it was only a story, but I had to ask. "Can I ride Enbar to the Otherworld—to see Mom?"

"No, my love, I wish you could. I would go with you. But even if you could, if your feet touched the ground, you would become instantly old and turn to dust."

As I looked back to where Knobby was supposed to be, I saw Anam pull into the driveway. I was beginning to understand why she would shut down this line of conversation.

"It's almost time for lunch. Let's finish this chair, eat, and then do the second coats." He spread out the freshly cleaned brushes and winked at me. "This stays between us."

Baylar's comment would have to wait, yet again.

8

The Welter

From my welter of Invisibles emerged seventeen individual ghosts. They often showed up when I went into Tory Island with Nog, like when I went with him to Hermit's Butcher Shop.

The shopkeeper reminded me of a brown-haired Santa Claus with his bushy mustache, beard, and twinkling eyes. Santa Hermit. I smiled, despite myself. The butcher's belly jiggled like jelly when he clapped Nog on the shoulder and grasped his hand.

"Ha. That wandering Angus of yours was sniffing around here this morning. Couldn't resist giving him some scraps. And here's some bones for when he finally shows up at home." He turned and retrieved a few neatly wrapped white packages. "Now, for Miss Anamary Cara, fillets of fresh trout, a whole chicken, and a wheel of brie. And for you, Nog, sausage. I made it yesterday. Try a pound. On me."

While they talked about the weather (it might snow), recipes (stuff the chicken with sausage and apples), and village news (Joy's nephew was looking for work), I looked around at fig preserves, French pâtés, and cookbooks. It reminded me of a store in the city where Dad used to get fancy food and wine as gifts for his clients. I remembered when Erin and I were nine, we went there and after seeing all the meat lined up in display cases, we decided to become vegans. It took about two days for me to realize that I couldn't resist hot dogs and ice cream. I wondered if Erin stuck with it. She was always so much more committed than I was.

"So, Bonnie," Hermit's voice returned me to the present. "What do you think of Tory Island?" When I shrugged, he suggested that I give it some time to grow on me. *Like mold*, I thought, and returned to the shelves. "Not really mold." Hermit's voice startled me. Had he been reading my mind? No, he was simply showing Nog the outside layer of a cheese wheel, which he had explained was not really mold at all. "It's the rind. That's where the ripening process starts. It's what gives each cheese its distinctive flavor."

Suddenly, two shadows appeared next to Hermit, leaning into the explanation. I recognized Tory in his teal-colored hat. "I've made a little rhyme for you, about your Uncle Seamus." He pointed to his companion, who looked like a Cheesehead in an oversized orange plaid beret—a tam. "Since he likes cheese and I like poems, it will help you name us."

Hermit and Nog were so engrossed in cheese rinds that they didn't notice me staring at Tory as he recited his verse.

When you try to name us
Be brave. And be courageous,
Even, I might say, be outrageous.
Don't be scared, and please don't blame us
Or think that we're some ignoramuses—
We're the great, we're the famous
Ancestors. Celebrate us!
Remember the names are Tory and Seamus.

Hermit mistook my gaping mouth for hunger and offered me a chunk of cheese. I shook my head as the Invisibles dissolved. Of course, they hitched a ride home, bringing with them the powerful aroma of aged cheddar.

Then there was Mamie. She mooed her name the first time we stopped at Mountainside Dairy. While I knew that milk came from cows, I didn't really know what that meant until we visited the dairy.

What an operation! Nog, of course, turned it into a lesson. The cows, he said, were Jerseys, meaning they came from the British island of Jersey. And how they got milked was nothing like a picture I had in an old book of a girl sitting next to a cow squirting milk from the cow's udders into a bucket. These cows were milked by machine, with suction cups attached to their udders. After only a few minutes, they returned to graze in a huge pasture and make more milk.

The milk they produced was yellow, not white. Nog said that was because of the high butterfat content. Anam raved about the fresh butter. Nog liked the cream to make ice cream, and I loved it for everything. It tasted so much better than milk at home. Nog said that's the difference between factory-made and straight from the cow.

Angus often showed up to scrounge any spillage he could get his tongue on, and the staff gave him little treats as well. They dressed like tacky cowhands and frumpy dairymaids with checkered scarves and straw hats. Their costumes reminded me of clowns, which creeped me out, because as a kid, I was afraid of them.

"*I'm M-A-A-A-M-M-I-E. M-o-o-o-o-v-e over.*" Her soft voice bawled in my ear while Nog placed his order one afternoon. I sidled closer to my uncle, who mistook my sidestep as shyness. He responded by wrapping a protective arm around my shoulders. I wished I could have told him it was Aunt Mamie that made me move closer, not my childish fear of clowns.

Mamie looked like butter—creamy yellow, soft, and kind of gooey around the edges. She often showed up with Cookie—they went together like milk and cookies!

One day, Anam came with us on errands so that she could stop at the Mill Shops to buy more yarn. The wool shop was named the Yin and Yang. Its logo was the tai chi symbol, in which a black comma with a white dot chases a white comma with a black dot.

"Isn't that clever?" Anam explained that the shopkeeper, Martha, was a shepherd and a weaver. "She keeps a black flock around back and a white one on the side. I call the shop the Ys, short for yin and yang."

"I call it the *EEss*," Nog broke in. "Like the legendary city of Ys, which is spelled Y-s but is pronounced EEss. It sank into the sea and turned the king's daughter into a mermaid."

"I like mermaids," I said, so I listened.

"Well, then, remember Clíona?"

"Yes, the church."

"Correct. Sometimes Clíona appears as a mermaid. Sometimes as a fairy, witch, or banshee." When Nog said *banshee*, Anam frowned. "But that's beside the point. Some say that one day Ys will rise from the sea, and when it does, the first person who hears the sound of the bell will become the new ruler. I like to think that if the bell rings at Clíona Church, it will announce the new head of Knobby's clan."

Anam rolled her eyes and proceeded to browse the skeins of wool. Martha had dyed some white wool into a rainbow of colors. While they talked about skeins and weights, another Invisible tangled her name cleverly across the counter with crimson yarn. *T-E-S-S*. I looked around and saw a stringy shadow with a bit of a reddish glow to her shimmer. She followed us back to the van, which I noticed was getting crowded, even though the Invisibles didn't really take up any room.

"What the yin and yang mean," Nog said as we headed home, "is that there is always an opposite meaning to everything. In everything good, there is a seed of evil. In everything evil, there is a seed of good. Like the Old Mill itself. Think about it. Mills are magic." I thought they were dingy. "They grind something old, like wheat or trees, into something new, like flour or lumber, to make something different, like bread or houses. They'll even grind your grudges into forgiveness."

I had a lot of grudges. Dad for leaving Mom and me. The truck driver for killing Mom. Dad for marrying Deb-Horror. Deb-Horror for making me move. Benjy for crying. The misfits at school for getting me in trouble. The teachers for calling me socially awkward. Anam for having me do so much cleaning. Nog for not telling me about Baylar. And of course, Baylar. I wasn't ready to give up any of my resentments—why would I? I nursed them like they were a pretty string of worry beads.

"It's just a story, you know," Nog said, as if he could read my thoughts. "To help you let go of negative thoughts. Of course, if you don't want to grind your grudges, you can slay them. Just stop by the ironsmith. He'll forge you some weapons so strong you can smash them to smithereens, as if they were dragons or demons."

Maybe I could get the ironsmith to make me something to slay Baylar, or armor to defend myself against her. I usually avoided the hag like a hornets' nest. But I went with Nog the day he picked up Anam's coat rack. While I was moving the seats in the rear of the van so that the rack would fit, Baylar tried to catch my attention by coughing and gesturing toward me with her broom. But I kept my head down, out of direct contact with her evil eye.

Then she hissed at me—hissed, like a cat. That's when another Invisible showed up like an unseen wall between her and me. He steered me to the front of the van with his strong shoulders and ushered me into the passenger seat. Rather than telling me his name, he just sat next to me—on the front seat—like a bodyguard. With a long face and neck, and a mop of hair hanging from his forehead, he looked like a chestnut horse.

Later, when we got home and put the coat rack in the barn with the other old furniture, the Invisible mimicked the sound that horses make and whinnied his name: *P-A-D-D-Y*. That was easy to remember. Nog called the area where we kept the horses a paddock.

Arthur showed up at the old cemetery, where—against my objections—Nog insisted on showing me Uncle Emmett's grave. Encircled by a weathered iron fence, the bleak collection of headstones overlooked the lake. At the main gate was an elegant statue of a woman whose body arced out of a tree trunk. I preferred to look at her, and not the old graves that Nog liked. With one branchlike arm reaching toward the sky, she stretched her neck up and toward the lake. The palm of the other hand was empty, but facing upward as if it once held something valuable. Her face was so eroded that she had only the hint of eyes and lips. An empty water fountain surrounded her feet. Beneath the statue were carved the letters *N-U-C-A*.

"What's Nuca?" I asked.

"Old Romanian family. From Transylvania."

"Transylvania? Like Dracula?" I clapped my hands over my eyes. "So, there are vampires here? Along with undead specters, bats, and spirit hounds? Of course!"

"Oh no, no, no. Long, long before Transylvania was associated with Dracula, it was a center of Celtic culture. I like to think of Nuca as a druid, a Celtic princess."

Another princess! I imagined her empty hand held a crystal ball. Perhaps she had seen such terrible things that tears erased her eyes and created the empty fountain at her feet; or perhaps the fountain poured forth happy fortunes. Before I could think about it any further, Nog pointed to Uncle

Emmett's grave a row behind her. Next to it were two headstones that were so old, nothing remained except the names Dobbin and Arthur.

I already knew Dobbin, but I started to point out Arthur. They were the invisible twin undertakers, but Nog thought I was pointing to real people studying the old grave markers.

"Photographers and genealogy buffs," he said. "They're always coming here. The former to record the living," Nog said, pointing to a man taking a picture of a child playing on a stone fox. "The latter, the dead. See that woman rubbing a headstone?" I did, fascinated that her black crayon transferred the marking of a winged cherub with its lifelike eyes onto white paper. "You'll see a lot of tourists this summer doing just that. Cemetery headstones hold a lot of information for genealogists."

On another trip, I encountered Jeanne. She hung out at the Rainbow Stream, where I often browsed books for magic spells that might help me understand the Invisibles, find some real friends, or prevent Anam from finding things to do. That was hopeless. There never were any kids my age there, just toddlers with their mothers. Jeanne blended into the crowd one day during storytelling hour, spelling her name with colorful alphabet blocks the children had left lying around. I remembered that she liked to read to children.

But of all the Invisibles, it was Kelty who was the most dramatic.

Nog had dropped Anam and me at the Crystal Keep while he ran errands. It was the first time we'd been back here since the day I arrived. It was a blustery day, so we hurried inside. Anam wanted to get some beads to make some lamp pulls. I wanted to check out everything, but especially the vials in the back.

Tiny brass bells jingled as we opened the door. The howling wind tore it from Anam's hand, causing the bells to clang. She struggled to pull it closed behind us. But once we were inside, bling shot in every direction. Everything twinkled, even the owner, Glenda. She appeared from a back room, carrying a box of trinkets and charms. With white braids coiled about her head and a snowy-feather scarf edged in seed pearls draped across her shoulders, she reminded me of Glinda, the good witch, in *The Wizard of Oz*, only older with almond-shaped eyes and tawny skin. I liked her immediately, unlike Baylar, who reminded me of Bastinda, the wicked witch.

Rows and rows of beads and stones, from amethyst to zircon, from the Arctic Circle to Zambia, crammed themselves into the tiny shop. There was even a real crystal ball that I imagined must have belonged to Nuca. I tiptoed my way up and down each aisle, fingering the cool beads that begged me to string them into jewelry, while Anam chatted with Glenda. Silver findings, gold clasps, and copper links promised to secure the baubles into treasures that I would drape around my neck, through my hair, from my ears, and around my arms. I touched my wrist where once I wore a friendship bracelet—it matched one that Erin had. We made them a few years ago when we discovered a bead shop in the city. I couldn't remember when I stopped wearing it, or what happened to it.

Against the back wall was the display case of brilliantly colored vials embellished with tiny gemstones. First, I looked around to see if there were any Invisibles back here. There weren't, though I was pretty sure I had seen one the day I arrived. With a mere pane of glass separating me from the exquisite collection, I examined each one, imagining which magic potion I would concoct for it.

Then I saw it—the object that would change everything. A pale blue crystal ampule. Its miniature facets refracted light into tiny rainbows. Wrapped in a fine silver filigree, it was capped with an aquamarine stone. Maybe I could fill it with a concoction that would make me beautiful and popular. It was only as big as my thumb, but I knew I had to have it.

In the midst of my rapture, Anam called to me—once, twice, thrice. "Time to go, Bonnie. Time to go." As I reluctantly stepped toward her and away from the vial, a gust of wind blew open the door to the shop, sending its little bells clanging like a fire alarm. The wind scooped beads and baubles into a kaleidoscope of turquoise, rose quartz, and pearls. It slammed into the display case in the back, shattering the glass and knocking the delicate vials in all directions.

Frozen with fear and surrounded by glass shards and beads, all the crashing and clanging got stuck in my head. I cradled my head in my arms and sunk to my knees. One high-pitched shriek rose above the wind, the glass, and the door chimes. I thought it was Anam. It wasn't. It was me. But Anam was screaming, too. She looked like that famous painting, *The Scream,* with her hands smeared against her face.

While yanking the door shut, Glenda kept yelling like she was a voice of reason far, far away. "You're okay. You're okay, Bonnie. But don't move. You're surrounded by glass. Anamary Cara, she's okay. Don't either of you move. Let me get a broom." She practically flew toward me like a good witch.

I was shaking so bad, I couldn't have moved even if I wanted to. I looked up, I looked around, and I looked down. There, on the floor leaning against my knee, was the blue vial. Without thinking, I bent over and picked it up. I was about to drop it in my pocket when a shadowy hand guided my palm upward toward Glenda, who was sweeping a clear path in my direction.

It doesn't belong to you, a woman's voice tinkled in my ear, distinct above the roar. Then she clearly added, *Yet.* I spun around and saw an aquamarine shadow over my right shoulder. Into my left ear she said, *Kelty.* Before I could react,

Glenda wrapped her arms around me.

"My dear girl!" She released me, checked me for any cuts, and swept the broken glass off of my jacket and out of my hair. Then she spotted the vial in my hand. "I'm so glad that you found this one. It's quite old, quite valuable. They say it holds a magic potion. It must be true since you're not hurt." Then she guided me back to the front of the store, where Anam hugged life back into me.

"Let's go next door to the Rainbow Stream and wait for Nog there," she said, smoothing my hair, her mouth still agape. "I thought you had ... that I had ... lost you."

I opened my mouth, but nothing came out. Anam probably thought I was stunned by the explosion. It wasn't that at all. Kelty was hovering behind Anam. She knew I was about to steal the vial. She stopped me, saying it wasn't mine—yet.

9

BAYLAR'S CURSE

A few days after my encounter with Kelty, Anam headed for New Grange on business. I had finished breakfast and was cleaning up the kitchen when Nog came in and helped me load the dishwasher and wipe down the counters.

"Looks like my lovely wife has left us with chores—beginning with cleaning the bureaus and closets in the guest rooms upstairs. She'll be gone all day. So how 'bout we do them together."

"Okay." I hesitated as the house creaked its *tap, tap, tap.* "But before we do, tell me about Baylar. Please?" I knew I had hit a nerve because he wouldn't look at me, choosing instead to study his fingernails. "Why did she say that I'm the reason Mom died? When I asked you last week, you said I needed to know about Knobby to understand her. So, you told me about Knobby. Now, Baylar. How could I have been the reason Mom died? I really need to know."

"Have a seat here, Bon." He scooted into the nook and patted the seat next to him. Taking a deep breath, he clamped his hands over mine and looked me square in the eye. "Of course, you didn't cause your mom's death." He took another deep breath and spoke slowly, hesitating between words. "Here's what happened. I'm going to tell it to you straight. On the day your mom died, your dad was supposed to take you to the zoo, so she could go shopping with Anam. But he had to cancel at the last minute, some meeting came up."

"Yeah," I tsked. "Of course, he had to cancel."

Nog smiled, but his face wasn't into it. "When you heard you weren't going to the zoo, you threw a temper tantrum. You really knew how to do that!" I still do. I thought about the hole I kicked in the wall at home. "Anyway, your mother tried calling me, to see if I could take you to the zoo, but I was in the library with my phone turned off. When she couldn't reach me, she called your aunt to cancel their plans. Anam said to bring you along, they would do something else. But since you really wanted to go to the zoo, it took a while to get you settled down and into the car ..."

His voice trailed off. His gaze did, too, landing somewhere beyond the window. A few seconds passed before he sniffled, sat up straight, cleared his throat, and looked directly at me. "Maybe she was distracted, or angry at your dad. But as she pulled onto the highway, she texted Anam to tell her she was on her way. All it took was a few seconds for her to look away, but that's all it takes. She was texting and driving. That's when the truck slammed into the car."

It took about five seconds for that last sentence to sink in. Tears burned my throat, but didn't escape to my eyes. "I thought ... Dad said ... everyone said ... " Nothing made sense. "What about the truck driver? I thought it was *his* fault."

Nog never let go of my hands or his gaze into my eyes. "The police investigated it thoroughly. All the evidence showed that your mom drove right in front of him. Witnesses said he tried to stop. Apparently, your mother never saw him coming."

I yanked my hands from his, and pressed them against my

head to keep it from exploding. "So, so my tantrum ..." My voice trembled into a quake. "Made Mom late ...." Then, in the horror of recognizing a truth that had been withheld from me all this time, my words and my heart shattered like the glass at the Keep. I squeezed my eyes shut against the bright white rage surrounding me. I gulped and forced myself to speak the unspeakable. "So, I really did ..."

"No!" Nog gently retrieved one shaking hand and then the other from my head. It didn't explode, but I thought my heart might. Once again, he held my hands firmly in his and locked my wild eyes into his calm ones. "No, no, no. You were just a baby, a little girl. Your mother was the adult. She made a big, big mistake. You did nothing wrong."

"Why didn't Dad tell me this? Why didn't you or Anam, or anyone ever tell me? Why was it a secret? Is there anything else I should know?" I yanked my hands away from his. Another grudge—this one against the whole family—planted itself in my heart.

"I guess we were all trying to protect you, Bonnie. It was just easier to say that she was hit by a truck. It absolved us all of any blame. See, we all felt responsible in a different way. Your dad because you were supposed to be with him. Me because I had turned off my phone. Anam because your mother was texting her when it happened." Nog's eyes filled with tears. He grabbed a handkerchief from his pocket and began to blot his eyes and blow his nose. It looked a lot like Knobby's, I realized as I waited for him to continue.

"Anam knew immediately that something had happened. When your mom didn't respond to her text or phone calls, she got frantic. She called 9-1-1. You know your aunt. She gets herself full of the what-ifs, and always sees the negative. That's why she says cellphones are dangerous." Well, that made sense, in a crazy way. "It was your mother who made a tragic mistake. We all had to come to terms with it, that it wasn't our fault. And certainly not yours. Not one bit of it."

The shimmering welter that assembled in the portal seemed to shake its collective head and weep in sympathy. I thought of telling Nog about them, but my heart was full of Mom. My uncle handed me a napkin to catch the tears that spilled from my eyes. I didn't even realize I was crying. "But why, why did Baylar say that?"

"Baylar never got over your mother's death. Ever since we were kids, she loved playing with her, babysitting her. I think Baylar even taught her to swim." The mismatch of that old witch playing with Mom must have shown on my face. "She's only a few years older than me, you know," Nog explained. "She insisted that your mom was special, destined for greatness. Everyone thought the attraction was a little odd, but harmless. After all, we all loved your mother. She was such a cute little girl."

Nog closed his eyes, obviously reconstructing Mom as a child. I did too, from my pictures. This all seemed very unfair. The house *tap-tapped*, the water hissed.

"Anyway, Baylar had it in her head—still does, apparently—that your mother was destined to take Knobby's place as head of the clan—its matriarch—once she learned all the stories and songs."

"Mom? Take Knobby's place?" An absurd image of her sitting in the eave with a pipe and a beer popped into my head. "No way."

"I guess that's how your mom felt, too. She wasn't interested in the legends. And as she got older, she wasn't interested in Baylar, either. Baylar didn't like that." We sat in silence for a few minutes, wiping our eyes and staring out the window. "Your mom was a beautiful, vivacious young woman, who loved living in the city. Not here. I wished you had known her."

Me too, admitting to myself for the first time that being

here with Nog and Anam allowed me to learn more about Mom than I would ever get from Dad. Or anyone else. These were the people who knew her best. Being around them gave me more of a sense of who I was.

I stared out the window for I don't know how long. It wasn't just the truck driver, or Dad, or Nog, or Anam. It was also me. It was my bad temper that set the ball rolling. *Companion Moon,* I exhaled, realizing I had been holding my breath. *Mom, I really need you now.* I missed her more than ever.

"Baylar told everyone that Knobby was waiting for your mom to return to Tory Island," Nog said, bringing me back to the kitchen. "But when she met your father, they fell in love, and did all the things young people in love are supposed to do. Got married. Had you." He reached for my hand and squeezed it. "She never came back. Baylar blamed your father for taking her away. Said he wasn't good enough for her. Baylar's prejudiced, you know. Not because your dad's Black, but that he isn't Irish. Can you imagine that? That he's not Irish! Even though his last name is. She doesn't realize that family and culture transcend race and nationality."

Nog paused for a minute before changing the subject. "Sometimes bad things just happen, Bonnie. But good things happen, too. While we were grief-stricken about your mother, we were elated, blessed really, that you weren't hurt. Your mom strapped you in right."

He squeezed my hands again and we just sat there for a few minutes. Then he continued.

"Now, the other thing about Baylar is that she has a second or third cousin, once- or twice-removed—a boy, Tony. Lives out in the Midwest. She thinks that since your mom died, Tony should take Knobby's place as head of the clan. So, I think she sees you as a threat to Tony. She wants you to leave and not come back."

I thought my head was going to burst. *I* was a *threat* to a kid I never met? Could this get any more bizarre?

"What's with her eye?" I demanded. "And don't tell me bats ate it."

"Ha! One story is that she's named after an old Irish tyrant whose evil eye can destroy a person. Now, I don't believe the evil eye bit." I did, recalling the icy-hot blasts she directed at me on that first day. "Honest truth, though, I don't know. It's been patched for as long as I've known her, which is practically my whole life. Probably a childhood injury. She had a tough life. No siblings. Father was an alcoholic and abandoned his family. Mother worked two jobs and died young. Baylar's a bit strange, but I think she's just misunderstood." It was so like Nog to give her the benefit of doubt.

I almost—almost—felt sorry for her.

"Tell you what, Bonnie. How about a walk down the labyrinth? That will soothe your soul." I bobbed my head. We layered on parkas, hats, and boots for a day that threatened snow. "In honor of your mom, let's play hooky. No chores today. Your Anam will understand."

* * *

As we walked to the lake, Nog filled in a lot of blanks. Like I knew that Mom and Anam were best friends, but he filled in the *forever* part. Their mothers were best friends who lived next door to each other and had their baby girls days apart.

The girls did everything together, like me and Erin. One day, they covered each other in peanut butter. Another, they stuck stones in their noses to look like monsters, only Mom's got stuck and had to be removed at the hospital. In high school, they played hooky to spend a day at the beach and got caught only because of bad sunburns. A few years after that, Mom crashed Anam's new car when they decided at the last minute to go to a concert.

"I guess she wasn't a very good driver." In making a joke, I was beginning to realize that Mom wasn't perfect. In fact, during that hour-long walk, Mom was turning into a real person, not an idealized version of who I wanted her to be.

"Companion Moon," I said, suddenly feeling very close to her.

"Companion Moon," Nog repeated.

We headed back in silence. I had a lot to absorb. When I looked up to the top eave of the house where Knobby hung out, I imagined Mom there with a pipe and a beer. That absurd thought prompted a question.

"Hey, Nog, are you going to be the next Knobby?"

He also looked at the eave and shook his head. "No, my love. That person will have the Sight, and I don't have the Sight." Cold bit into our faces and wind howled at our backs. "But I do have the appetite, and the chill in my bones." He laughed at his own joke. "Let's hurry along and have some lunch by the fire."

Nog threw together a hearty stew from leftovers while I crawled around the hearth, as Anam had taught me, to get the fire going. As I sliced some bread and cheese unbidden, I realized I was in tune with the daily rhythm here. Nog ladled lunch into sturdy earthenware bowls that looked like they were a hundred years old. Cupping one between my hands, I invited the aroma and steaminess into my heart. I imagined Mom sitting here like this when she was a girl, and I felt like she was right there beside me. Nog and I slurped in quietude for a few minutes with the house sounding its *tap, tap, tap*.

"Nog," I broke the silence, "if you're not the new patriarch, who is?"

"Ah, great question. I don't know. It's up to Knobby. Here's what will happen, though, when he decides." Nog put down his bowl and cleared his throat. "Close your eyes and picture this."

The promise of a story drew Angus, the cats, and the welter into our circle. The house *tap tapped*. The water hissed.

"It is a bright and cloudless night. A full moon is rising. Everything is quiet—*dead* quiet, you might say." Nog coughed to emphasize his pun. "Knobby is sitting under the eave like alabaster, pale and translucent ..."

Yep. That's what I'd seen, although it no longer seemed scary. Even with my eyes closed, I could sense my uncle waving his hands.

"He's in suspended animation," Nog said, his voice rising and falling as he got into the act. "He's neither cold nor hot, neither conscious nor unconscious. His realm is endless twilight—the gloaming, I call it—where he waits for the full moon to bloom in his lake."

"Your lake."

"Our lake." I knew Nog's smile without looking. "Now imagine a flutter breaking the icy silence." I didn't have to imagine anything—a rustle through the kitchen curtains raised the hair on my neck, exactly like when I felt the first Invisible in the van. "A bat alights on Knobby's shoulder ..."

"Stop," I balked. I was in no mood for this. "Why is it always bats?"

"Ha! They are so misunderstood," he said, mumbling to himself more than to me. "Bats are essential to this legend. They are guardians of the night, the symbol of family ties, messengers from the Otherworld. They communicate with Knobby in wordless whispers when they perch on his shoulder. That's what gave rise to the legend that bats ate his hair." He rubbed his own bald head.

"Enough, Nog." I clapped my hands around my ears.

"*You're* the one who asked *me* to tell *you* about Knobby choosing his successor."

"Then get on with the story."

Nog described Nana, saying she would bustle about,

tamping tobacco into Knobby's pipe. It sounded like the one in the office, where the computer was. Sometimes, when I was doing my lessons, I would run my thumb across the pipe's smooth stem that leaned slightly forward from a finger-worn shank.

"You're making this up, Nog. There's no way you know what they said and did."

"Well, okay, I'm embellishing the story a little. But this is how the legend goes. Nana would hand the pipe to Knobby with a wink and a curtsy. Then she'd fill his mug with beer and his soul with love. But she's gone now. Unlike Knobby, she crossed over eons ago. With her gone, the cold pipe smolders in his memory, never to be extinguished, never to be relit. Like the beer. It will never be consumed, his thirst never quenched. Thus, he sits, alone, ever hidden from mortal view."

That last line got me a little concerned since he wasn't hidden from my view. I was tempted to tell Nog that, but the Invisibles drew closer. *Shhh*, they warned. *Don't say you can see Knobby.* Kelty's pale blue shimmered out of the welter and cautioned, *Not yet.*

"Not yet?" This was the second time she had used those words. "Then when?"

Nog stopped, thinking that I was talking to him. Realizing I had to be careful talking to an Invisible when somebody was around, I opened my eyes and backtracked.

"I meant not yet smoking or drinking. Until when?" I was proud of my quick recovery. "When will he not be hidden from mortal view? And what, exactly, do you mean by mortal view?" I knew that mortal meant human, and since I could see Knobby, did that make me non-human? That would explain why I didn't fit in anywhere.

"Eh, that mere human eyes cannot penetrate the haze that clouds him from our view." Maybe I had superpower eyes. I adjusted my glasses a bit and the welter nodded in a sweeping breeze that rumpled the curtains, which, in turn, ruffled Nog's attention. Clicking his fingers to and fro in front of his semi-closed eyes, Nog retraced his narration to the point of digression.

"Where was I? Oh yes. Perched alone in the eave, he wonders if it might be time to become an ancestor. Give up the ghost, so to speak. But that would be hard for a hero."

Knobby didn't look like a hero to me. He looked like a skinny old man.

"Back in the day," Nog continued, always seeming to know what I was thinking, "he was a fierce warrior, back before he laid down his shillelagh." He paused. "*Shuh-LAY-lee*," he pronounced it. Let me explain that."

He said that some people think a shillelagh is a walking stick. Grabbing a broom by the hearth, he stood as tall as his five-foot, 10-inch frame would allow.

"Unlike this broom, Knobby's shillelagh was a symbol of power, handmade from blackthorn, which the Irish call the Chieftain Tree." In the afternoon light, he did look a little like his famed ancestor. He stroked the broom's length like he might pet Angus.

"Blackthorn's magical, you know. Its roots, fruits, bark, and sap are used to make medicines and potions to protect the user as well as cast spells on the enemy."

While I pondered blackthorn as a potion ingredient for my coveted crystal vial, Nog turned the broom bristles up. "The top, the knob, was really the bottom, the root." Grasping the broom and using the bristles for leverage, he swung his make-believe shillelagh in a wide figure-eight. My chin dropped and my eyes widened as I watched my uncle, armed with a broom, do battle against some unseen enemy. The welter fell back in pretended fright, while I struggled not to laugh. "This knobby limb is how Knobby got his name. The man and his shillelagh, after all, were one and the same."

Holding the broom out in front of his chest, Nog danced an odd little jig. He raised his make-believe shillelagh upward with his right hand while jabbing his left forward and scissor-stepping his feet.

"Now, when Knobby chooses his successor, he'll use his shillelagh to convene a *céilí* with the following incantation." His voice dropped an octave and doubled in decibels as he intoned, "The spirits above are the spirits divine. The spirits below are the spirits of wine! *Céad míle fáilte!*"

I stopped breathing, the house stopped *tap tapping*, and the welter held its collective breath. Finally, the house creaked, the welter exhaled, and I managed to find my voice.

"What?"

"*Céad míle fáilte.*" He pronounced it slowly for me. "*Kayd mi-lə FULT-chə.* It's a blessing. It means a hundred thousand welcomes. It's also like saying abracadabra. It's magic."

Nog pointed to a needlepoint tapestry hanging by the front door. I could see it from where I sat. Obviously, I'd noticed it before. I knew that Aunt Luna had made it, but I was confused.

"What does that thing by the door have to do with Knobby?"

"*Céad míle fáilte.* That's how Knobby will convene a *céilí* while the Strawberry Moon rises. A hundred thousand ancestors—and one mortal successor—will suddenly appear."

"Under the eave? With a hundred thousand ancestors—and one mortal? You're weird, Nog."

"Actually, the *céilí* is in the attic, not under the eave." Of course. Where the undead live. Another reason not to go there. I shook my head. "And yes," he said, stamping his make-believe shillelagh on the floor, "a hundred thousand ancestors can fit in the attic."

"No wonder Anam doesn't want you talking about all this."

"Speaking of which, let's fix a nice dinner for her. She'll be home soon. We can tell her what we talked about today—the accident, I mean. She'll be relieved to have everything out in the open. She'll have even more stories about your mom."

I was glad to be done with Nog's stories for now. Anam had a few tales, but it wasn't the words that stuck with me. It was what she did when she came home an hour later, loaded down with shopping bags.

"What am I missing?" Anam asked, when she noticed we had set the table for a candlelit dinner. "What have you two been up to?" She looked from Nog to me. Nog took both her hands in his.

"We had a long talk about Maura. Maura's death." After a long second, she dropped Nog's hands and reached over for mine. She drew me into an embrace that was different from any I could remember in my whole life. Not like Dad's and certainly not Deborrah's. Anam didn't hug me, she held me. It reminded me of the protective way I held Benjy when he was born. It reminded me of Momma. Momma—I hadn't called my mother that in years. Even though it was babyish, it was what I called her in my heart. I felt her in Anam's arms. In that instant, for the first time that I could remember, I let someone hold me. My *soul friend* held me. And I held her back.

That night, long after a dinner that included lots of stories about Mom and Anam, I retrieved the ring. It used to be so big that I would slip it on my thumb. But that night, it fit neatly on my left ring finger. Securing it within my folded hands and turning it inward so I could feel the cool gemstone against my palm, I sat on the moonlit window seat and cradled the treasure between my chin and chest.

With head bent and eyes closed, I tried to make sense of everything I'd learned that day. I laughed when I pictured Mom and Anam covered in peanut butter, then cried when I came back to Baylar. Her words had pierced my heart with fire. I held the ring closer, if that was even possible. Did I screw up Knobby's plan to name Mom the new family ruler? What would happen next? I didn't want to prevent Knobby from crossing over. But I didn't want to deal with some kid named Tony, either. And my only weapon was a broom, a make-believe shillelagh?

When I opened my eyes, the welter fluttered into view, not as a jumbled mess, but as individual Invisibles, most of whom I could now identify by name. How did this happen? I had been ghosted by every single friend I had ever known, and now I had ghost friends.

The newest one was Maggie. I knew her instantly because she looked like the snake on my treasure box. She was elegant and slender, with a burgundy stripe down her back and a white forelock directly above her forehead. Just like the snake on my treasure box.

10

a Basket
of Woe

Just as January had slipped into February, February
pushed into March with mind-numbing slowness.

Along with never-ending chores was a mountain of
school-work. Sometimes they overlapped, like with Nog's
furniture lessons and a project on my ancestors. Or Anam
teaching me basic bookkeeping using Excel. That counted for
math and computer skills.

As much as I liked going to school this way, I missed other
kids. And I missed not having the digital technology to do
research, create graphics, or do my reports as videos.

Like for my geography project on ice ages, glaciers, and
lakes. What I really wanted to do was a video blog—a vlog. I
had started learning videography at my old school. Instead of
writing my report, I wanted to shoot a video of me explaining
how 10,000 years ago, glaciers from the last ice age carved out
valleys that filled with water when the ice began to melt. At
that point, I'd gesture to a panoramic view of the lake and cut
to an illustration of the percentage of the world covered by
glaciers. I'd animate it to show the glaciers receding. Then I
would cut back to present time and explain how the presence

of glaciers thousands of years ago affected plants and animals today. Dad always said that pictures are worth a thousand words.

But my complaints about old technology fell on deaf ears.

We kept a journal of my lessons and projects, which Nog sent off to the teacher who coordinated my homeschooling. I went from failing everything to straight As.

We watched old movies on DVDs. Emphasis on old. No streaming. No Netflix. Sometimes Nog would put music on an old record player. "Stereo system," he called it. He liked jazz, Anam liked classical. That's when she would crochet afghans. She tried to teach me, but we both got very frustrated. So, I made beaded necklaces. One night, I dropped all the beads and they scattered across the parlor. I started to cry.

"Let me help you," Anam said. "It's not that big a deal." But it was. It was like everyone I ever knew were beads on the broken necklace. Even if I could gather them all up, they'd never be restrung in the same way. And there were always the missing ones—Mom, Erin, Jenny, Sara. Would I ever find Erin? Even if we could restring our friendship, would we be the same?

I found comfort in the horses—Epona, Rowan, and Enbar—and the barn's earthy sweet smell. But cleaning it was the hardest work I'd ever done, and even stinkier than changing Benjy's diapers. After just a few days helping Nog and Anam haul out soiled hay, I understood how they had lost so much weight.

One day, after we had swept away all the cobwebs and before Nog returned with bales of new hay, Anam tilted her head way back and looked up to the rafters. She closed her eyes, clasped her hands over her heart—she did that a lot—and raised her eyes upward. She looked like a painting in the museum where she used to work. In spontaneous imitation, I did the same—without the hands over my heart. If I gazed in just the right way, would I become Anam?

That was a scary thought. So was the sudden memory of Mom, Anam, and I sitting around a table eating ice cream. I must have been four. How could I remember that? But it wasn't really remembering. It was more like that déjà vu episode the night I arrived. I just saw it.

"When I grow up," I had said, putting my spoon down and looking directly at Anam, "I want to be just like you. I used to think I wanted to be like Momma, but now I want to be you."

"Me?" she said. "Why on earth would you want to be like me?"

"'Cus you have a job, and a car, and can go anywhere you want. And you bought me ice cream."

Mom laughed as she wrapped me in her arms and kissed my freckles. "Why don't you want to be you?"

I didn't have an answer then, and I didn't have one now. But as I stood in the barn, I wrapped my arms around myself, almost feeling my mother's embrace, like when Anam held me a few weeks ago. I no longer wanted to be my aunt—she reminded me too much of my stepmother. Change my clothes, comb my hair, do my chores, smile. But we did share a dislike of Baylar, even though she did like all of Baylar's old stuff. Well, not all of it.

One day, the old hag arrived with a tangle of bikes in the bed of her beat-up pickup truck. A snarl of dark shadows crowded into the cab with her. As she rumbled up the driveway, I saw Anam glaring out the kitchen window.

"What ... on ... earth?" she muttered over and over as Nog directed Baylar to dump the load by the barn. She was out the door as soon as Baylar and her wicked welter pulled away. "That woman is nothing but trouble, Nog. Now what? What are these shenanigans all about?"

"Bikes! We need bikes for guests to ride into town."

"We can't afford bikes." Anam was always counting

money. She didn't care that Nog bought the whole lot for 50 bucks. "How about you spend 50 bucks finding someone to fix the noises in the attic?" She marched back toward the kitchen without even waiting for a response.

It didn't take long for the handyman in my uncle to salvage a half dozen bikes, using the others for spare parts. He let me help paint and polish the frames, and attach new seats, baskets, and bells. I added streamers to a couple of kid-sized ones. Far from fancy, they were what Nog called "classic."

"If people want anything fancier, they'll bring their own," he figured. A bright red one fit me perfectly, so I claimed it. Even though the driveway was too muddy for me to use just yet, I asked Dad to send me my helmet.

Spring arrived on March 20, followed by Easter. When I suggested that we dye eggs, Anam and Nog got all excited. We assembled a couple dozen eggs, wax sticks, and dye. Funny, I didn't mind the vinegar at all for this project.

Nog wrote *Companion Moon* on one egg, and dyed it silver. Anam wrote *Maura* on one egg and her own name on another, then stenciled them both with bits of lace. She colored them emerald green. I scribbled my own name on an egg and dunked it in dark purple, my favorite color.

Nog then decided to honor the ancestors and wrote family names on more than a dozen eggs. He chose gold for Nana and Knobby, and we all decided that Angus needed a black one. Then he asked me what color to dye each of the others.

With that, the welter exploded into a racket of yakety yak, with favorite colors flying like bats out of a cave. "Stop!" I commanded without realizing I was talking to the Invisibles. Nog and Anam paused and looked at me. I recovered nicely. "Let me think a minute."

Luna quieted them down. She wanted sky blue. Baron, dark blue, like his sailor's outfit. Aloysius, royal blue, like a computer screen. I repeated their preferences slowly, as if I were thinking about it. Kelty, pale blue, like the vial. Dobbin and Arthur, lavender, like soap. Maggie, burgundy. Gramp, forest green. Mamie, buttery yellow. Cookie, rich chocolate. Tess, crimson. Edmund, apple red. Seamus, a deep cheddar orange. Tory, teal. Jack, violet, like the color that resulted from spinning red and blue plates. Jeanne, multicolored, like a library shelf.

"My goodness," Anam said. "What precise colors. And so many!"

I was afraid to say where they came from. I didn't want to invite questions about my sanity.

We spent hours mixing the colors to the right hues and made a giant color wheel of the dye baths, with red at the top and the warmer colors to its right, all the way around to violet on the left. We put black in the middle. Each name emerged from a dye bath like magic. And the darker the color, the more stunning the magic. We had just enough for us, the ancestors, Angus, Mo, and Willy.

When we nestled all the eggs together, they reminded me of an Invisibles' basket of yakety yak.

The next morning, we got dressed up and went to the old Clíona Church. Sitting atop the stone bell tower was the statue of an eagle, which Nog said symbolized the Otherworld because it flies so high.

The incense-infused air made me dizzy. The stained-glass windows looked like Easter eggs. Not only did they depict saints like Brendan, but also angels that looked like fairies; demons that looked like witches; and mermaids, snakes, horses, fish, and birds.

Nog made the pictures into a lesson while we waited for the Easter service to begin. He pointed to a picture of St. Brendan in a boat with so many companions that it looked like it should sink. I counted 17.

"Legend has it," he said, "that when Brendan embarked on

his mystical journey, he took 17 companions."

"Seventeen? I'd be happy with one."

The Invisibles just laughed, like a basket of yakety yak.

Nog then counted nine waves around the little boat, and said that when Clíona tried to leave the Otherworld, she was washed back with a ninth wave.

After we recited a few prayers and sang some psalms, the minister preached about finding new life. That sounded good, but I wanted my old life. At the end of the service, he asked for contributions to the fund to repair the old bells in the carillon. Afterward, villagers clumped around the snowy grounds. But it was too cold to talk much to anyone. Besides, it was mostly old people, young couples, and little babies. No kids my age.

On the way home, I thought about the minister's sermon. Finding a new life. I was stuck in a new one and missed the old one. It was all so unfair.

The Invisibles sighed like a basket of woe.

11

GhOST
GIRL

Even though the calendar said spring had arrived, the weather vacillated between outright nasty and intolerably gray. Although businesses were opening up in Tory Island, there was nothing going on. In the city, I could go to a movie, hang out with Erin, or binge-watch *High School Musical*. But not here. If things didn't change soon, I thought I'd go crazy. Maybe I'd run away. But to where? And how would I get there? I was so bored that I wanted to scream.

Then, like a miracle, a springlike morning arrived, full of fresh warmth and sunshine that dazzled off the blankets of old snow. Nog opened the windows and a soft breeze fluttered through the kitchen. We finished our spinach omelets to the chirpings of early robins. Anam seemed to have abandoned her list and Nog his stories. We simply sat there smiling, smitten with a huge case of spring fever.

"Can I go into the village?" I didn't even realize what was going to come out of my mouth until I heard the words myself. Anam and Nog just stared at me. Although we went into the village of Tory Island a few times a week, I was itching to be on my own. Dad had sent me some money that was burning a hole in my pocket. "It's a nice day and I'm caught up on my schoolwork. I'd like to go to Rainbow Stream. Get something new to read." Downloading books was frustrating here with the archaic connection. And while the Stream had a strong Wi-Fi connection, I preferred the look, feel, and smell of a paperback, rolling it back into itself to consume the story. "They're open today. It's Friday."

Anam took a deep breath. Before she could enumerate the reasons it was a bad idea, Nog saved the day. "That's a great idea! Don't you agree, My Cara?"

"Well, I'm not sure ... not sure I'm up for that."

"Oh, I don't mean for us, I mean for Bonnie." Nog turned with a wink. Anam's eyes ping-ponged from Nog to me and back like she was missing something. He put his hand over hers. "It's only a couple miles. The walk would do her good, get some fresh air. She certainly can't get lost. And it gives us a little time alone."

"Time alone?" Anam frowned at Nog. "I have to work on the budget."

Nog's heavy brow lifted with a sudden idea. "You know, you can pick up some linseed oil that I ordered from Baylar for ..." My eyes widened. No, not Baylar. Anything but Baylar. The expression on my face probably told him that was not a good idea. "Come to think of it, that might be a little awkward to carry home."

"Linseed oil?" Anam tried to wrestle the conversation back under control.

"For the attic. Baylar suggested rubbing it into the floors in the attic."

"I don't want you in the attic."

"Well then, maybe Bonnie can pick up ..." Nog arched his eyebrows and danced his eyes around the kitchen looking for an object to finish his thought.

"Thread." Anam announced. She had caved! Her shoulders

sagged just a second before she continued. "That's an excellent idea. I need to finish the curtains for the downstairs suite." She shifted her attention to me. "Bonnie, how about if you pick up a spool of navy-blue thread at Joy's. That would be a huge help. I don't have time to go into town today just for that."

"Absolutely!" Before she could change her mind, I cleared my plate and ran upstairs to pull colorful socks over my leggings and a heavy sweater over my T-shirt. It would look nice under my quilted vest. I added a scarf. Brushing my wild hair, I looked at myself in the mirror. I looked fabulous! I galloped downstairs, anxious to finally be outside and on my own.

Anam handed me a few dollars that I tucked into my pocket as I darted toward the back door. Nog called it the vestibule because it was more like a room than a door. The hand-hewn oak door opened to the expanse of what would soon be lawns, gardens, and pathways to the barn and lake. Framing it was the huge coat rack from Four Fences where everything a guest could want for a day's excursion was neatly arranged.

"Hats, maps, books, and sprays; sundries, sherry, wine from berries," Nog would sing as he added accouterments to the collection. Anam often said that he obsessed. He smiled away such criticism, saying he preferred the word "prepared."

"Hat," Anam called out as I reached the door. "I don't want you getting a sunburn."

"For real? Sunburn?" Freckles maybe. Even with my father's darker skin, nothing—not even a hat—could halt their incessant march across my nose. But sunburn? I'd never had a sunburn, except once at the beach, as a little girl, the time Dad took a picture of Mom and me squinting into the sun. Not in early spring in the middle of the backwoods.

"Hat. The sun is very bright this time of year, especially reflecting off the snow."

Knowing that once Anam made up her mind, there was no talking her out of it, I gave in, resenting that I always ended up obeying. I hate hats, so I grabbed the ugliest one on the coat rack and slung it over the hair I had just brushed into fullness.

"You be careful," Anam called as I waved from the first curve in the driveway, which was so muddy that it seemed ready to suck me under. My sneakers were already wet and dirty, and I was tempted to go back and replace them with boots. But when I looked back at the house, instead of Anam's surveillance, I saw a different set of eyes—Knobby's. He was watching me from the invisible porch where he smoked his unlit pipe.

I blinked hard and looked again. He was gone. I wanted to think I had imagined it, but I knew I hadn't.

Instead of letting Knobby ruin this day of independence, I took a deep breath, yanked off my hat, and crammed it into my vest pocket. I turned my face into the fullness of the sun and blew a few cold-air clouds. I was on my own, just as I had been on the train. Free from adult company and rules. The breeze lifted my hair and my spirits. When I got to the *Companion Moon* sign, I stopped. *Pay attention,* I told Mom with a smile. *I love you.*

Beyond the driveway, the road evened out. I waved to Miss Eileen, the pink-faced, white-haired woman who ran the Fish House, Anam and Nog's favorite restaurant. She stood in an opened window, blending into the lace curtains that fluttered around her. The sign in the front was a friendly, hand-drawn salmon.

"Best restaurant around," Nog would always say. "No one ever leaves there hungry."

His other favorite restaurant was a few hundred yards ahead on the other side. The Fiery Pig, a BBQ joint. Smokey was the cocoa-skinned pit master, who smoked chicken, turkey, ducks, and ribs, but whole pigs were his specialty. He and Nog were good friends, often talking for hours about secret blends of oak and apple woods. But not today. Today was my day.

Pausing at the Old Mill, I thought, *I'll keep my grudges, thank you very much.*

When I arrived at the village, I noticed that the warm, sunny day had drawn a few people to outdoor tables at the Voyager. Kath flourished a greeting as she poured coffee for her customers. Maybe I would buy a cookie on my way home.

Bypassing Joy's—I'd get the thread on my way back—I headed straight for Rainbow Stream, where a cluster of boys and girls, all about my age, were horsing around on the sidewalk. Kids! Was today a school holiday? *Aha*, they must be playing hooky. That's what I would want to do. I fluffed my hair before I got to the doorway.

"Hi," I said.

"Hey," said one guy with longish hair and glasses. Cute, I thought. A couple of boys lifted their chins in lazy response. The girls shrugged in silence. Since none of them seemed interested in talking to me, I swallowed my loneliness and went inside, heading straight for the fantasy section.

I lost myself among eccentric beasts, mythical creatures, wizards, and witches. Looking for a new adventure, I slipped a few books in and out of their places in the stacks, inhaling their book-ness, absorbing memories of Mom reading to me. Dad always called books food for the soul.

Inside, the air was still and the room silent. Sunlight filtered through the front windows, lifting specks of dust into a protoplasm stream. It was so quiet that I could hear my own breath. So quiet that ...

"Boo!"

I screamed. The room was filled with laughter, led by the boy with long hair, the one I thought was cute. All those kids were around him, laughing at me, their taunts indistinguishable as they echoed in the otherwise empty store.

"Ghost girl!"

"Look at those glasses!"

"The better to see ghosts with, my ghoul!"

"Are you looking for books that teach you how to talk to ghosts?"

"She doesn't need to learn how to talk to them, she lives with them."

"Where she talks to bats! Don't let the bats eat your hair."

"Looks like bats live in your hair."

I wanted to disappear, to run away, to throw up. Holding up my hat, which he had grabbed from my pocket, the first boy jeered.

"A ratty hat for batty hair."

"Batty girl! Ratty girl!"

"Monster girl! Look! She's got green teeth!" I flicked my tongue over my braces and sensed the spinach stuck there. They laughed hysterically at their own stupid jokes.

"Ghost girl!" Their voices became one. "Ghost girl! Ghost girl!"

Gulping for air, I ducked my flushed face into my chest and ran out the door. I didn't remember a single thing about my mad dash home until somewhere near Mourning Stream, where I tripped, sprawling my skinny self face-first into shame and anger.

Humiliated, I looked around to make sure no one had seen me. My hands were muddied and my right knee was scraped, right through my new leggings. That's when I realized I was crying. Not just tears leaking from my eyes, but full-body sobs. I tried wiping away the tears, but I only smeared them with my dirty hands. I cried so hard that I couldn't remember how to stop.

I did remember Nog's stupid story about weapons that could smash dragons or demons to smithereens. That's what I wanted, so that I could smash those kids into nothingness.

When I got to the *Companion Moon* sign, I dropped onto the cold earth. Thoughts of Mom flooded over me. Her face, smile, hair, and scent. Sobs began anew, first as a hiccup, then as a soft peal, and finally, a tormented bawl. Was I that much of a misfit? Was I that ugly? Would I ever have friends? Would I ever belong?

After a few minutes, the wind murmured *Naannaa,* and a quiet sigh embraced me. It was smooth, like the worn stem of the pipe on Nog's desk. Comforting and comfortable, it had to be Nana, the ancestral mother who cradled me. Suddenly, I broke loose. Why was she holding me? Why was it not Mom? Wasn't Mom an ancestor? How come she wasn't an Invisible? Where was she?

"Why did you have to die?" I asked, craving answers. I looked to the sign for answers. Of course, there weren't any.

I didn't even know what death meant, but I captured a few memory bubbles and played them like scenes from a bad movie. Mom was driving. I could see her thick hair from the back seat. There was a scream of brakes and a crash of metal. Then sirens everywhere. Somebody pulled me out. I was howling. A few days later, hundreds of people I didn't know showed up for a service I didn't understand. Dad called it a funeral. The only thing I remembered was Dad holding my hand while Nog cried. Dad asked him if he believed in an afterlife.

"After life? You call this life?" Nog sobbed. "This is hell. Is there life after hell, you mean? There damned well better be."

I don't know why I remembered that, but I did wonder if this was hell. Is that why I couldn't see Mom, even though I could communicate with all the other Invisibles? Or was she in a different Otherworld? Where did I fit in? Not with Dad's replacement family. Yeah, he loved me, but he was always too busy with someone else. I shuddered, chewed my thumb, and cried harder.

I looked up at the sign again. I closed my eyes and let the sun dry my tears. Then I looked around to make sure no one was watching. I wrenched my T-shirt from under my sweater and used it to wipe my face and blow my nose. Then I stretched my socks over my knees to cover the tear.

Pay attention, I told Mom. *I need you. I really, really need you now.*

12

UNRAVELING
THREADS

"What do you mean you forgot the thread?" My aunt's anger filled the kitchen when I arrived home from the village empty-handed and hatless. "That was the reason—the only reason—I agreed to let you go to town."

"I just forgot." I pushed past her.

"Come back here." She ordered, blocking my exit. "Why is your face so red? You're sunburned! No, you're not, you're flushed. Are you all right? Did something happen? Where's your hat?"

"I don't know." I didn't give a rat about a hat for batty hair. I shrugged. What could I say? Mean kids took it? I was too ashamed to look at her.

"What do you mean, you don't know? Your leggings—they're ripped. Did you fall? Were you in a fight? Have you been crying? What's going on?" Again, I attempted to escape. Why couldn't she just leave me alone?

"Where's the money I gave you?" I reached into my pocket. It was gone. It probably fell out when the boy with the glasses pulled the hat from my pocket. How could I explain *that*? "Answer me."

"It's not fair," I blurted, wiping my hands across my face.

"What's not fair?"

"Life. Me being here. You yelling at me." I maneuvered around her, inching closer to the stairs.

"Yelling at you? I'm not yelling at you. I'm concerned." She didn't act concerned. She acted like a nosy busybody, like Deb-Horror. "Life's not fair, Bonnie. Life is about dealing with what is handed to you, being responsible, doing the right thing. I asked you to do one thing. And you *forgot*." She made air quotes with her fingers around *forgot*, as she emphasized the *F* with upper teeth clenched against her bottom lip. "Then you come home with no money and torn clothes, looking like you've been in a street fight. But you say nothing is wrong? So, tell me then, what happened?"

"Nothing. Leave me alone." This response usually worked with my stepmother, sometimes even with my dad. But it clearly was not working here. "I don't feel well. I'm going upstairs."

I didn't know until I reached the staircase that Nog had been watching from what he called his portal. He stepped aside in an exaggerated gesture as I stomped past him and up the stairs. My knee hurt with every step. It took everything to hold back the tears. I slammed the door, stuck out my tongue to the world, and threw myself on my bed.

"Let her go, my love," I heard Nog say to Anam. I often eavesdropped on them. I wasn't really being sneaky, but sound traveled in this old house, especially when I was right above the conversation. Sometimes, when I knew they were talking about me, I would tiptoe to the door and crack it open. So that's what I did. Nog was still talking. "Something's off. Let it go for the time being."

"Let it go?" I didn't have to eavesdrop. Anam was nearly shouting, something she never did. "No way. She lied."

"She lied? Why did you say that? About what?"

"No hat. No money. Torn clothes. And she didn't 'just forget' to pick up the thread. Something happened. And she won't say what. That's a lie in my book."

"Whoa, my dear, slow down. Okay, okay, I agree, something happened. Obviously, she's upset. But maybe she's not ready to talk about it. Maybe she needs to figure things out in her head first?"

"But what if she did something wrong? What if she's upset because she got caught? Remember the shoplifting incident? Maybe ... I don't want to say it, Nog. But maybe ..." She lowered her voice so that I had to strain to hear it. "Maybe Joy caught her taking thread?"

"Thread?" Nog pronounced the word like it had three syllables. I could hear the question mark and pictured him lifting his brow and shaking his head. "Shoplifting *thread*?"

Before either could utter another word, I was out the door and screaming from the top of the stairs.

"I did not take anything!" I shrieked "Nothing! Ever!" I slammed myself back into my room. So that was it. The shoplifting incident. Just because some of my supposed friends stole some cheap jewelry at the mall, I would always be haunted by association. I shook with anger. But beneath the battered ego, something else was nagging at me.

"Ana," I heard Nog say in response to Anam's pleas for me to come down. "Let it go. If something serious happened, someone would have called us. Yes, something is wrong, but we need to give her a chance to work it out. She's 12. Reminds me of her mother at that age. Moody as all get-out. Middle school is full of moody kids, just like all the kids I taught. She'll calm down. Maybe then she'll open up. Here, let me give you a hand with laundry."

"I'd rather you help me with the budget," Anam countered. "These numbers aren't working, Nog." Before long, their voices muffled into chitchat. I got up and studied myself in the mirror, trying to tame my hair and reconcile myself to my face. That's when I saw the spinach stuck in my braces. The kids were right. I did have green teeth. I threw myself down on my bed, like a rock had landed on my heart. It hurt so much, I couldn't swallow. It was more than being called names by some stupid kids, but I couldn't identify it.

After a while, Nog tap-tapped on my door, urging me to come down for lunch. I grunted that I wasn't interested. Besides, I would've thrown up if I ate anything. More than that, I couldn't stand to face Anam, who automatically thought I did something wrong, just as Deb-Horror always did. When the kids were arrested at the mall, she immediately asked if I had ever stolen anything. It really hurt that she even thought that. And it hurt even more that Anam did, too.

Suddenly, truth stabbed my heart and I bolted up straight. I finally realized what had been bothering me. What if Kelty hadn't stopped me from taking the crystal vial at the Keep? Would I have dropped it into my jacket pocket? Or if I had been at the mall, would I have stood up to the clique or just left? I was afraid, really afraid, that I would have gone along with them. Did that make me a thief in my heart? And what about the times that I made fun of kids—the good kids, the ones I really wanted to hang out with? Did that make me no better than the kids at the bookstore? Or the times I lied to Deb-Horror and Dad about what I did with my friends after school. Was I a fraud, a thief, and a liar as well as a misfit? The afternoon dragged on. I was consumed by darkness, and it had nothing to do with sunshine slipping away.

Nog came knocking again. "Bonnie, come on downstairs."

"I'm not hungry."

"That's okay, but this is not an invitation. You don't have to eat, but you need to sit with us." I complied—because I always did—and silently picked over my food as my aunt and uncle jabbered about chores. Afterward, Nog tried to interest me in a movie and Anam suggested a new beading project. After an hour or so of trying to focus on arranging seed pearls, I asked to be excused, went to bed, and cried myself to sleep.

From my room above the kitchen, I awoke hours later to the subtle aroma of coffee. It was way too early to get up, and I didn't want to face my aunt and uncle after yesterday's fiasco. My face still burned. I wasn't sure if it was the tears, sunburn, humiliation, or dejection. I ran and reran the incident with the kids at the bookstore. How could I be so stupid as to think I would be accepted? Or so naive as to think I was any better than them? I snuggled deeper into my soft bedding and willed myself to not cry as I tried to return to sleep.

But behind the morning's coffee was another smell. Neither good nor bad, it was sort of sour and oddly comforting. Nog must have smelled it too, because I heard his deliberately quiet slip-slap down the stairs.

"Bread!" His hoarse whisper told me he didn't want to disturb me, but his enthusiasm was too exuberant to contain.

"Shhh," Anam hushed him. "Don't wake Bonnie."

As I had done the night before, I listened, especially since I heard my name.

"I thought you gave up on bread, Miss Moon," Nog whispered. "I'm delighted you didn't."

"I want our guests to enjoy fresh bread in the morning," Anam replied. "You know, the *breakfast* in 'bed and breakfast'? The last time I was at the Voyager, I asked Kath her secret. She told me to use yeast cakes, not dry yeast. She also said I have to feed the dough properly so that the sugars from the flour wake up the yeast. And you'll love this, Nog. She suggested I think of bread as a child, not a project. And as it grows, it burps out the gas. You'll know it's cool enough to eat when it whispers *crackle, crackle, crackle*."

"Ha! I do like that. But why are you up so early?"

"I couldn't sleep after yesterday's commotion. Bonnie has

me so worried. So, I decided to experiment."

"I like experiments."

It got quiet. I knew they were kissing.

"About Bonnie ...." Nog began. Yeah, I knew they'd get around to talking about me. I strained to listen.

"Maybe I was wrong to suspect shoplifting," Anam began. *Oh no,* I thought, now wide awake. Not that again. "But something happened."

"I agree. Something did happen. But we need to trust her, to be patient."

"Nog, I'm trying to be patient. I don't understand children. You know, it's ironic that Kath told me to think of bread as a child and not a project. I've been treating Bonnie like a project. No one deserves to be treated like something you have to fix. But that's what I've been doing. And just because I made it through adolescence doesn't make me an expert on girls, or young teens, whatever she is."

"No, but now you're becoming an expert on bread," Nog said as he scraped a chair across the floor, changing the subject. "That's an excellent project. Mind if I cook pancakes? Maybe Bonnie will smell breakfast and come eat." Pancakes. My stomach growled. I hadn't eaten since yesterday's breakfast.

"Good idea. I think we still have blueberries in the freezer. I'm sure we still have a few pints from what I put up last summer." I could hear Nog rummaging. "Hand me the maple syrup," Anam instructed. "I'll warm it up over here by the fire." Quiet noises persisted until Nog cleared his throat.

"I'm concerned about her, my dear. I was thinking about what you just said, about treating her like a child, not a project. I've always enjoyed being her uncle. But now I feel like her father." He paused. "Wow. I can't believe I just said I feel like Ben. That's one man I don't like. I never understood how he could pursue his girlfriends instead of staying with Maura after Bonnie was born. It was almost like he felt neglected when Maura fell more in love with Bonnie than with him. And he couldn't handle being number two."

Dad left because Mom loved me more than him? Was that my fault, too? Nog really had my attention. I never understood Dad's girlfriends, either. I remembered being a little girl in bed at night hearing Mom and Dad argue. When Mom cried, I did, too.

"Well," Anam said hesitantly, "I can understand why Maura—and other women—fell for him. He's so handsome and personable and successful."

"To be honest," Nog sighed. "I'm actually a bit jealous of him."

"You? Jealous? Of Ben?" I could easily imagine Anam's moon face accentuated with wide-open eyes.

"Yes, in a way. I admit it. Wealthy, successful, adorned with beautiful women on his arms. But I still have the only woman I have ever loved. I love you, Anamary Cara. You're worth more than anything to me. And just because I love spending time with the love of my life, I assume others feel the same."

"You're so sweet, Nog. You know," Anam continued after what I assumed was a kissing break, "when Maura and Ben asked us to be Bonnie's godparents, I really thought it was symbolic. That there would never be a reason for us to assume responsibility for her. Granted, we didn't expect Maura ..." To die, is what she didn't say as her voice trailed off. Then she recovered. "I just don't know what to do with her. Even though we both really wanted to have her come live with us, I realize now I wasn't ready for it. At least you spent time with kids as a teacher. I didn't. I'm trying, Nog. I'm trying. But I don't understand her."

As hard as I tried, I couldn't hear Nog's response. But I did hear something about "fosterage," calling it an old Celtic tradition and an "honor to Maura." My being here was an honor to Mom? I needed to pay attention. About then, I smelled the pancakes. I *was* hungry, and eventually, I would have to face my aunt and uncle. I threw off my blanket, went to the bathroom, and pulled on some sweats.

"Just think," I heard Nog muse as I crept downstairs, "if I hadn't persuaded you to come here to relax, put your feet up ..."

"Put my feet up! Humph. With bats."

"Do we have to talk about bats?" I groaned as I stepped into the kitchen.

"No bats." Nog shared a look with Anam that implied they were ready to accommodate me. They busied themselves around the kitchen while I poured some milk and sat in the nook with my arms wrapped around my knees. Ouch, my knee.

"Your dad called last night, Bonnie, after you went to bed." Anam stopped and looked directly at me. "He was concerned. Hadn't heard from you in a few days, so he tried calling and texting you last night. I told him we had worn you out, that you'd call him today. Okay?" Nodding, I wondered what else she had told him. "They're going to try to come in August, for your birthday."

"Yeah," I rolled my eyes. I wouldn't bet on it.

"I'm making bread," she changed the subject. "Right now, the dough needs to rest. Good timing. Let's eat."

"I was just reminding your aunt how I convinced her to live here rather than sell this house." Nog placed pancakes and syrup on the table. Anam poured more coffee for them and settled into her chair in the nook. Even though I had heard the story before, I appreciated that my uncle had deliberately turned the conversation away from my disastrous trip.

Tory Island, he reminded me, was growing into a getaway town. They had hired an architect and some local builders to convert the old house into a modern inn, one that he told Anam would attract an investor. But his goal was to keep it.

Little by little, Nog spruced up the yard while Anam designed a dream kitchen. It would impress the buyer, they agreed. Same thing with the master suite. They always stayed at the Avalon. Eventually, though, they spent a few nights here, then a few weeks. Anam loved shopping in the village while Nog painted, trimmed, and polished. Anam's buddy, Angus, certainly knew the difference between going to town and going home to the city. With his head out the window of the car, he joyfully ran errands with his mistress, although she suspected he would rather trot his way to the village and grub rewards for his efforts.

Angus, sensing that the story was about him, ambled from nowhere into the kitchen. He looked lovingly at Anam, then curled himself next to her. She reached down and scratched his neck. I would say that he purred, except that I realized that sound came from Mo and Willy, who always seemed to appear rather than arrive.

"Not only did I fall in love with Angus, I fell in love with this place," she begrudgingly admitted.

"Ours is a charmed life," Nog concluded, refreshing his coffee. "This transformation—of the house and our lives ...." He paused, seemingly at a loss for words, a rarity for the man. "You know, Bonnie," he used my name but looked at his wife, "what happened was magic. I am humbled to be the innkeeper here." Overhead, the house heaved a *tap tap creeaakkkkk*. We all looked up. Then he concluded, "It's a restful spot, an island. For you, too."

"Why do you call everything an island, Nog?"

"Because we're all on a mystical journey, Bon. Remember what I said about the labyrinth and Brendan's *immram*? Islands provide shelter from the storm, places to replenish ourselves and our supplies on our journey through life."

"And what a journey!" Anam added, looking over at the animals, who were now playfully chasing each other and the Invisibles around the hearth. Anam glanced upward with the echo of a *tap tap creeaakkkkk.*

"You've got to do something about the attic."

"Yes, dear." Nog rather liked the rasps and groans. They made the house sound alive. He rose and rinsed their cups while Anam placed the bread in the big oven. She then drew a kettle of water and poured it into the cast iron pot that hung within the ancient fireplace. Nog called it her cauldron. She called it common sense. Hissing filled the chamber.

"I'm going to shower while the bread bakes," Anam said. "No jumping around. That means you, Angus."

I swear he smiled. I picked at my pancakes until I heard the water running upstairs.

"About yesterday," I started with downcast, tear-filled eyes.

"Yes, Bonnie, about yesterday?"

"Kids, some kids at Rainbow Stream, they made fun of me," I sobbed. "They called me names and laughed at me. Called me Ghost Girl, and said bats lived in my hair. They said I was looking for books that would teach me to talk to ghosts. They took my hat. I think that's when the money fell out."

Nog drew up next to me. "That wasn't very nice of them." He leaned over and handed me a handkerchief. He always had one in his pocket. "They should have been in school, Bon. Tells you something about kids hanging around in town instead of being at school." Wrapping his arm around my shoulders, he waited for me to blot my tears before asking, "What did you do?"

"I ran away."

"Well, that's okay. Sometimes the best thing to do is walk away from your tormentors." We sat quietly for a few minutes. I listened to the house noises, Anam's shower, and the hissing cauldron.

"Why did they say those things, Nog? Do they know about Knobby? How do they know?"

"You see, Bonnie, Tory Island is full of stories. And a lot of them are about Knobby. One is about the Clíona Church. Legend has it that when Knobby passes over to the Other-world, he will proclaim that he has found a successor by ringing the carillon—bells that haven't rung in centuries. And then the eagle will fly away. Some say the Avalon is haunted by a bevy of female ghosts. And, of course, many people claim that the old graveyard is haunted."

Well, yes. If it hadn't been for Arthur and Dobbin there, I might have found the place spooky. "You see, a lot of locals—kids, especially—tell tales. About the Avalon, this house, Baylar, that she has an evil eye or that she communicates with the devil." I could believe that, especially the evil eye thing.

"But that's what they are—stories. Local legends. Like the one about this house. It's been in the family for centuries, ever since Knobby built his first campsite. Uncle Emmett, you know, was the last to live here. But as he got old and bothered by arthritis, he couldn't keep up with it. He was a bit of a loner, bent over, walked with a cane. He was known to be cranky sometimes. Probably because he was always in a lot of pain. That's probably when kids first started making up stories. After he went into assisted living, the house sat empty for years and got even more run-down. You can understand why people called it the Ghost House. You know, if you grew up here, you would probably say those things, too. And maybe—I'm not saying you would—but maybe you would have made fun of a new kid who lived in a house that allegedly was haunted. Maybe?"

"How did you know?" I gulped.

"Know what?"

"That me and my so-called friends at the new school made

fun of other kids. Not about a haunted house." The tears started anew. "I made fun of a new girl. I think she was poor. I told her she should get some cool clothes like mine. I made her cry. I made her feel like I do now. I'm so ashamed. I am sorry about that, so sorry." I sobbed. "I got in trouble for that. I figured Dad told you."

"No, my love. I knew nothing about that. I don't think you give your dad and Deborrah enough credit." He let that sink in. "You know, I was a teacher. And that experience taught me kids can be cruel. I think I know the boy, the instigator. Long hair and glasses?" I nodded. "I see him around town all the time when he should be in school. I'll talk to his folks."

"Please, Nog, don't."

"Oh, yes, Bonnie. We can't let that behavior go unnoticed. In some ways, maybe you were like him. But good kids learn you don't have to be that way. Remember the stories of Brendan and Máel Dúin? They had to forgive themselves before they could forgive others. Of course, you're sorry for the way you acted back at your school. You can't change that, or what happened to you yesterday. But I bet you won't deliberately hurt someone's feelings again, even though others may hurt yours."

I thought about the kids. I didn't think I could forgive them.

"It's all in the journey of life," Nog said. "A journey where past, present, and future are like the three leaves on a shamrock." He held up three fingers of his left hand and enumerated them with his right index finger. "And really, all you have is the present. That's where you have freedom to live."

"Wait. What you just said. That's what Porter said. And that the future's a mystery."

Nog nodded.

We sat in silence. The house *tap tapped*. The moment was right to tell Nog about the ghosts, when Anam startled me by placing her hands on my shoulders. I had not heard her arrive.

"And the future's not ours to see," she whisper-sang in my ear. "That's from an old song that your Grandma Maggie used to sing." As she turned me gently to face her, Maggie shimmered behind her in characteristic burgundy. "That's why I like old things so much. I can see the past, touch it, understand it. Unlike the future."

I thought of my dollhouse again, the one that Erin and I played with. It was proof of my simple, previous life. I had never thought of my aunt's musty antiques as a way of understanding life. But now I did, sort of.

"If I think of life as an adventure, like coming here was for me, for you," she placed her hands on my shoulders, "for all of us—then I can face the future. We find meaning in everyday adventures. That's how we find meaning in life. I think maybe you found some meaning yesterday."

Sitting next to me, she lifted my chin, bringing my eyes to hers. "Do this." She placed both hands in her lap. I did the same. Then she drew them up to her neck as she inhaled. She extended her hands and held her breath for a couple of seconds then exhaled, bringing her hands back to her lap. "Come on, do this with me." I followed her lead, but without the hands. "Again." I don't know why, but I felt calmer, stronger. "I learned to do this—deep breathing, it's called—after your mom died. It was the only way I could calm myself down." Then she grinned. "I had to do it a lot when we moved here." We did it a few more times, and then she leaned in and stroked my tangled tresses. "Your hair is lovely, Bonnie, but it is a bit unruly. Maybe we can trim it back a bit. Would you like that?" I shrugged.

"Then nobody will say that bats live in there," Nog said.

"No bats!" I emphasized. Silently I added, no zombies or vampires, either. But ghosts were okay. My welter was proof of that. Nog beamed with an idea.

"Why don't you two go on into New Grange. Get your hair done, pick up some thread on the way home." He winked at Anam. "I've got enough to do around here." With that, the house groaned and we all looked up, even the welter. "Starting with rubbing linseed oil on the floor of the attic. That's what Baylar suggested. I thought I would ..."

"No," Anam ordered. "I don't want you in the attic. I'm afraid you'll fall through." I laughed at the image of Nog crashing through the ceiling. "If Baylar won't do it, get someone else. It's so noisy, especially late at night. What will our guests think?"

"They'll think we have ghosts." Nog was attempting to have the last word before Anam glared him into silence. "What? They're just the past fluttering through the eaves to a silent melody."

13

ISLAND
OF WOMEN

I couldn't believe I was getting my hair done with Anam—at a *beauty parlor*, no less. Not a spa or salon like I would do in the city. I had to admit, though, that since Anam's hair had a wow factor of about a zillion and mine had been called a bat's nest, the beauty parlor was a good alternative. And it meant a trip to New Grange, the closest city. I'd only been there once before, to go to the orthodontist. It was an hour's drive. Beyond Tory Island.

No Invisibles accompanied us. They only showed up in the car when Nog was driving. And while their absence felt a little strange, the trip without Nog gave us a little room for our soul friendship to deepen. I was beginning to understand the *anam cara* thing. In addition to hair, we talked about makeup and clothes, the kind of conversation I used to have with Erin, Jenny, and Sara. The kind I wanted to have with Mom. The kind that always disintegrated into an argument with Deb-Horror.

Deb-Horror. Maybe Nog was right. Maybe I didn't give her enough credit.

I was accustomed to chic stylists at hip salons, so when the middle-aged Kitty came at me with her cat-eye glasses and retro bouffant hairdo clipped with a red bow, I cringed. "You've got gorgeous tresses," she assured me as she fluffed my hair and pulled it to one side and then the other. "Nice bone structure, too. Let's see if we can play that up."

Then she washed my hair and turned me away from the mirror, like they do on a TV makeover. Even though she swore she wouldn't do anything drastic, I expected that her scissors would render me as bald as Nog. But when she spun me around to see the results, my hands flew to my cheeks in wonder. Instead of cutting inches off my hair, she strategically cut shape into it. I looked more like Rihanna or Zendaya than I did me. Kitty had transformed what the kids called a bat's nest into a sophisticated sweep of loose curly bangs and tapered shoulder-length hair. She showed me how to twist it up into a topknot or make bouncy curls. I couldn't stop smiling—even my braces looked better.

And I kept on smiling, because we then stopped at the New Grange Mall. The mall! I didn't need to buy anything in the neon wonderland, I just needed to be there, to belong someplace familiar. Anam suggested that I get new leggings and a stylish hat. We found a lilac crocheted turn-brim hat that showed off my curls nicely. Not only did it replace the one I lost, but I liked the way I looked in it. It went a long way toward smoothing things out with my soul friend. I glanced at her while we were driving home. Although I no longer wanted to be her, I realized I was liking her, trusting her, more. But still I wondered, what would it be like to be me?

In the following weeks, we ran more errands together, too, but the best solution for smoothing those bumps was the Crystal Keep. On one of our many runs there, Anam found a handful of sea-glass discs that we both liked. We bought a set of tools and made key fobs for all the guest rooms. We worked on that together at night and hung the keys in a colorful display by the office.

With the leftovers, we made wind chimes, and then hung them on the veranda. As the days warmed, the chimes tinkled in the spring breeze. I often curled into a newly painted chair—usually the azure blue one—to polish bits and pieces of brass and glass for the house. Or if my chores and schoolwork were done, finger and toenails for me.

My painted nails reminded me of the Avalon Inn, the hotel that Anam called a Painted Lady. Whenever we passed it, Anam would sigh and fold her hands in front of her chest.

"Oh, Bonnie, we need to do tea there. You'll love the decor. Lots of local antiques."

Even though I now understood why Anam loved old things, I still didn't. But I did like her Painted Lady and the way the colors popped. I dreamed of having a purple house with lime and turquoise trim. Or maybe a yellow house with pink trim. So that's how I painted my nails.

One day, she made good on the tea thing. We got all dressed up. She even let me wear some makeup that covered a few pimples that had appeared on my chin and forehead. After I fastened a sparkly beaded necklace that I had made, I pried open my treasure box and slipped on Mom's ring. Admiring myself in the mirror, I had to admit that I almost looked pretty. But I also felt like a fraud, like my insides didn't match my outsides. I put the ring back. That was too private.

When we got to the Painted Lady—the Avalon—a hostess ushered us into a dining room hushed with deep rose carpeting and sprinkled with small clusters of women, just women. She steered us through clouds of waitresses in pastel, puffy-sleeved dresses, frilly aprons, and lacy bonnets. We were seated in tufted wingback chairs around a linen-covered table festooned with gardenias, glass-ensconced candles, and silver napkin holders. It was like a scene out of an old movie and I was a glamorous actress.

Anam ordered tea while I gawked at chandeliers dripping with crystal, thickly folded draperies sashed with gold, and sheer curtains beyond which was a fountain-splashed court-yard. A few Invisibles chased each other among the curtains, fluttering them ever so slightly. *Aha!* The Avalon wasn't haunted. It was just the aunts playing hide and seek.

A young woman appeared with a tea cart and asked about our preferences. She looked like me, with the same rich café au lait skin, though hers was a few shades darker. Less cream, Dad would say. And unlike my pimpled complexion, hers was flawless. Long fingers bore several colorful rings—I noted, however, that none was an emerald. She had twisted her mahogany hair into an updo, a look I wanted to imitate. Subtle coral lipstick framed pearly straight teeth (she probably had worn braces, I thought, running my tongue over my own rigid scaffolding). Deep brown eyes, no glasses. She probably wore contacts. I straightened my boring wireframes. Dad promised I could get contacts when I turned 16.

Watching an older me pour tea into our miniature cups, I barely heard Anam ordering eggs, cheese, sausage, walnuts, cucumbers, bananas, and chocolate. It sounded so good that my appetite announced itself with a grumble. I ignored it, though, because time stood still while I sensed my future. Here was someone I would like to be. When I smiled, the grownup me smiled back.

While we sipped tea, Anam talked about the different hotels in the city where she used to go for tea. The older me returned with dainty plates of even daintier morsels. I blinked a few times, trying to figure out what was in front of me. Intimidated by the elegance and soft conversation, I whispered, "What is this?"

Anam sat up like an expert, and discreetly identified the mystery items. "Cucumber goat-cheese sandwiches, sausage rolls, lemon curd scones, and banana walnut éclairs."

Goat cheese and curds? I thought she had ordered sausage and eggs. *God save me*, I prayed silently to whatever deities might oversee this island of women. Then I took a deep breath. Even though I'd eaten nothing like this, I was hungry. I nibbled on a sausage roll. It was much better than I expected. I looked sheepishly at Anam, who smiled approvingly. The cucumber sandwich, while bland, offered a pleasant contrast to the spicy meat. The éclairs and scones were great, but they were so tiny they just made me hungrier.

"Hey, Anam," I ventured on the way home. "If we do this again, can I order the food? And can we order more of it?"

14

the weary traveler

"Batten down the hatches," Nog shouted as he stomped in the vestibule. It was late afternoon in mid-April and I was chopping vegetables for Anam's stuffed chicken breasts. I looked outside and saw trees swaying in the wind as ominous thunderheads eclipsed the late day sun. "Anamary, get the candles and flashlights! Bonnie, turn off all the electrical equipment! Where's Angus? We got a nasty storm coming in from the west. I just got the horses in the barn." A resounding *boom* underscored the urgency in his voice.

Anam pulled out an emergency kit from a kitchen cabinet and plopped it in the middle of the floor. She grabbed her red cloak from the far side of the vestibule. "I'll find Angus."

"No, you won't." Nog stopped her. "He knows to come home. It's too late to go out there." *Boom!* One crackling flash of lightning and simultaneous roar of thunder plunged the entire house into darkness and shook it silent of taps and hums. Rain battered. Wind howled. Windows rattled. The welter whooshed. I stiffened. As Anam and Nog spun into survival mode, I choked back fear as the house groaned a renewed urgency with its *tap tap creeaakkkkk*. The door thudded.

"Good lord, dog!" Anam opened the door for stinky Angus.

Nog disappeared, then reappeared from the hallway with an armful of towels and tossed them to Anam, who quickly rubbed Angus dry. "Need to check the house for open windows, anything leaking." He grabbed a flashlight and shouted over the din. "You all stay right here and build up the fire!"

Like I was going anywhere. Right.

Within minutes, we were all hunkered in the flickering warmth of the kitchen while the storm raged outside.

"We've gotten used to this," he said.

"Well, never really used to it," Anam added. "The first time it was pretty terrifying. I know exactly how you feel. I'll warn you, we're at the end of the power grid, so it could be hours—or even days—before the electricity is back on."

The house *tap tap creeaakkkked.*

It took about an hour before the storm moved on, leaving us in its dark wake for hours. Anam ditched her dinner plans in favor of a chicken stew cooked over the fire in the hearth. Its aroma wafted slowly, then it beckoned us to the fire to sit, eat, and stay safe and warm. Despite the coziness, I felt isolated. I was scared. Even the phone had gone dead. It was bad enough that we had terrible cell reception here, though it was a ready excuse not to answer when Dad called. Now I wanted to call him and tell him I was scared. But we couldn't even call the power company to find out when the lights might come on again. I needed to do something about this lack of connectivity.

"How about a story?" Nog suggested after Anam plated some cookies. She wasn't big on desserts, so this seemed like a special occasion. "Back in the day, my Aunt Kelty—oh, was she ever a legendary storyteller and musician—she would play the piano, lead us in song, or tell a story. Shorten the night, is what she would call it, in those long-ago days before television and internet."

Sure enough, Kelty fluttered to the piano and struck a few keys that I alone heard. She was soon joined by Dobbin, Jeanne, and the uncles. In no time at all, Seamus nibbled on leftover cheese as Nog cleared the dishes. Gramp stoked the fire into a brighter burn. Cookie helped herself to cookies. When she noticed a few were already gone, Anam glared at Nog and me.

"You two are shameless. Did you eat them already?" She had already convicted us of the crime of stealing cookies. We responded with simultaneous shrugs, vigorous head shakes, and hands held high in the air. "I suppose you're going to tell me that a ghost ate them."

I gagged, then quickly covered that reaction with a cough.

"What cookies, Ana My Cara?" While Nog continued to protest, I watched Cookie laugh and replenish the cookies.

"Those." Anam pointed with her right index finger to the platter, which was now full of cookies. "I *thought* I had put them out." She mumbled something to herself.

"Maybe we really do have a ghost." Nog grinned and reached for a glass of water by his chair. But it wasn't there. Jack was balancing it on his forehead. I tried hard not to laugh. When Nog put on his glasses and looked again, it was right where he thought it should be.

"Storm or no storm, when all the kids and adults were huddled around at the end of the day, like we are now, Kelty would entertain us," Nog said. "I do remember a few of her tales." I noticed that Baron had taken over the rocker like he owned it. He did, he informed me with a salute.

"Of course." I did it again. I was talking to ghosts.

"Of course, what, Bonnie?"

"Of course, you remember some stories." I had to be more careful. "I want to know more about the ancestors." I really meant the Invisibles. Besides, a story might take away some of my uneasiness. Nog cleared his throat, but before he began, he directed his gaze at me.

"I'm going to tell you a very important story," he advised. *"The Tale of the Weary Traveler.* Legend has it that it really happened here, about a hundred years ago. It's imperative that you remember it." Anam and I rolled our eyes.

"Okay."

Nog reached over to the coffee table and took one of the candles, a long taper. Holding it like a torch in his right hand, he rose to his feet. Theatrically brandishing it, he began the tale in a very deep voice.

It was a dark and stormy night ...

Nog zigzagged the candle beneath his chin, transforming himself into a Halloween-like ghoul. The flickering light deepened and exaggerated his round nose. Shielding the light with his left hand, and widening his eyes in anticipatory glee, he sustained the silence for several seconds while he glanced around the darkened room and let the muffled rain outside drench our senses. Then he continued.

There once was a traveling man named Johnny. He was cold and tired and far from home. He came upon an inn—perhaps even this one—seeking shelter from the storm. Now, Johnny, he was a funny man and he talked like this...

Nog stepped to the left as he switched the candle from his left hand to his right. He screwed his mouth to the right, grotesquely aligning the left corner of his mouth with a nose elongated by the candle flickering beneath it. Speaking from the pinched corner of his mouth, Nog became Johnny. His facial contortions caused a lisp.

Kind, thir. Do you have a room for me? I'm cold and tired, and far from home.

Untwisting his face and holding the candle normally in front of his chest, Nog became himself again and resumed his role as storyteller.

"Now the innkeeper was a funny man, too," he said. Nog stepped to the right and shifted the candle to indicate that he was now another speaker. Contorting his face in the opposite direction, he mimicked the innkeeper's voice. He talked like this...

Yeth, thir, we have a room for a cold and tired traveler
on a night thuch as thith.

The wind and rain blew outside. Nog stepped left and shifted the candle yet again. He transformed his face back into Johnny's. Johnny then spoke from the pinched right corner of Nog's twisted mouth.

Thank you, kind thir.

The innkeeper spoke from the pinched left corner of Nog's mouth, as he gestured toward an imaginary room.

Thith ith your room.

Switching the taper from one hand to the other and stepping from left to right, Nog, as innkeeper, handed the candle to Johnny, the traveler. Stepping thus from one character into another, he not only told the tale of the weary traveler, but he also became it. Johnny spoke from the right side of Nog's mouth.

Good night, thir.

The innkeeper spoke from the left side of Nog's mouth.

Good night, thir.

Johnny, as portrayed by Nog, blew and blew from the right corner of his mouth to extinguish the flame that he held in front of his face.

Whew, whew.

But because Johnny was a funny man, he couldn't blow it out. As Nog demonstrated Johnny's frustration, Anam laughed. I hooted. The house applauded with its *tap tap creeaakkkkk.* Johnny pleaded.

*Could thomebody pleathe blow out the candle tho I can
go to thleep?*

Taking the candle, the innkeeper blew and blew from the left corner of his mouth.

Whew, whew.

But he could not extinguish the flame. Johnny begged for help.

*Could thomebody pleathe blow out the candle tho I can
go to thleep?*

Nog then shifted the candle and his mouth to indicate that the innkeeper was speaking.

Let me call my wife.

Now, of course, his wife was a funny woman, and she spoke with a severe underbite that Nog portrayed by shoving his jaw forward. He stepped back when he spoke as her.

Yeth, my huthband.

The innkeeper responded by stepping to the right and twisting his mouth to the left.

Can you blow out the candle tho our guetht can go to thleep?

Yeth, of courth, my huthband.

Nog, as the wife, stepped back. She huffed and puffed upwards.

Whew, whew.

Alas, she could not extinguish the flame. The traveler pleaded by stepping to the right, holding the candle to the left, and twisting his face toward it.

Could thomebody pleathe blow out the candle tho I can go to thleep?

Again, Nog switched the candle and his face to indicate that he was again speaking as the innkeeper.

Let me call my thon.

Now the innkeeper's son was a funny boy, too. Nog withdrew his jaw sharply to become the son with a severe overbite. He spoke through buckteeth.

Yeth, father?

The innkeeper spoke through the left side of Nog's mouth.

Can you blow out the candle tho our guetht can go to thleep?

The wife asked through the upper side of Nog's mouth.

Can you blow out the candle tho our guetht can go to thleep?

Johnny pleaded from the right side of Nog's mouth.

*Could thomebody pleathe blow out the candle tho I can
go to thleep?*

The son spoke patiently from the exaggerated downward
side of Nog's mouth.

Yeth, father. Yeth, mother.

He quickly licked his thumb and forefinger, pinched the
wick, and extinguished the flame.

Good night.

As Nog snuffed out the flame, the lights came back on.
Angus barked. The house creaked. Strangely, I felt like I
belonged.

"It certainly has been a long day. Would somebody please
turn out the light so *I* can go to sleep?" Nog laughed as he
extinguished candles and started for the stairs. I held him back
for a minute.

"That was a fun story, Nog, but why is it important?"

"Because one day, you may have to welcome the weary
traveler. And you must be ready."

15

Bonnie, Bonnie Banks

A few days later, I powered on the computer and said good morning to Aloysius, who greeted me by spelling his name on the screen. It was a gesture that was now as reassuring as Mamie mooing whenever I poured milk into cereal.

I had to finish up several school projects. Nog and I kept a portfolio of projects, essays, and tests. We had gone over it the day before, and I was impressed with how much I had learned. I had about a month before everything was due to my teacher, and was about to finish up my glacier project. Once again, I wished I could do it as a vlog. If only I had a real camera, some editing software, and high-speed internet access.

In the midst of my daydream, I saw Anam intercept Nog as he returned from early chores. Her round face was pinched into a square. A pencil (who uses a *pencil*?) stuck out of a messy bun like an exclamation point. Her appearance signaled panic. The feeling spread to me. It started in my gut, bounced up to my eyeballs, then down to my toes, and then back to my gut, where it sat. And grew.

"We've got trouble, Nog." Nog was looking for coffee, not

trouble. Anam followed him into the kitchen, her hands clutching several pages of numbers that she waved in front of him. Her red glasses added fire to the urgency. I had a feeling I knew what was coming. I'm not a math genius, but I understood negative numbers, and there were a lot of them on Anam's spreadsheets.

Nog lowered his chin and lifted his bushy eyebrows to meet her gaze.

"What's wrong, Ana My Cara? Come sit down. No trouble we can't fix with coffee."

With two mugs of coffee between them, Anam laid out her accounting. Nog slipped on his reading glasses and followed his wife's fingers up and down the columns. The dilemma, she declared in a shaky, though controlled, voice, was quite simple. "At this rate, we don't have enough guests registered to cover our expenses. If we can't get some money coming in, we won't break even let alone get our investment back."

Nog toggled his attention between Anam's ledgers and her eyes. Water sizzled above the hearth. The welter fluttered into the shadows of Nog's portal one by one. The house creaked its *tap tap tap.*

"I hate to say it, Nog. I really do. But it's time we talk about pulling the plug. We don't have any more savings to tap into and we're mortgaged to the brink. At least we can get our money back if we sell the house."

Nog, uncharacteristically silent, simply rotated his head from side to side. He wasn't giving up on his dream. Not yet. Not without a fight.

Most of the reservations for the upcoming summer were from a few friends and business associates Anam and Nog had in the city. The rest were overflows from the Avalon and other hotels in the village. Our first two guests were coming two weeks after Memorial Day, six weeks away. Then no one for another two weeks.

"We need more people," Anam said, her voice barely audible. "A lot more people."

The welter gasped. The house *tap tapped*. I had formulated an idea after the storm that would solve their guest problem and my frustration with old-fashioned technology. This was my moment.

"I can help." I sauntered to the refrigerator, imitating a cheerful Nog. "No trouble we can't fix with milk." Mamie nodded approvingly. Anam and Nog stared at me as I scooched into the breakfast nook across from them. Still speechless, Nog took off his spectacles and eyeballed me. His big eyes grew huge and his big ears even huger as I continued. "We need to do some upgrades and marketing."

Unlike Nog, Anam was quick to respond.

"Upgrades? Whatever you have in mind, we can't afford it. And marketing? What do you know about marketing?"

"Dad." His name had the force of a secret weapon. He would be so proud of me. "I've learned from the best."

Tearing a blank sheet of paper from Anam's sacred notebook, I outlined my strategy. They could entice more guests and offer them a better experience by first upgrading to high-speed internet, installing a router, and getting a cellphone signal booster. Although I had had it with missed calls and poor signals, I deliberately omitted the benefits to me.

"Routers? Boosters?" Anam shook her head. "I don't like the sound of that. We're running out of money, Bonnie. We can't afford upgrades." Once she made up her mind, I would not change it, so I had to get to the point immediately.

"Actually, to make money, you have to spend money, and we're only talking a few hundred dollars—a lot less than some of the other improvements you've already done. About the same as new bikes or ... curtains." Anam flinched, like I had bonked her on the head. There always seemed to be money for curtains. "Your ISP, sorry, your internet provider could tell you exactly how much in just one phone call. All you need is a couple of guest bookings to cover the expense. Best of all, these upgrades will make it easier for people to find us."

Did I just say *us*? As if to confirm I had, the welter sifted into the nook. They crowded around Nog and Anam. Even Angus, Mo, and Willy circled in. Everyone looked at me. I sat a little taller and channeled Dad.

"Once people get here, they'll be happier because they'll be able to use their own devices for phone calls, internet access, and streaming. Long-term, we can use it in our advertising. You know ..." Arcing my right arm in one direction and my left in the other, I said in Dad's dynamic voice, "Secure Wi-Fi to complement the rustic surroundings."

"Can you help me install Wi-Fi in my station wagon?" Nog asked after a few seconds of silence.

"Absolutely." Good, I had him onboard. "Then we need to develop a social presence."

"Eh ...?" Anam blinked a few times. "Social presence? What do you mean?"

"Facebook. Instagram. Twitter. Blog. Search engine opti ... optima ..." I was stuttering. This was not the time to lose my edge over the pronunciation of a word I hardly knew, but Dad used it, so I had to. I took a deep breath. "Optimization. Search engine optimization."

"What are you talking about?" Anam protested. "Search engine opti ... whatever you call it, sounds expensive and we just don't have the resources. Besides, we already have a website."

"Well," I proceeded slowly. I didn't dare tell her how dreadfully boring the site was. "For starters, it doesn't help to have a website if no one can find it. It would be easier for people to find us if they were already on Facebook. And every-one," *except you,* I wanted to add, "is on Facebook. It won't replace the website. In fact, it'll make it easier to find and liven it up. We can update it every day with pictures and stories." *And my vlog.* "Then when people do come, they can *Like* us. And they will post pictures and share them with their friends. That will increase visibility." I really sounded like Dad. "And that doesn't cost us anything!"

"I, um ..." Anam scrunched her mouth and nose, twisting them from side to side, like the innkeepers in Nog's story. "I, um ... I don't know, don't know how ..."

"I bet *you* do," Nog grinned at me.

"I do." My insides danced. "And while we're at it, we need to invest in a guest reservation and management system."

I had spent the previous day researching software that would integrate reservations with social platforms and process credit cards. Anam had been keeping track of reservations on index cards that she kept filed in a shoe box. A shoe box!

"Guests can see availability and prices and select their rooms online." I paused long enough to let this all sink in, but not long enough for Anam to start objecting. "Your index cards and checklist leave too much to chance. What if you spill coffee on them? Or what happens when someone calls and you're not home? They might not bother leaving a message and just call a different inn. Then you've not only lost a guest, but future guests as well."

"But," Anam sputtered, "I must talk to every guest by phone. Get a feel for them and their needs, you know, like diet and, oh, I don't know, maybe they need to avoid stairs."

"Maybe we can ask those questions through the reservation system," Nog said, touching Anam's arm. "Or you can do that with a personalized confirmation call." He nodded, encouraging me to continue.

"Guests can make reservations at their convenience, even in the middle of the night. But first, we need to be connected to the Cloud." Luna gleefully tossed and tousled her edges at the mention of clouds. "Not *that* kind of cloud." Anam and Nog followed my eyes toward the invisible Luna, then drifted back to me in confusion. I pinched my ghost-distracted self.

"I meant, not clouds, like up in the sky. But the Cloud. You know, data storage?" Obviously, they didn't know. "Let me show you how this all works."

For the rest of the day, I outlined what we needed, stressing the urgency of getting things done immediately if we were to start registering more guests. We ate Anam's latest experiment in bread, cheese (Seamus cheered), cookies (Cookie clapped), ice cream (Mamie licked her lips), and snacks from every cabinet, using nearly every plate. That amused Jack, though I was careful to keep my chuckles to myself. Gramp fed the fire. It took a few pots of coffee, a carton of milk, some arguing, and lots of laughing, but by midnight, we had a plan.

The next morning, we compiled a list of FAQs. I came up with #CompanionMoon for Twitter. Anam wrote the *About* page, nixing everything Nog wanted to say about his ancestors, although he thought it would be "charming to imbue a lingering sense of family."

"Absolutely not!" Anam said. "Sounds too much like ghosts and we will have no mention of them at all around guests." The welter collectively sighed. "Not even a hint of any of that malarkey."

Nog took pictures of us, Angus, the cats and horses, the veranda, the lawn chairs (so savage in their bright colors), and of course, the lake. Nog came up with a stay-three-nights, get-one-free offer. They worked out promotions with the Fish House and The Fiery Pig.

Anam wrote a post about homey breakfasts with freshly baked muffins, local berries, and fresh cream. I wrote about the lake itself:

Escape the city and find yourself at Companion Moon. On the banks of a glacial lake, where infinite shades of green and blue melt into black and contradictory textures fold themselves into shallow inlets. Relax along its sloping banks, where slender spires of pine and thick massifs of deciduous trees descend into flowering bushes of pink, amethyst, copper, and red. Paddle, swim, and sunbathe for hours, or ride a complimentary bike into the nearby village for lunch.

I nailed it. Nog wrote a big A+ across the draft. He said I was a natural writer, "as good as your dad." He paused then added, "Maybe even better." A few days later, I used it as the script for my first vlog.

"A what?" Anam asked when I told her my plan.

"A vlog. A video blog. A journal that I'll post online using movies that I make on my phone. I'm a girl who codes, you know." She didn't know, so we left it at that. I suggested calling the blog "The Bonnie, Bonnie Banks of the Moon" in honor of the inn and of Mom, who used to sing me a song that went,

By yon bonnie, bonnie banks an' by yon bonnie,
  bonnie braes
Where the sun shines bright on Loch Lomon'

Nog filled in the words I didn't know. He said it was an old Scottish ballad. We found a free version of the song to play in the background. I listened over and over. But the words weren't as important to me as Mom telling me it was why she named me Bonnie. It's Scottish for *pretty*. I remembered that Nog told me my middle name means *bright* and *shining*. My last name says I'm a warrior. And I come from a loving family. I was beginning to feel better about myself and like my name fit me.

Our launch rocked! I finally had something to text Erin about. Not only did she respond, but she *called*. Told me how much she had missed me. We talked for an hour. She still lived in the same house and went to the same school. While she found that mind-numbingly boring, I thought it was perfection. Jenny moved away when her mother got a new job in California. She rarely saw Sara, who was busy babysitting and putting money aside for dance lessons.

I told her I had become a mean kid at my new school. She got me to laugh at myself when I told her about the kids making fun of me. She said she loved me, she missed me, that I was still her BFF. When we hung up, I cried. It doesn't take much these days to start that going. But it was a happy cry, one of relief. Not pain.

Erin shared the page and vlog with her parents, who said they would bring the family up for a few days. Dad was so proud that he bought me a video camera with autofocus and dual-image stabilization—and a tripod. He hyped the inn to his friends and associates. One asked about facilities for a business meeting. Nog said yes, and immediately began to clear out and paint the room in the barn that we had used to clean furniture. It became another item on Nog's ever-expanding to-do list. If I didn't hear him snore every night, I'd have sworn that he didn't have time to sleep.

Within days, we had a presence and bookings. We were finally on the way to making money. And I was breaking out of my isolation.

16

LIFESAVERS

With reservations coming in, the opening became real. Everything inside was pretty much done. Refinished furniture, afghans, and decor were in place. Now, we had a lot to do outside. Like plant flowers in the window boxes that Nog built. We painted them cherry red, which stood out against the earthy stone façade of the house. Anam and I planted white impatiens into them. Anam envisioned that they would spill out of their containers, giving Companion Moon a "cozy cot-tage look."

"Deborrah says that cozy really just means small." As soon as I said that, I realized that I no longer thought of Deborrah's negative connotation of cozy. In fact, I no longer thought of her as Deb-Horror.

"I used to think like that too," Anam replied with a smile. "But cozy also means full of character. And just think how much more work a big house would be."

We laughed. Then Anam said, "I think we can now afford some housekeepers. Especially when the guests arrive." I liked that.

Then there were the boats. Nog bought two rowboats and

a canoe that he housed in the boathouse—another Nogism. It was really a shed, but "boathouse" sounded so much more romantic. He named the vessels after his women—Mag, Mar, and Mor—mother, wife, and sister. The rowboats, Mag and Mar, required a lot of upkeep. The canoe, Mor, was named for Maura, because it was "elegant and maintenance-free."

"Does that mean that Mag and Mar are inelegant?" I tested him, a sign that I was getting a sense of humor. I also couldn't resist the urge to be mischievous. "Is that why you call them *dinghies*?"

"No," he winked during what was nearly a daily ritual of picking pine needles, leaves, and twigs from inside the row-boats' hulls. "Just high maintenance." He had painted Mar's prow with a bird, Mor's with a tree, and Mag's with a snake. No sooner had he pointed out the snake, than a striped reptile wriggled out of the grass and shaped itself into an "M." I recognized it as Maggie. Nog traced an index finger above the long burgundy stripe down the reptile's back. Furrowing his brow, he stuck his finger upward, shaking it slightly, indicating he was about to tell me something important.

"Most people would think this is a harmless garter snake. But this one," he followed the reddish stripe to the white mark by either eye, "this is the rarer eastern ribbon snake. Your Grandma Maggie called it her totem animal. Said it represents staying grounded during times of change—and that she did, always on an even keel." He gestured toward the image on the boat, then looked to the horizon. "She used to have a beautiful black enameled box with one of these as an inlaid design. I wonder what happened to it."

"I have it! Up in my room. Grandma Maggie gave it to Mom. Dad gave it to me." I wanted to add that the Invisible Maggie also had a burgundy stripe and whitish eyes. Instead, we shared a long look and a smile. "I'll show it to you later."

After the boats were cleared of debris, we tested their

seaworthiness. Nog taught me how to row, use a compass, and read the water. He also taught me water safety and survival skills, like wearing a life vest and how to tread water. "You're a natural," he complimented me after a trip out to Bull Rock. "Just like your mom." I loved being compared to Mom, just as I now realized I was a lot like Dad. Smart and successful.

Then there was the raft. Last year, Nog worked out a deal with a few guys in the village to build a raft about 25 yards offshore, out toward Bull Rock. "Guests need a raft to swim to," was his rationale. That was because he had a raft to swim to when he came here as a kid. Although work on it began as soon as the lake thawed, the project took a lot more time—and money—than Nog expected. Anam would cluck disapproval as the bills started rolling in.

"Now you've gone and done it, Nog," she proclaimed one evening after a day trip to New Grange. Laying a sheath of paper on the table and patting it emphatically, she captured Nog's attention. She took a deep breath. "This raft is going to cost us even more money. I just spent the afternoon getting licenses and scheduling inspections. The Board of Health will not certify us to have a swimming area without a lifeguard."

"Then we'll get a lifeguard."

Anam sighed. "And just where will we find a lifeguard at this late date?"

I leapt to the rescue. "Joy! Didn't she say her nephew is a lifeguard?" My aunt and uncle looked at each other, then me.

"You're a bright girl, Bonnie." Nog said. "That just might work."

"That could solve a few more problems," Anam nodded after a minute or two. "We had to get more insurance for the bikes and boats, too. A lifeguard could lower those costs a little—for the boats, anyway."

A few days later, when the raft was finally moored, Anam sat in the bright blue Adirondack chair and smiled. Really smiled. I smiled, too, because they hired Joy's nephew James, who was every bit as good-looking in person as he was in the picture I saw the day I arrived.

He caused a bit of a stir when he came for the interview, rumbling up the driveway on a moped. While Anam hugged the sides of her face in dismay—again like that *Scream* painting—I ran to the window by the front door in time to see him dismount. Not only was James tall, but he looked totally awesome in a black leather sector jacket that made his broad shoulders look even stronger. Matching leather boots added at least an inch of height. In one smooth movement with his right hand, he unstrapped his full-face helmet, removed it, tucked it under his left arm, and peeled off his gloves. Hello. The helmet had mussed up his reddish-brown surfer hair, complete with a blond streak. In two steps, he landed on the porch and rang the door chime. I let its warmth echo for about 10 seconds before I opened the door.

"I'm James," he said as he extended his hand. I grasped it firmly. His eyes were sharp and black, like a raven's. His jaw sprouted a wispy beard. Bright teeth flashed against naturally dark skin. He certainly did not have to work on a tan.

"Bonnie," I managed to identify myself without a stammer. I was so glad that I had spent a few minutes on my hair, clothes, and jewelry. "Nice bike."

"Nice necklace," he replied, noting my simple strand of rainbow beads.

"Nice necklace," I replied, noting his turquoise choker and silver star earring. Wow.

Anam calmed down a bit when he came in and peeled off his jacket, revealing a crisp blue shirt and neat jeans. I hung back in the portal to observe the interview—and more of James. He answered all their questions with appropriately placed "Yes, sirs," and "No, ma'ams" before Nog took him out to the lake. Anam followed them with big eyes, then turned to me.

"Well," was all she said. She paced a bit and mumbled something about motorcycles, but I said nothing, using the interlude to run upstairs to apply some lip gloss and recomb my hair. When the guys got back, Anam sat them in the parlor with lemonade. They spent the next hour discussing hours, wages, and responsibilities. James handed Nog his Red Cross Lifeguard Certification and a list of references; Nog handed him a file of regulations.

"If it all checks out," he concluded, "we'd be happy to have you on board."

As I walked James to his bike, I suggested that I take his picture and post it on our website as soon as Nog gave him the thumbs up, which he did a few days later. I really just wanted a picture of him. I snapped one with the lake as a background, to feature him as the newest member of the Companion Moon team. I also took a selfie with him alongside his moped. I sent that one to Erin.

"Rad!" she replied. "You landed a lifeguard."

A few days later, Nog and Anam hired him—the same day that Anam reported we were in the black with reservations up 50 percent, and Facebook likes up to 500.

"This has earned us all a reward," Nog proclaimed at dinner that night. We were one week from opening day. "Hey, Miss Moon, let's take tomorrow off. A whole day, just for us, before the guests arrive."

She started to object, but Nog said that because of our new reservation system and his new smartphone, we didn't have to worry about missing a potential guest. He beamed at me in appreciation.

"We can take the horses on the old road around the western shore. I've been meaning to explore back there. Maybe build a little picnic area on the edge of our property. You know, where the bridge is. We can pack a lunch. What do you say, Ana My Cara?"

I turned to my aunt with pleading eyes. Other than a few laps around the paddock, I hadn't had a chance to ride the horses. Nog's idea got me stoked.

Anam nodded in approval. Early the next morning, she created a picnic from leftovers while Nog and I headed to the barn. Although past their prime, the horses were perfect for easy rides and lots of affection. Nog spoiled them as if they were his own.

As he assembled the tack, I spun in circles, looking up to the rafters, as I had done months ago in imitation of Anam. She arrived with saddlebags that Nog deftly attached to his favorite, Epona, an old sorrel with a proud, flowing mane. Anam preferred the gentleness of Rowan, a dappled gray. Enbar, with white coat, amber eyes, and a youthful good nature, was perfect for me.

As we saddled up, Anam said that *Enbar* was an old Irish word for imagination. Nog had told me that Enbar of the Flowing Mane was a magic horse in Celtic mythology. Running above the sea and ground, he transported the rider to *Tír na nÓg,* the land of eternal youth, the Otherworld—as long as your feet didn't touch the ground. Since my feet, of course, would eventually touch the ground, I went with Anam's definition.

Sometimes when I rode Enbar around the corral, I was a cowgirl. At other times, a warrior queen, or a princess—Knobby's princess—on a unicorn. It was always in a perfect world, my own *Tír na nÓg.* Wind in my face, hair streaming behind me, I sped across land and sea, forever free. Enbar didn't really go fast enough for my tangled hair to stream. And it was always tucked into the helmet that Anam insisted I wear. But in my imagination, I galloped unburdened.

We rode to the lower western shore on a dirt road that bordered a thick, marshy terrain. To the right, an old wooden bridge nestled itself beyond the water's edge. A small stream trickled its way through ferns, catching flecks of sunlight and transforming them into tiny kaleidoscopes.

"The water here comes from an underground well," Nog said as we paused.

Delighted that I could play puns with Nog, I replied, "Well. That sounds like a deep story."

"It is," he grinned. "It's fed by groundwater and then feeds the lake. Anywhere one element—in this case water—meets another element—earth—that place is neither. It's a magical no man's land, a portal, an opening into another dimension." He looked around, then dismounted. "And I think this dimension tastes like lunch."

Anam spread a blanket on the dry ground by the bridge and began to unpack lunch. Nog walked around, adding chores to his unending to-do list, which, unlike Anam's, he kept in his head.

"We need a picnic table over here. And look," he pointed to a cluster of trees with smooth, light brown bark and deep, serrated green leaves tinged with red. "Nine hazel trees. Why, that's magical! The Well of Wisdom is surrounded by nine hazel trees that grow close to water. I'll add a little bench in the midst of them."

"A little bench would be perfect," Anam agreed as she lowered herself to the ground. "I'm a bit sore from riding. But before you start yet another project, please find someone to do something about the noises in the attic. I'm sure they're not mice or bats, but I don't like all those noises. And I don't think the guests will, either. Besides, I'm concerned that the ceiling is going to cave in."

"The ceiling's not going to cave in. The floor is very sound. In fact, when I went up there yesterday ..."

"Nog!" Anam stood in abrupt anger. "You promised." With the quickness of a summer thunderstorm, Nog's face darkened and his voice barked.

"I never promised not to go up there. Never. It's just an attic with a perfectly sound floor, some old furniture, cobwebs, and very familiar memories of being a king, a knight, a cowboy. It's *my* attic. *My* belfry. I've oiled and polished the floors. They're quite safe. And believe me, there are no bats in *my* belfry!"

Sitting on the blanket, I looked from one to the other. Nog had been to the attic. Of course. All those times that he would appear in the portal, I figured—and I'm sure Anam did too—that he had been outside or in the cellar. Instead, he had probably been in the attic.

I couldn't get over seeing my aunt and uncle argue. When I saw tears filling Anam's eyes, I tried to become invisible. Vague memories of Mom and Dad fighting churned in my stomach. I chewed my cuticles.

Now I was really curious about the forbidden upstairs. It still scared me, not only because Anam had forbidden me to go up there but also because that's where Knobby was. And he wasn't friendly like the Invisibles. He just brooded. But Nog had just said it was safe.

"Nog," Anam's voice trembled, "Please. I can't have you getting hurt. Please, please, don't go up there. Promise me."

"I can't promise you that, Ana. I can't. I can promise you there's nothing wrong with the floor. And I can promise to be careful. But my entire childhood, my whole life, is tied to the attic. You have to trust me."

Realizing she had lost the battle, Anam closed her eyes and took a few deep breaths. Opening them, she quietly gathered the picnic leftovers and packed them into the saddlebags. It was a sour ending to a sweet day. Angus met us about halfway home, breaking the uncomfortable silence with a silly polka in the grass.

As the inn came into view, so did the welter. Although I scrutinized the attic for signs of Knobby, he wasn't there. But a few things started to make sense. Nog went to the attic to think about Knobby and the ancestors. His work up there had caused the *tap, tap, tap*.

The welter, however, shook its collective head, suggesting otherwise.

17

IⴹⴹRAⴹ

"Where's Angus?" Anam charged into the kitchen, flapping her arms while I finished what had been a quiet breakfast.

Of all days for him to get loose! We were on a 24-hour countdown to opening day. The sun was barely up, and already there were too many things to do. Anam had made a big deal of washing him last night and giving us strict instructions not to let him out.

"Bonnie," she called over her shoulder as she headed toward her bread-making station. "Go find Angus."

Anam wasn't the only one with things to do.

After submitting my schoolwork portfolio, I'd been going nonstop cleaning guest rooms, hanging new wooden hangers in all the closets, and stocking each guest bathroom with soaps, shampoos, lotions, and toilet paper. I had polished silverware and dusted furniture. In the library, I had set up a guest book, and in the dining room, I had arranged dishes and silverware for a breakfast bar on the sideboard. I glanced over at it. It looked so inviting with its colorful plates and mugs. I needed to take a picture of it. That reminded me that I hadn't even had time to work on my vlog. We had a little countdown clock running on the website, which told me we really needed something current and relevant.

"I need to post ..."

"No, you don't need to post." She fluttered her floured hands around in the air. "That's frivolous right now."

"Frivolous?" I gasped. I eyed my camera and tripod sitting in the office. We had agreed during our meeting yesterday that I would post a vlog of us getting ready for opening day—Anam baking bread, Nog cleaning boats and bikes, me arranging flowers around the house in the vases from Four Fences. A groan within the old walls echoed my despair.

"How can you call my work frivolous? I'm the one who saved the inn. I'm the one who got guests coming!"

"You're right, Bonnie." Anam's shoulders sagged. "I'm sorry, but I'm really nervous." We were all nervous, but she didn't have to treat my contributions as irrelevant. "Your social—whatevers—accomplished what we needed them to do. So just find Angus, then you'll have time to post something."

She turned back to kneading bread, leaving me feeling dismissed. Although we had come a long way in figuring out our relationship, I still resented that she didn't suggest or compromise. And I always obeyed. For once—just once—I'd like to ignore her command. In defiance, I jerked my whole body and stuck out my tongue, as I used to do with Deb-Horror. I hadn't done that in a long time. Remembering how good it felt, I did it again.

Anam was more intent on thumping down dough, its yeasty mass pulsating with each punch. The house pulsed, too. *Tap tap creeaakkkkk,* it throbbed. Anam's single braid swayed back and forth in rhythm with the creaking and her kneading. A vague cloud of microscopic flour hung in the air. Steam from the cauldron hissed in the silence between us.

"You're treating me like an indentured servant," I sassed,

chewing on a cuticle. That got her attention.

"Indentured servant?" She spun to face me, eyes as round as her face. With elbows tucked, floured hands curled into soft fists, and jean-clad legs planted a foot apart, she looked nothing like the aunt I knew as a child. "Where did you get *that* idea?" She looked around, perhaps suspecting Nog had put me up to this.

"In history." That was true, sort of. "You're making me work off my stay here."

"Working off your stay here?" She scoffed. "That's really funny. We're all working off our stay here. That's what being a family—a *loving family*—is all about. Stop acting like a little girl."

"Don't call me a little girl."

"Then please, Bonnie, don't act like one. Start being a grown-up. And stop sucking—chewing—your thumb. You're too old for that." Feeling my cheeks redden in shame, I slid my hands behind my back. "Right now, it's your job to find Angus because you're a part of this operation, part of this family. Not because you're some kind of servant." She planted a floured hand on my clench-fisted sulk. "Remember what Nog said the night you arrived? You belong here."

Inhaling deeply, Anam looked taller than her five feet, four inches. Without a word, she turned to the sink, washed her hands, and shook them dry.

Then she reached one hand into a bright yellow jar and the other into an earthenware crock. "Here you go, a muffin for you. Dog cookies for Angus." Accepting the goodies softened my fists and got Cookie's attention. "Now go. The sooner you find Angus, the sooner you can do your, your posting." With one long braid flung over her shoulder, her stern eyes directed me toward Nog's portal. "Better wear a jacket. It's cool now, but it's going to get warm."

I grabbed Angus's leash and a windbreaker from the coat

rack. Off to the far side, a deep red mantle hung separately. I stared at it for a second. It was Anam's and not for sharing, although I was tempted to take it, just to spite her. But I instinctively knew better. I trudged across the veranda, through the heather shrubs, and past the vividly painted Adirondack chairs that would soon encourage guests to enjoy a cup of coffee, plan a day's hike, or just dreamily gaze upon the lake.

Entering the barn, I noticed that Nog had spread fresh hay. I ground my heels into the clay floor and looked around. Inhaling the sweetness, I looked up—not that Angus would be up in the rafters, but because when I stood with my head raised and eyes closed, it made me dizzy, sort of like spinning then stopping. It reminded me of church. Maybe I should pray. Since I didn't know any prayers for lost dogs, I made one up.

"Please, God, whoever you are, help me find Angus. And while you're at it, help me find where I belong." Anam and Nog said I belonged here. But I didn't feel like it. I looked around and whispered, "Companion Moon."

Neither God nor Mom answered, but there was a rustle in the far corner. Lolling in freshly mucked stalls, the cats roused themselves. Willy's markings camouflaged him in the matted hay while Mo, whose black fur turned a rich sable brown in the sunlight, blinked her green eyes from a sunny spot in the far corner. She was more dignified than Willy, whose life revolved around chasing bugs. Sometimes, they would climb into the rafters and leap from pillar to pillar. But not today.

"Hey, kitties. Where's Angus?" Only Willy deigned to respond with a weak mew before resettling into a nap. That was silly, conversing with a cat. Dogs, maybe, but not cats. Except when they wanted food, of course. Dogs, on the other hand, seem to get it. With a yip or a wag, they suggest answers. Horses, too. You have to be able to communicate with a horse to ride one.

Horses. Maybe Angus would be with them. Following a

trail of hooves, I trotted to the paddock. If this were a day with nothing to do, I would groom Enbar and imagine myself on a journey. From where I stood, it was clear that Angus was not there, but I tried anyway. "Cookies, Angus!"

Disappointed that biscuits were not apples, the horses simply ignored me. I slogged back to the rack where tuned and polished bicycles awaited riders. The one I had been using seemed too small. How did that happen? Had Nog changed the seat? I found a larger one that fit me better and grabbed my helmet.

"I'm going into the village," I shouted to the unseen but watchful Anam. Nog heard and stepped out from the shadows of the barn. I think he was working on the business center.

"Good day for an *immram*," he called.

"No, just looking for Angus."

"Perhaps. But maybe you will find the meaning to life on your journey to find Angus."

I shrugged as I headed down the driveway.

The helmet had become my symbol of independence and the driveway was my road to freedom. I'd been to town by myself a few times since the Ghost Girl incident. On gentle glides down it, the progression of spring mesmerized me. As much as I missed the city, there it was winter, then spring. Nothing in between. Here, it was all in between. Ugly gray branches ripened into yellow fuzz, then glowed neon as tiny emerald buds popped open into sunny forsythia. In May, azalea blooms appeared in unending arrays of colors before plumping into forest green.

The bigger bike was clunkier than the one I was used to. Maneuvering it down the stone-edged driveway, I glanced up at the inn and noticed the impatiens spilling out of the bright window boxes. Anam was right. It looked cozy. And creepy— Knobby appeared under the eave long enough to nod. Then he disappeared.

As I pedaled past hedges that marked the property line, I spotted Miss Eileen weeding flowers in front of the Fish House. It, too, looked cozy. Smokey was buzzing wood at the back of The Fiery Pig. Since Angus often hunted for scraps at both places, I whistled for him.

Not only had Nog taught me how to whistle, but he also said that whistling is an ancient language. I didn't know if that was true—it was hard to tell with Nog. But Angus often responded to a whistle when words wouldn't do. And since Nog also said that whistling brought good luck, I trilled again and again. Miss Eileen wiggled her fingers at me. Smokey turned, waved, and returned to his island of pigs. No dog.

I pedaled past the Mountainside Dairy, where Angus often stopped for stray dollops of fresh cream. He wasn't there, but Mamie was. She joined me.

When I paused at the Mill Shops, I let my imagination do battle with Nog's monsters. With my bike as a warrior horse, I armed myself with weapons from the ironsmith that were so powerful I could turn Mourning Stream into fire. I thought about my grudges. "Don't grind my grudges," I said aloud, but added silently, *not yet*. That's when I heard the wind whoosh, but nothing moved. I looked around and realized that more of the Invisibles were with me. I was glad for the company.

In the village, Kath was sweeping the sidewalk in front of the Voyager, causing debris to swirl into little pockets along the curb. I waved before skidding to a stop at the sight of the boy who led the Ghost Girl taunts. He was hanging out by himself on a bench across from the café.

I hadn't seen him since that incident, and my first instinct was to get the heck out of there, but Edmund scrawled his name in the dust that had accumulated at my feet. I noticed that several of the uncles had joined him. Fortified by their presence, I dismounted and did the deep breathing that Anam had taught me. I realized that I felt sorry for someone who was so thirsty for attention that he enjoyed making fun of me, and probably other kids, too. I walked right up to him.

"Remember me? I'm Ghost Girl." He curled his lip in response but before any words could escape his foul mouth, I leveled my eyes on his. "Get this straight. If you ever pick on me again, you'll answer to my crew." I gestured to either side of me. "My ghosts. They're real. They will haunt you to stone." The wind picked up just enough to jolt him into a shiver. He grunted and turned away. The welter applauded. Maybe I didn't need any magic potions after all. Maybe my welter was my potion. I smirked as I strutted back to my bike.

Next, I tried Hermit's. Angus wasn't there, but Seamus was. He grabbed a hunk of cheese and joined us. So did Kelty and Jeanne at the Crystal Keep and Rainbow Stream.

Then I saw Baylar sweeping her sidewalk with her snarl of murky Invisibles.

"You," she muttered in a voice barely above a whisper, wagging her bony finger as she had done the day we met. "You should be ashamed of yourself, you little troublemaker."

Emboldened by my crew, I took a few deep breaths and walked right up to her.

"You," I sassed right back, wagging *my* finger in *her* face. "You ought to be ashamed of *yourself* picking on me. You're a bully, and you should mind your own business. You've got enough trouble of your own." I waved dismissively toward her dark shadows. "You shouldn't have tried to make me feel bad for something I didn't do. I was just a little kid who did nothing wrong. You're an adult who *is* doing something wrong. You and your cousin Tony should mind your own business."

Baylar stared at me, but instead of feeling stabbed by a bolt of lightning, I was filled with a warm sense of purpose and felt an inch taller. Maybe I actually was an inch taller, because I could look her straight in the eyes. Or the good eye anyway. Her evil eye didn't affect me anymore. Her Invisibles disappeared while mine cheered me on.

"How do you like that?" I asked them aloud. Baylar thought I was talking to her. She spit on the ground and walked inside her shop.

My heart skipped when I saw James lounging on the bench in front of Joy's. His long, tanned legs stretched lazily onto the sidewalk and my imagination. Placing my helmet in the basket, I fluffed my hair and discreetly dug out some cherry lip balm from my jeans. Flicking a dab on my lips, I smiled.

"Hi, James."

"Hey." He whipped off sunglasses that were totally for show on this overcast morning. Rubbing his sleepy eyes awake, he sat up straight. "Yeah, hey, hi, Bonnie. I guess we'll be seeing a lot of each other this summer." His dazzling grin warmed my heart. "I saw my picture on your blog. I like it. I was going to head out to your place this morning to check everything out. Maybe I'll see you then."

"Yeah, maybe." My heart cooled. "But first I have to find Angus. The dog."

"You have a dog? What kind?"

"Mixed breed. So mixed, in fact, that I think he's just mixed up." James laughed at my attempted joke.

"Well, okay. If not today, tomorrow?" As I bobbled my head in agreement, he replaced his shades, stretched his legs a little farther, and resettled into his nap. Joy was right. He did seem to work on his tan, if nothing else. He might be lazy, but he sure was cute. Luna fluttered in agreement.

I rode toward the edge of town and glanced down at the pitiful beach. A young family played in the sand, taking pictures of each other. That's when I noticed a gravelly trail that led from it west toward Companion Moon. I'd never been on it and I wouldn't today, either. Although it looked like it might be shorter, it didn't look bike worthy. And if Angus were indeed taking it home, he would be impossibly ahead of me.

Then I noticed someone in a long, red, hooded cape

moving along the path. I shivered. Not only did I stay away from strangers on strange paths, but there was also something about the stranger that was, I don't know, weird.

Riding up the hill, I circled past the old cemetery, where Angus sometimes hunted chipmunks. Coasting to a stop, I wasn't sure that I wanted to go in there alone. Porter had said that the secret to understanding life is to first understand death. I understood neither, instead feeling a bit apprehensive at this island of sorrow. Nog told me that confidence hides a kernel of fear, and fear hides a kernel of courage. So, I drew up some courage, dismounted, and laid my bike on the grass next to the statue of Nuca.

I followed her visionless eyes a few hundred feet toward the barely discernible lakeshore trail to see if perhaps Angus had taken it. I saw only the woman in the red cloak. At first, I thought it was Anam, wearing her red cloak. What? Did she not trust me to find Angus after making such a big fuss about it? But this woman was much taller. And there was no way Anam would be out strolling the lakefront. While I studied her, she paused and glanced around, almost as if she too, were looking for something. Her dog, perhaps? Lifting her face to the sky, she pivoted to look around. As she turned toward me, I stepped back into the shadow of a tree. I didn't want her watching me watching her.

Besides, I really did have a dog to catch. I readied a whistle, but stopped. Even though Nog had said that whistling past a graveyard meant that you were acting brave even if you weren't, I took a deep breath, whistled, and called for Angus in a soft voice. A few photographers and genealogy buffs were haunting the graves that were huddled between ancient oaks and sprawling crabapple trees. They glanced toward me and one another.

"My dog," I said to no one in particular. "I'm looking for my dog." Had I just called Angus *my* dog? I was embarrassed to admit that I did indeed. But they were too busy capturing pictures and grave rubbings of once frightening angels of death and eroded epitaphs. A walk around the cemetery would make a good vlog. I made a mental note to come back with my camera.

When no dog emerged from the headstones, I grabbed my bike. Before I could mount it, however, a distinctly feminine voice stopped me in my tracks. "Take 17 companions," she advised—not through my ears but from inside my head. Seventeen companions? I looked around, but no one was paying attention to me, let alone talking to me. I must have been imagining it. As I grabbed my bike, the voice continued. "You will find what you seek."

"Who said that?" The historians and photographers looked at me again. My eyes landed on Nuca's name and I got that itching on the back of my neck. She wasn't like the Invisibles. First, they all seemed like people and Nuca was stone. Second, they were all related to Nog, and they all started by telling me their names. This was more like I was hearing the words of a fortuneteller inside my head, and I didn't like it one bit. Hurrying away, I noticed Arthur and Dobbin, who had been hanging out between the headstones. They shrugged their shadowy shoulders and joined the welter that was amassing behind me.

I stepped into the bike's frame and pushed off toward the inn. It seemed like hours, but I guessed that Anam's final batch of bread probably was still in the oven. Pausing before the last uphill climb, I rested next to the *Companion Moon* sign.

Pay attention, I told Mom. *I need you.*

In the clearing, Nog had tucked a little white bench. Neatly pruned bushes hugged either side of it. Angus often sunned himself here after chasing a rabbit. He would kick his paws skyward and roll from one side to the other, twisting his hips to an unheard polka. But not today. I plopped on the bench, arms sagging between splayed knees.

"Angus! I have biscuits. Come here, good dog." Nothing but the sifting of leaves as a bird took to flight. I plucked a sprig of mint and chewed on it while I fixed my gaze between the unseen and nowhere. What did Nuca's words mean? I didn't have 17 companions, and all I wanted was to go home.

Home. Not to the inn and not to Dad's. Home. The one of Christmases and birthdays, when Dad lived with us and took us to the beach, where Mom kissed away bumps and bruises, where I opened the door every day to belonging, instead of aloneness. My shoulders wilted. I didn't want to look for a dog. I wanted to pick flowers and post a vlog. A rustle in the brush brought me back to the present.

"Angus?" No dog, just another critter living an unseen life. I ate a muffin. Cookie appeared and got most of the crumbs before the ants did. Giant ants. They had no choice but to find food—theirs is a world of digest and decay. Mine was a world of following orders and finding a dog. I headed back up the driveway.

18

ninth wave

Nog waved and headed my way as I pedaled up the driveway. "Angus must be across the lake," he called.

"Check over by the bridge." he suggested. "Hug the shoreline. Take Mor, the canoe." Steering me toward the boat, he ex-plained his logic. "It's small enough for you to handle alone, big enough to bring the dog back, and," he smiled, "it's named after your mother."

He had faith in me. Apparently, so did Anam, who waved from the kitchen window. I felt a little grown-up.

"Your provisions." Nog gave me a cooler filled with a peanut butter sandwich on Anam's freshly baked bread, fruit, and water. I added the cookies and muffins I had brought with me to town. He handed me sunscreen, and we stashed it all in the bow. Then we traded my helmet for my new hat and my windbreaker for a life jacket. Once he got me in the canoe, I noticed Maggie was with me. I felt secure. But I asked Nog anyway if he could join me.

"I'd love to," he shrugged, "but you know my wife has a list a mile long. Wants me to be around if the housekeepers need help moving furniture. They're coming," he glanced at his watch, "in about an hour. And, of course, I'm supposed to do something about the noises in the attic." He winked. "Even though I'm not supposed to go up there." Handing me a paddle, he raised his right hand to his head in a salute. He reminded me of Baron.

"If Angus is out there, that's where you'll find him. You know, when Saint Brendan sailed the seas looking for the Otherworld, he found it beyond the ninth wave. Just like Clíona—remember her?" I thought of the church and nodded. "When she left the Otherworld, she was washed back with a ninth wave."

"Why the ninth?" I was stalling. "Why not the eighth or tenth?"

"Now that's an excellent question," Nog beamed. "Nine is an important number in all the world cultures—Indian, Chinese, Egyptian, Greek, Aztec, Mayan. In Norse mythology, the universe is divided into nine worlds. Think about how we use the number in everyday language. A pregnancy lasts nine months. We say a cat has nine lives, or a stitch in time saves nine."

"Yeah," I said. "Or being on Cloud Nine."

"Exactly! Remember when we went on the picnic?" Of course I did, especially the argument. Before I could dwell on that, Nog continued. "When I noticed the hazel trees, I said that the Well of Wisdom is surrounded by nine hazel trees that grow close to water. Nine is also three times three, and three is sacred in Celtic mythology. Think of the three-leafed shamrock."

"Is this now a math lesson?" Nog turned everything into a lesson. He grinned.

"No need to, Bon. You've passed math with an A. Bottom line is that the Ninth Wave separates the Earth from the Otherworld." He saluted again. "To the Ninth Wave."

I returned the gesture as he gently shoved the boat into

the water. Although he would return to his errands, I knew he would keep his awareness with me. Besides, he had his new phone, and the house had a boosted signal. So, I could call him if there were a problem. I also knew that he had dropped an electric motor into one of the rowboats so that he could race to fetch me in no time. But we both knew that wouldn't be necessary. Then he turned toward Anam, who was watching the watcher.

Unlike many of Nog's aggrandizements, this body of water really was a lake. Not a pond. It was at least a mile wide and a few miles long. And certainly not the briny deep. In fact, it wasn't deep at all. If I hugged the shoreline as Nog instructed and the boat capsized, I'd be standing in water that reached my waist. But I knew that wouldn't happen.

But I pretended otherwise. Sometimes it was an ocean of mist, spouting clouds from its surface, or a sea of glass in the windless morning. Or sporadically sprinkled with sparkling diamonds, it was a lagoon within an enchanted forest where I set off to the west to fight monsters, wrest treasures, discover new worlds, encounter a prince, save a maiden, and oh yeah, find a dog.

Schools of perch, bass, and trout circled about in opposite directions just offshore, testifying to the lake's reputation as a fisherman's paradise. A vacationer's refuge. Or a girl's undoing—if she were to encounter a legendary monster that dwelled in its depths. I didn't believe that, but it was fun to pretend.

The lake was one of my classrooms. Nog taught me geography, geology, and biology by walking around it; astronomy and astrology by observing the sky above it; and history by telling me what was buried in it. We studied my ancestors, world events, and even Irish fairy tales. Then I wrote up summaries, which counted for English. When I had turned everything in to my teacher for credit, I realized it had been my best school year ever.

On that morning, the smooth pewter surface transformed itself into a rippled teal, creating a kaleidoscope of sky and flowers that reminded me of the millefiori beads at the Crystal Keep. I wanted to scoop them all up, string them on silver, then drape them around my head and neck. I was a young goddess cast out upon the main, fleeing a dragon, under the spell of ...

"A magic potion," I said aloud, inspired by little bubbles, little fish, flotsam, flecks, and algae that brewed in slowly stirring currents. *A magic potion for a crystal vial,* Kelty seemed to whisper in my ear. I craved bewitchment; I was, after all, a princess. Maybe. And maybe I was too old for such a pretense, but princess was better than dog hunter.

I lowered the paddle and peered into Nog's Otherworld. Deep within the lake's reflection were the buried legends of our ancestors, but I saw only underwater grasses. Braking toward the water's edge, I paused to scan the shore. My body was growing strong—a new phenomenon—and my skinny midsection was getting curvy. Once flaccid arms now responded to my will as I set the course and plied away.

The sun completely edged out the clouds and pleasant coolness gave way to sticky warmth. After a bit, I slackened the pace and as I rounded Bull Rock, I whistled. The welter cheered me on. I whistled again. And again. I called for Angus, again and again. Alerted to crinklings in the brush, I looked in one direction, then another. But they were just that. Crinklings.

Careful not to upset the balance, I rested the oar across the hull and then engaged my shoulders to rotate my head in one direction then the other. I shrugged up and down, back and forth, easing the tension across my upper back. Very cautiously, I twisted my hips to relieve my lower back. I wiggled my way into sit dancing. If my friends could see me now, they would most certainly tease me. Lulled by the slip-slap of soft waves, I sought old comforts in memories of them.

Friends. Erin told me that she never saw Sara anymore because of her dance lessons. I covered my eyes in the recalled shame of dance lessons. I had begged Dad to let me take classes with Sara at Miss Susie's. Even though I was nowhere near as good as Sara, I did practice every day. Every single day.

For the recital, we wore costumes with swirly scarves. But Dad missed my recital, sending Deborrah instead. A burning sourness replaced the warmth of memories. That afternoon, I left my slippers at the studio and never went back.

Dad had complained about wasting money, saying he knew I wouldn't stick with it. How could I tell him it was because everyone else had family there except me? I felt a little guilty thinking about Deborrah. Maybe Nog was right. I didn't give her enough credit. Maybe I needed to forgive her. I said a silent goodbye to Jenny and Sara. I would probably never see them again. But I would see Erin.

After drifting for a few minutes, I reset my paddle. A couple of strokes brought me full circle to the exact point where I had sat minutes before. That's when I noticed I wasn't alone. Not only was Maggie with me, but the entire welter had managed to fit itself into the boat, like an obscure crew guiding me to safe harbor. A bit of that déjà vu thing overtook me, like I had been here before. In the van, when Nog and Anam picked me up at the station, I had seen myself in a small boat in a troubled sea. But this was a calm lake. I shook my head to clear that image, then laughed out loud. I used to be afraid of the Invisibles. Uneasy. Like maybe I was nuts. Now I found comfort in their presence.

"Welcome aboard," I said aloud, calling all 17 of them by name. Out here, I didn't have to worry about anyone hearing me. I felt like Santa—Santa Hermit, in fact. "Come, Baron," I called to the sailor who led the crew. "Come, Luna, come Tess,

Aloysius, and Jack. On, Seamus; on, Edmund; on, Tory, and Gramp. To the *céilí*, Maggie, Mamie, and Cookie. To the Otherworld, Paddy, Dobbin, Arthur, and Jeanne. Dash with me, Kelty, dash with me all."

I giggled at my little ditty. So did the welter, except for Tory. He tried to dampen my mood by whispering, "Save yourself. Release your grudges." I playfully swatted him away, causing the canoe to wobble a little. I quickly steadied it and admonished him.

"Don't rock my boat." He shrugged in response. I saw the bridge where I had picnicked with Nog and Anam and angled toward it. After wedging the canoe into a muddy strip, I stood and stepped over the side, planting one foot in a spongy mud flat, and hopping the other onto firm land. I stretched my body top to toe before securing the boat to a tree. After fastening my life jacket into the hull, I walked over to the bridge.

I noticed that Nog had painted it a pale blue. It reminded me of a Claude Monet painting at Anam's museum. Although this real-life picture didn't have water lilies, it did have a small stream trickling through ferns beneath it, catching flecks of sunlight and transforming them into tiny prisms. There was another big difference—my bridge had muddy pawprints all over it. *Aha!*—Angus had been here.

I walked up to its apex, a good vantage point for spotting an errant dog. Folding my elbows on top of the rail, I gazed north and south. I didn't see Angus, but I noticed that Nog had been busy. He'd already built a bench amid the purple asters, buttercups, and clover that sloped gently to the water's edge.

I looked to the other side. With the sun nearly overhead, my squat shadow mimicked me. I flapped my arms, she flapped hers. I extended them overhead, she stretched with me. I wiggled, she wiggled. I jumped, she jumped. Following our lead, the welter danced shadowlessly in the breeze. We all scoured the brush for any sign of the wandering Angus. If only

I could find him and head home.

Home? Had I just called the inn home? Being somewhere and belonging were two different things. Only a few hours ago, Anam told me I belonged here. Sure, she and Nog did their best to help me fit in, but I didn't *belong*. I belonged in my old life. I belonged with Mom. I begrudged everyone and everything that prevented that—Dad, Deb-Horror, Baylar, old friends, new school, bullies. I was a misfit. I was lonely. I couldn't even admit to myself how lonely I was. A flood of memories gushed out of me. I tried right there on the bridge to cram everything back in, but like the vast and unexpected troubles Pandora unleashed, misery clung to me like vapors of fog over the lake. Giving in to my deepest grudge—I didn't want to be here—I crumbled into sobs.

I don't know how long I stood there, but at some point, whether it was physical exhaustion, the sunshine on my forehead, or just being cried out, my mood brightened a bit. I wiped my face with my hands, then looking around to be sure no one could see me, blew my nose into my shirt. My head bobbled in a defiant shake, loosening the hat. I took it off and let my tangled hair fall. In my periphery it blinked auburn—sort of like Mom's—sparkling with diamonds bouncing off the water.

Hunger replaced tears. To Anam's lunch, I added fresh blackberries from a nearby bush. The sweet fruit and a sudden burst of butterflies brightened my spirits. Forsaking my search for Angus, I danced with the iridescent lepidopterans—that's the official name for butterflies and moths. A bright green one landed on my arm. When I looked closely, I noticed it wasn't a butterfly at all. It was a moth, a Luna moth. One day, I would make a dress from Luna silk. It would be as green as emeralds and as fine as silver, casting a net upon me that would reach up, up, up to the highest sky. The Invisible Luna nodded approval. And since the elongated tails of the moth's hindwings confused the sonar detection used by bats to find food, my gown would protect me from those fearsome creatures.

The moths spun themselves into my magnificently cloaked prince. He and I had ridden Enbar to a gala in a magnificent castle in the midst of these hazel trees that Nog said surrounded the Well of Wisdom.

The sun exaggerated my gangly limbs as I danced with my prince, who became one with my lengthening shadow. My snotty shirt was now a gown of goddess proportions and my hair streamed with silver-strung diamonds encircled by radiant butterflies. Thus transformed, I twirled and swayed until our shadows extended into the enchanted forest that teemed with dragons that we had tamed, and ogres that we had transformed into loyal subjects. Victorious, we jumped onto Nog's nifty bench.

A rustle beyond the palace stopped the dance. As prince and butterflies dissolved into a dark umbra, the Invisibles separated into their individual entities to encircle the meadow where I stood. My shadow had lengthened into a taller version of myself, telling me that time had passed. What if I wasn't alone? What if it was the hooded woman I saw on the low road? What if it got dark? As the rustles grew louder, I struggled with the intersection of reality and imagination.

A mist rose from the sod and attached itself to the edges of my shadow. Then my ankles. Then, wetness everywhere. The wet, wagging Angus, encircled by birds, was spinning himself dry just beyond my reach.

"Angus," I yelled, "Come here, you dumb dog." In his mouth was a long stick, a peace branch, perhaps. I considered playing toss and catch, but then thought better of the situation. What if he ran again? Instead, I pulled a biscuit from my pocket. "I have cookies for you."

Staying one step ahead of his hunger, I playfully grabbed

the stick's other end and drew him toward the boat so I could retrieve the leash. He complied in his half-smiling way, wet coat gleaming silver in the afternoon sun.

As I handed him a biscuit, he dropped the thick twig. I clipped the leash to the collar and held it in my tight fist. Done! I could not afford to let him escape. Once restrained, he sat with me on a slip of beach while I reprimanded him.

"Do you know how long I've been looking for you?" I scolded, tapping each word for emphasis. "Do you know I had to sail the seas and fight off dragons to find you?" He simply cocked his black head to the right. A butterfly captured my attention. "And give up the prince of my dreams for you?"

He cocked his head again, this time to the left. Then he sat up, locked onto my gaze, and shifted it to the stick.

"Oh, you want to play catch, do you?" I teased him. He shook his head, releasing the last of his wetness, and looked back at me. "No. We've played enough catch for one day."

If I were to hurry, I could make it back to pick flowers to start the vlog. But, I slyly deduced, if I took my time, it would be too late to do anything but shower and eat. The latter seemed a just reward. I'd work on the vlog tomorrow. I'd focus on guests arriving. "Let's eat, Angus."

Sitting together on the edge of the lake, I played with the branch as we shared the rest of Anam's bake-a-thon. I took off my shoes and let the water lap about my heels and calves. Birds chirped. Fish splashed. Angus nuzzled into me, paws over eyes, haunches curled into himself. I closed my eyes. In exhaustion and relief, a dreamlike state crept into the fringes of my mind. Angus, Nog, Anam, Dad, Mom. The picture Dad took at the beach, of Mom and me covered with sand, sun hats obscuring faces that sported matching freckles. Mom crouching with a giggling toddler between her arms and legs. A bonny day on a bonny beach—a bonny day in a bonny life. Bonnie banks. Bonny waves. Bonny toes ...

Wet toes. In that instant, immediately before sleep, when consciousness steps into an abyss, I jerked. Yuck! Angus was licking my toes. Yikes! I had let go of the leash, but Angus showed no interest in running away. He uncurled himself, stood, and shook himself dry. He raised his head toward the inn. I could see it across the fetch, tucked up into rolling green lawns, basking in the afternoon sun. Its quaint and rustic beauty caught me by surprise.

I took one whiff of Angus and realized he would need a bath when we got back. I brightened. That would be Anam's job. Although she often pretended to begrudge the task, I knew she really enjoyed it. I stood, using Angus's branch for support. Nice walking stick. I kept it. I raised it with my right hand into the air. Now I was a queen, a ruler, and this was my scepter. Planting my left hand on my hip, I aimed my stick to the southeast and declared, "Come, Angus. Let us go forth."

I texted Nog to tell him we were heading home and then settled my charge in the bow and myself in the stern, careful not to let go of the leash. I thrust an oar into the soft margin of beach and leaned into it, pressing our combined weight into the mud and releasing us back into the sea. Freed from the hold of land and accompanied by my welter of Invisibles and a dog, I allowed myself to be drawn by the magnetism of Companion Moon.

19

Day is Done

nam sent me straight to the shower while she tended to Angus. I took my time lathering top to toe. Sinking into my window seat cushion, I toweled my hair dry and watched Nog step outside for his evening ritual of contemplation and gratitude. Pausing at the head of his labyrinth, he turned and looked up toward his Companion Moon. No longer did he dash toward the lake through a tangle of weeds and memory. In-stead, he wandered and wondered over a meticulously groom-ed walkway, dotted with quaint benches and patches of flow-ers.

While Anam and I often joined Nog on these evening walks, tonight he was understandably alone; tomorrow was opening day, the culmination of his dream. Although I had chosen a hot shower over the adventure trail, I questioned my choice when I saw the setting sun sifting through the overhead boughs. It would soon blaze rosy-orange across the lake, burnishing Nog's brow and swelling in his barreled chest as he hooked calloused hands into beltless loops. I think this was one of those times when he needed alone time to meditate on his blessings with the humility of having listened to his heart, imagined with his wits, and toiled with his body. Few men are so blessed, he often proclaimed. Then he would bow his head and say, "Amen."

"Day is done," I heard Anam say to Angus, amidst the clatter of dishes and pots, from my little room above the kitchen. It reminded me of a tune Nog often whistled. "Taps," he called it. *Day is done*, the song goes, *Gone the sun, From the lake, From the hill, From the sky. All is well, Safely rest. God is nigh.* It was written during the Civil War to tell the troops it was time to go to bed. I was tired, but certainly not ready for bed. From my perch, I noticed Nog tramp toward the house, elfin in step yet stalwart in stature. I think he was whistling.

Shoulders strained from rowing, I stretched lean arms up and overhead, lifting long, damp hair up and out, allowing the natural curls to fall across bronzed shoulders. Rising from my seat, I caught myself in the mirror. I hardly recognized the girl who slowly smiled back at me. She looked more like the waitress at the Avalon than the sad little girl with the sad little life who arrived here only a few months ago. Although I was hungry and tired, I lingered over what to wear, until aromas reminded me that dinner awaited. I settled on a nice blouse and a sporty skirt.

"O, Ana My Cara, my love, my dear, what's for dinner?" I heard Nog sing as he came through the portal. "I'm as hungry as a bear."

She ticked off the dinner menu. Salmon, baby peas and carrots, fresh sourdough bread, and strawberry shortcake. Now I was famished.

"Where's Bonnie?" he asked.

"Upstairs. She seems to be done showering. Poor girl. She's had a long day. I'm sure she'll sleep like the dreaming Angus." On cue, Angus grumbled so loud that I could hear it up here.

"Me, too!" Nog proclaimed. "My turn to wash up. Then let's eat."

Sun-flushed, damp, and buoyant, I met my uncle at the top of the age-worn stairs, which were wide enough for us to pass each other, but narrow enough for him to give me a quick hug.

"Thanks for finding Angus, my dear girl. That was one of the most important things that needed to be done today." I was sure there were other important things to do, like posting a blog, but I hugged him back and dawdled downstairs.

"Smells good, Anam." I took in her scrubbed face, silken hair, white blouse, and light blue skirt. We almost matched.

"Wow, you look nice," we said in unison to the other. She encircled me with unfettered arms, inhaling the freshness of soap and shampoo. "You've become quite the young lady."

Angus rolled on the hearth, sat up, tilted his freshly washed head, and seemed to smile in agreement. He lifted a contented paw from his nose to his brow, almost a salute.

"Can you help me set the table? Tonight's a celebration. I'm using all the good stuff." She had laid out fine china, crystal goblets, monogrammed silverware, and a linen tablecloth with hand-tatted edging. I smiled when I noticed she had done my job of placing wildflowers in little glass vases. "All of this came from Aunt Luna." Anam's moon face widened as she thought of Nog's aunt. I smiled as Luna inspected each item, knowing that I knew more about her than Anam did. "Did we ever tell you about crazy Aunt Luna?" I nodded.

"Years ago, she left me all her handcrafts, along with the patterns and techniques that created them. I had little use for them back then." In those days, Anam treated the quaint crafts as folk art, telling friends and colleagues that she might one day display them in a museum. This house had become that showcase. She pointed to a leatherbound book in the tidy little library off the parlor.

"They're all in that book," she said. "Someday, it will be yours. Now, though, I would give anything for another session with her. She was a wisp of a woman with pewter-flecked hair braided from crown to nape. She and Aunt Mamie were very close. Did we tell you about her?" I nodded as Mamie peeked out from the nook. "Mamie used to pack a flask of whiskey in her purse. Then she'd nod off in the midst of a lively conversation." Anam snickered. "Her fondness for the bottle wasn't as well hidden as she thought." With that, Mamie waved a bottle of whiskey in the air, demonstrating that she liked it more than milk! The upstairs creaked. A whoosh, a rasp, a squeak. I still found all the noises startling.

"Are there bats up there, Anam? Nog swears it's birds, or the house settling, but ..., I don't know. Sometimes it scares me to think they are bats." Ghosts, okay, but not bats.

With a nudge and a wink, she whispered, "I don't think so, Bonnie. But I let Nog think I do. But still, don't go up there. I don't trust the floor."

"No problem," I giggled. "I hate bats."

"Bats?" Nog made a dramatic entrance, hooking his thumbs and fluttering his hands as if he were shadow-miming a flying creature. "A flitter mouse. Maybe one bringing us a missive." Anam and I shared a glance. "A symbol of family ties and rebirth. You shouldn't fear the unknown, wife and niece. Fear interferes with the mind's power ..."

"Good God, Nog," Anam interrupted. "Enough of the bats. The only ones I want in this house sound like *Die Fledermaus*." She fluttered her arms as if conducting Strauss's operetta. "Speaking of which, Nog, put some music on. Let's eat."

"What a festive table," Nog said as we gathered around it. "I recognize all these pieces. We used them only for special occasions. Tonight, for sure, is one. Luna learned the needlecrafts from her grandmother—or was it her great-aunt? Tess, I believe," Nog said, more to himself than to us.

"Tess was a descendant of Gramp's second cousin, once-removed," I recited. While Nog beamed with approval, Tess appeared, teasing me with several three-foot-long chains of uneven crochet stitches that I had tucked into a basket in the parlor weeks ago. She left one out for Nog to find, which he picked up.

"Aha. I see you've been practicing. Tess revered the art as a family trust, as if each twist of the yarn and loop of the hook wove a tragic story of love and survival. Someday—when I'm old—I'll write a book."

Nog handed the chain to me. "Your mom would be proud." I wrapped it around my hair, tying it into a ponytail. "I think Anam planted a delicate seed in you. One day those baby chains will grow, just like life's loopy twists and turns weave the tapestry of life. You are now part of that web, Bon, one whose strands tie Tess to Luna, Luna to Anam, and Anam to you." The aunts applauded.

"To Luna," Anam lifted a glass before setting it on the table.

"To us!" Nog said, reaching for a slender bottle sitting on the hutch. The remainder of the welter sifted in one by one.

"Got this from Hermit." Nog held a tall, thin bottle high in the air. "Strawberry wine. His wife made it from local berries." He uncorked the bottle. A fruity essence filled the air as he ceremoniously poured three antique glasses with a pale liquid.

"In celebration of the inn and tonight's full moon—the Strawberry Moon, in fact—we drink of the past, present, and future. And Bonnie, my dear, you have earned a taste of this elixir of the gods." I had never tasted wine, or any kind of alcohol. With wide eyes, I looked to Anam, who nodded. My mood rallied. This was indeed something special.

"To the spirits above, the life divine," Nog toasted. "To the life below, the spirits of wine."

I sipped the wine. Not sweet, not sour. Definitely fruity. Nog and Anam exchanged looks as they watched my mouth dance, eyes water, and body flush. My brain tingled. Neither child nor woman, I felt like both. Wow.

"*Sláinte,*" Nog said.

"What's that?" I asked.

"*Sláinte. SLAHN-chə.* Say it after me."

"*Sláinte.*" It was a fun word to say.

""*Sláinte.* To your health!"

Dinner deliciously proceeded. I had learned to like salmon. Unlike the dry stuff I'd tried in restaurants, Anam made hers with a pesto crust on the outside and soft pinky flakiness inside. The peas and carrots snapped slightly when I bit into them.

"Wonderful bread, Anam," I said as I cut a chunk of fresh sourdough and slathered it with sweet butter. "I think you got it right. I think it's better than the Voyager Café."

She sparkled, just like the wine that complemented each course.

"Oh!" Anam suddenly remembered, as she stood to bring the strawberry shortcake to the table. "James came by today while you were out." While I was out. Right. Dismissed was more like it. But I perked up. "He asked about you. Said he saw you this morning. He's a very nice young man. I think Nog's right, that he likes you." I bit my lip, straightened my glasses, and sat up a little taller. Maybe it was the wine, but I felt more grown-up. Somebody liked me. Then Anam dashed the daydream by saying, "Keep in mind, Bonnie, he's a little old for you."

We talked about early chores. Nog would sweep the porches, then he and I would leave at nine o'clock to fetch two families coming in on the train. One had a 10-year-old boy, the other a 14-year-old girl. I looked forward to riding bikes with them, going to Rainbow Stream. Maybe the girl would like the Crystal Keep. While I daydreamed, Anam continued. She would set a bar of coffee, tea, fruit, and muffins. She would also secure Angus so that he'd be on the porch to greet guests. As he slept by the hearth, his freshly scrubbed ears perked ever so slightly at the mention of his name and his role.

The old house groaned, as if to remind Anam about one last item.

"Can't you do anything about the noises in the attic, Nog? Anything at all?"

"But you told me not to go up there."

"And I know you do."

"I'll go talk to the old bats—or ghosts, whatever they are— and tell them to be respectful. After all ..."

"You will not refer to bats and ghosts when the guests arrive." Anam commanded. Nog winked at me and nodded to his wife. With dishes washed and floor swept, we all gave in to the day's fatigue. Anam and Nog wrapped themselves in each other's arms.

"Sleep tight," Anam said, kissing my forehead. "May night transform you into morning bright."

"All is well," Nog proclaimed. "Safely rest. God is nigh." He drank in his surroundings as he drained the last of the wine. His dream had come true. "Let's go to bed."

20

STRAWBERRY MOON

What is it that dogs dream? Angus, who was supposed to be indoors, was outdoors with me. He seemed to be suspended in a silver net between silent moon shadows and daring exploits known only to him. I could see— or more accur-ately I could sense—his rhythmic breath interspersed with adventure. Twitch, quiver, whine—that gentle harmony be-tween mundane and exotic that sleeping animals achieve as they chase a rabbit or beg a biscuit.

It was hard to imagine that I had spent an interminable day finding what now appeared to be a lazy old dog. Paws over eyes and haunches curled into the straw in the corner of the barn, he lay next to Rowan, who unlike him, led a simple life. All the old mare ever wanted or needed was right there. Enbar, on the other hand, always wanted one more apple. And Epona had an adventurous streak, like the sorrel in the Zelda series. Maybe if Erin came this summer, we could play Zelda like we used to. Maybe Nog and Anam would let us go on a ride.

Switching my newly acquired walking stick from one hand to the other like a baton, I considered grabbing Angus before he ran away again. But I was too comfortable sitting on the moon-softened stone stairs that Nog had rescued from near obliteration by plucking weeds and encouraging herbs and whimsical wildflowers to define their edges. To the casual visitor, the tiny doorstep seemed arbitrary. To me, it was a secret entrance. In reality, it was neither. Unlike the wide and inviting veranda, this was a narrow and rarely used simple pine gateway into Nog's portal.

My butt fit nicely into a depression worn by generations of footsteps. The night's delicate fragrance had drawn me to this secluded stoop. I was tired but sleepless. Too bad Nog was asleep. He might have sat with me, silent for once, without tall tales or nostalgic ramblings of who used to do what, where, and when. And perhaps, who could see them now.

Looming overhead, the barn was silhouetted by the moon-brightened sky. Willy and Mo silently joined me, as cats are wont to do. With wet licks and kisses they groomed each other, then melted into one seamless bundle of fur alongside my thigh. Stroking them, I soaked in their purrs. Again, I thought of getting Angus. But with scents of chamomile and mint wafting, my body wouldn't move. My shoulders ached from rowing, my legs from pedaling, and my heart from the longings I kept tucked inside. I rested the stick on the stout retaining wall and, with arms wrapped about my knees to support my chin, I gazed at the moon. It looked like a silver apple drifting westward in the nearly midnight sky. But it wasn't the Apple Moon, it was the Strawberry Moon. Like strawberry wine. A rite of initiation, Nog had called it. He could be so daft.

Under the far eave, he and Anam tugged at bedding amid light snores that sifted through the open window. Night birds sang. While everything appeared so still, so simple, so perfect, it was so complicated. It was like what Nog said while we cleared the adventure trail. That thinking about the ancestors made life seem so simple. He also said that coming here would change everything.

It didn't. Mom was still dead. I was still a misfit. And instead of spending the day on my vlog, I had been banished to finding the dog that always returned. I looked at the Strawberry Moon, closed my eyes, and pictured Mom there with me. *Pay attention,* I told her. *I need you.*

The moon's spotlight shifted the shadows in the barn and, like a light switch, exposed the tufts on the top of Angus's head. Aroused, he uncurled himself from the sweet hay and unbidden, trotted over to me, ears piqued, head tilted to the side, and eyes locked on mine. All alert and fresh smelling, he seemed poised to take action.

"I thought you were dreaming, Angus." He danced gingerly from side to side, head lolling to one side and then the other, as if to deliberately distract me, because in one second, he snatched the stick he had found earlier and taunted me with it. "Don't you dare go running off now, you dog! I will not go looking for you again, not ever!" He paused, picked up the pace of his dance, and whined subtly. "Okay, maybe not ever, but certainly not tonight!" He whined, and signaled the door with a deliberate nod.

"Oh, you want to go in. Okay." It was time for me, too. As much as I was enjoying the full moon and light breezes, I really was tired.

I opened the door into Nog's portal. Straight ahead was a door to the foyer and the front stairway. To the right, a short hallway led to the kitchen. To the left were two doors—behind one was a flight of stairs to the basement. Behind the other, the stairs to the attic. I started toward the front stairs, but Angus blocked my passage with the stick. He nudged me to the left, toward the attic.

"I don't think so," I whispered. He was insistent in that way animals can be. His whining grew louder. "Shhh! No, Angus. Shhh." I glanced up. "You'll wake Nog and Anam. Shhh." I tried to usher him toward the kitchen, but he still blocked my path. He bobbed his head toward the forbidden door.

"No! Not the attic." He just sat there, glaring first at me, then the door. "Come on," I urged him toward the kitchen. "Want a biscuit?"

Tempting as that was, Angus stood his ground and stared at the knob. It's hard to discipline a loveable animal, especially when you're tired and trying to be very quiet. What would Nog say? Never mind that, what would Anam say? I shuddered to think of that. She would be mad, really mad, if I let Angus into the attic.

He whined. The bed creaked upstairs. What to do? Catch hell for being up so late, or catch hell for giving Angus his way? I tried the knob. It didn't budge.

"See, Angus, it's locked." I was relieved, yet questioned the sanity of using logic with an animal. He whimpered. The bed creaked. I sweat. I tried the knob again and it clicked open. Angus immediately pushed past me and started up the stairs. He turned and looked at me. *Come on*, he seemed to be saying, with what seemed to be a grin. He extended the branch. I took it.

Looking up the stairway, I was surprised to see how illuminated it was. Maybe Nog had left a light on. Casting judgment aside, I followed my curiosity. Guided by Angus and trailed by cats, I ascended first to the landing opposite the master suite, and then to the attic—Nog's belfry, which was apparently as bat-less as it was bell-less.

Large, thronelike chairs grounded each end of the otherwise barren house-sized room. Several chairs, alternately highlighted and eclipsed by softly shifting light, lined the walls between them. The moon traced an arc across oaken beams. Churchlike light streamed through wavy, age-stained windows that, despite discernible swirls of dust tucked into the corners of tattersall panes, were remarkably transparent.

No wonder Nog came up here. It reminded me of Miss Susie's after a recital—peaceful, yet energized, like the last dancer had left the stage, the last applause had echoed to silence, and the last attendee peeked into the darkened theater hoping for one last encore. My pupils dilated to take in greater details. The lofty chair at the far end beckoned.

In a fear-drenched moment, a touch above my right eye stopped me dead. I brushed a trembling finger across my right temple. Yuck. A cobweb. Wiping it away thawed first my breath, and then my right foot, allowing it to move toward the chair. The ball of my forward foot landed on the floor with a *tap* as the rear one poised midair. I froze anew. Unable to hold the pose for long, I slowly brought the other foot down. *Tap.* Both feet together. *Tap tap.* I stepped up and down in a silly march. *Tap, tap, tap.* Of course! The sounds that emanated from here were probably Nog himself as he tiptoed around.

Sighing in relief and amusement, I spun in spontaneous circles, recapturing dance positions and transitions learned long ago at Miss Susie's, but with a flair that had been absent in those days. With the moon as my spotlight, this was my recital. I pretended that I was wearing swirly scarves and high-laced boots.

It didn't matter that Dad wasn't here. I wanted to dance. I had to dance. Fragile cobwebs streamed outward in an ethereal costume that resembled my welter's billowing curtains as I swiveled, struck a pose, held it, shifted to the other foot, leapt, landed, and spun once more. My stick became a magic wand and I was dancing with my prince once more.

After I whirled myself dizzy, I stopped to center my balance. Balance. That's what Miss Susie insisted on for dancing and Nog for boating. Balance. I closed my eyes, picturing my belly button pressed into the small of my back, shoulders squared, chin parallel to the floor. I twirled again and again, with a giddy, yet steady poise. Until my prince stepped on my toes. "Angus!" I covered my mouth for fear of waking Nog and Anam.

We danced a few more rounds until the long day, the spinning, and the wine caught up with me. Chairs ringed the perimeter in no particular pattern, like the Invisibles had ringed the meadow. Dark and light, light and dark. It reminded me of the quilt on my bed, the one where the two sides of the same square seemed the same, but were really opposite. Nog told me magic happens when two things that can't possibly happen at the same time really are happening. Dark and light, light and dark. The room spun like magic.

Angus ushered me to the overstuffed chair nestled under the window. Looking out the window, I saw not the barn and yard, but a moonscape of bright contours and dark angles. Light and dark. Dark and light. Quilt and bed. Bed and sleep. Drawing in a deep breath, I extended my arms up over my head, then cuddled myself as I fell into the chair. It was as if I were sitting on a throne.

"I am the Queen of the World," I whispered. Angus positioned himself at my feet and cocked his head to the side. Willy and Mo appeared, of course, with no notice. "And you are my subjects," I told the assembly, my royal staff raised authoritatively. Mo jumped into my lap while Willy settled on the armrest.

The day's scenarios played themselves over and over, in sequence, out of sequence, in still life and panoramic views. Crickets and moonbeams filled the night. Dragons and princes filled my thoughts. Palaces, lakes, bridges, and boats. Specters and scepters. Mom and Dad. Anam and Nog. Angus and James. Angus's whine and waves of nine. Boats and sun. Freckles and fun, jewels a-run. Mom, sticks, stories, and stones. Momma, waves, baby, and toes. Momma and church. Elixir of wine.

Spirits above, spirits divine. Angus and Enbar and Baylar as one.

"Pay attention," Porter instructed as I mounted the white horse that turned red in that second before sleep.

21

CÉILÍ

ngus was cuddled against my feet, with Mo perched on one arm of a magnificent chair and Willy on the other.

A vague *tap tap creeaakkkkk* nudged me into a consciousness of spirits above and spirits divine, of silver apples and strawberry wine, of strawberry roans and strawberry moons. Of glittering moons and silver cocoons. I sensed I had been here before, washed upon the banks of a large moonlit palace after surviving a storm. Like that fragment of a dream the day I arrived.

"Pay attention." An unseen voice that smelled like after-shave spoke somewhere above and behind me, but I could not move—not to see the speaker, not to rub my eyes, not to open my mouth. My eyes still worked, though, and as I looked around, I was horrified to realize I was in the attic.

But it wasn't the attic. I mean, it was, but it was all different. I tried to remember how I got here. But before I could focus on that, the room that Angus had led me to was gone. It was like I was watching one of those 3D room makeovers on a humongous, high-def screen. In one jump-cut, heavy wooden beams had dissolved into pillars of silver that rose from a parquet sea. In another, bare walls melted into lavish textiles and bejeweled draperies that shimmered in the moonlight streaming through the window. But the sounds were familiar. *Tap tap creeaakkkkk. Tap tap creeaakkkkk.*

The Invisibles fluttered into full view. Like the room, they were morphing from their ethereal forms into real people as they entered this expansive hall, which Nog would probably call an island of ancestors. Baron led the parade wearing a sailor's outfit. He winked at me and saluted. Behind him was a handsome soldier—Grandpa John! Aloysius followed as a fussy, yet proud, old gent in a threadbare suit. Tess's crimson shimmer was replaced by a curly-haired woman whose red gown matched her hair. Maggie wiggled in with her burgundy-striped snake outfit and white shock of hair. Luna had traded her azure aura for bluish white hair that blended into a sky-blue satin gown. Seamus still smelled like cheese.

Before I could figure out anybody else, a different entity altogether materialized—an alabaster old man at the far end of the hall. The back of my neck prickled. It was Knobby! I wanted to tell Nog, but then I would have to tell him I was in the attic. And seeing our dead ancestors. Before I could resolve that predicament, the old man focused his eyes on me, arms extended, like he was expecting a gift. I willed myself to respond, but my limbs were stone and a spell sealed my lips.

"Pay attention." That voice ... it was Porter, the trainman. "You're in good hands now, young lady." He gently lifted the stick from my lap. When I looked at it, though, the simple branch had become a silver wand, etched with intricate designs and embellished with glass flowers. "Remember," he gently touched my shoulder. "The secret to life is to first understand death."

Death? Was I dead? I wanted to ask, but I could not speak. Dissolving through what appeared to be a thick TV plasma that separated me from Knobby, Porter reappeared on the other side and handed my stick, or wand, or whatever it was to the little old man who grew to about 10 feet tall when he stood.

In the second that Knobby accepted the branch into his outstretched hands, a bat flittered onto his shoulder. So, there were bats in the attic! Then the old man raised the wand moonward with his right hand while jabbing his left forward and scissor-stepping his feet. Like Nog had done with the broom, his make-believe shillelagh. The stick Angus had given me, and that I had brought up with me to the attic, became Knobby's real shillelagh. He pulsed it upward to punctuate each syllable of a booming voice.

The spirits above
are the spirits divine.
The spirits below
are the spirits of wine!

Knobby was convening a *céilí*. A dense throb sucked the air out of the room as I struggled to breathe. Was I dead? How else could I survive with no air, in a place full of the dead.

Céad míle fáilte!

Nana entered. I recognized her stately grace. The matri-arch *tap tap creeaakkkkked* her way across the shiny floor, while the welter continued to jostle, argue good-naturedly, and call each other by name. She curtsied and blew a kiss at her husband, just as Nog had described in his story. Gramp then lit a fire where no hearth had been.

Around it appeared nine girls, all about my age, in swirly scarves and high-laced boots, like I wore in my recital, but more elegant. I called them fire girls, and I wanted so badly to join them as they hummed and swayed to the tinkling of a piano—wasn't it the one in the downstairs parlor? How did it get here?

A petite woman with short silver hair smoothed her aquamarine suit before sitting down at the keyboard. With gentle caresses of the keys, she began to charm the old man into a faint smile. Then she looked at me and said, *Not yet.* It was Kelty. *Breathe,* she said without speaking. I did, long and slow like Anam had taught me. Then she sang in perfect pitch without even seeming to try.

> *By yon bonnie, bonnie banks an' by yon bonnie,*
>   *bonnie braes*
> *Where the sun shines bright on Loch Lomon'*
> *Where me an' my true love will never meet again*
> *On the bonnie, bonnie banks o' Loch Lomon'.*

My song! A gathering chorus of the very young, the very old, and everyone in between emerged in clusters and clusters along with children in bunches and bunches. The room swelled to make room for multitudes of vaguely familiar people. I wanted to join them, lonely as I was, but I couldn't move. And even if I could, I was separated from them by a veiled wall.

> *O ye'll tak' the high road, and Ah'll tak' the low road*
> *And Ah'll be in Scotlan' afore ye*
> *For me an' my true love will ne'er meet again*
> *On yon bonnie, bonnie banks o' Loch Lomon'.*

The attic was rocking like the biggest party I could ever imagine. Would it wake Nog and Anam? Maggie appeared with food in platters and platters, bowls and bowls, pitchers and pitchers. It was piled high on long, long tables. Before anyone consumed anything, though, Luna appeared and hushed the attic. "Bless us," she whispered. I swear she looked right at me. "Let us remember the ancestors, their legends, the descendants yet to come, and the one who will lead us."

After a moment of silence, the noise of the crowd rushed back like the wind of a sudden thunderstorm. The partygoers clustered in the center of the ever-expanding room, begging for the legends, dances, and songs of old. Kelty returned to her keyboard.

"Story! Story! Story!" the multitude called. Kelty nodded in delightful deliberation of the thunderous calls. *"The Tale of the Weary Traveler,"* someone suggested.

"Ah, yes," she nodded. "Tonight, indeed, is the night of the weary traveler."

Saluting Knobby and Nana, Kelty summoned the fire girls. "First," she intoned, *"The Dance of the Weary Traveler."* Her fingers teased an ethereal tune from the keys as the fire girls circled. Elbows tucked to their sides and forearms bent upward, they moved up and down, in and out, as the rhythm created its own words.

Surge to the center, ebb in a squeak.
Tap tap. Creeaakkkkk. Tap tap. Creeaakkkkk.

They were dancing to the sounds of the old house. No, they *were* the sounds of the old house. Miss Susie never taught me this dance, yet I seemed to know it. Still paralyzed and separated, I absorbed the tableau in the silent company of Angus, Willy, and Mo.

The dancers stopped. The welter sat. The voices died. The moonlight dimmed. A breeze sifted a chill from the rafters as Kelty lowered her voice an octave and began.

It was a dark and stormy night ...

"Oooh," the crowd chanted, sounding like the ghosts they were, then hushed. I knew this story. Just as Nog had done the night of the storm, Kelty brandished a taper and zigzagged it beneath her chin. Like Nog, she transformed herself into a make-believe ghoul. The flickering flame exaggerated a face deeply etched with lines of laughter and sadness. Shielding the light with her other hand, and eyes widened in anticipation, she sustained the silence for several seconds as she scouted the room, seeming to search for someone. She looked right at me.

> *A traveling man named Johnny was cold and tired and needed a place to stay. Now, Johnny, he was a funny man, and he talked like this...*

Kelty switched the candle from one hand to the other, screwing her mouth to the right, left, up, and down to imitate Johnny, the innkeeper, his wife, and their son. *Whew, whew,* she demonstrated while switching the taper from one hand to the other as the characters tried to extinguish the flame. She stepped from one into another, just as Nog had done, becoming the tale of the weary traveler.

Amidst the laughter, a new voice emerged from the shadow. A woman wearing a red cloak had entered the attic unnoticed.

> *I am cold and tired ...*

Not only did she not talk funny, but she also sounded familiar. She even looked familiar. It was the woman I had seen that morning trudging up the trail. The cloak I could now see was Anam's—the one by the vestibule. But it wasn't Anam's body. This woman was taller. Although her voice was weak, it hinted at knowing the story and she played along.

> *... and I need a place to stay.*

Her voice ... her voice. So familiar. The woman shrugged out of the cloak's red cowl, revealing long, thick auburn hair, deepest green eyes, and elegant hands. They all knew her—and I did, too.

"Momma!" I desperately called to her, but my voice was frozen.

22

momma

Nana stepped in to embrace my mother with a deep sigh. Hushed voices called *Maura, Maura, Maura.* Her fine features, heavy hair, and expressive eyes were unchanged, as if she had been secreted away, sealed in a treasure chest, asleep at the bottom of the sea. Missing, though, was the broad smile; in its place was sadness.

Swaying her head, her shoulders, and her hips gently, she choreographed a slower, dreamier version of the *tap tap creeaakkkkk.* Maggie stepped in. She looked like an older version of Mom.

"Welcome, my child." She held Mom like Anam had held me. "We are here to celebrate your life and the passing of the shillelagh." Maggie kissed her daughter, but she looked at me. I watched as she playfully stroked Mom's hair, just as Mom had done to mine many years ago. I strained to break myself free, to tear open the curtain that separated us.

"Here," Maggie gestured around the attic. "Here, in the land of eternal youth, we grant you shelter from the storm. Here, no one is hungry or thirsty." I realized this sounded like *Tír na nÓg.* Had I ridden Enbar here? Had my feet not touched the ground? I remembered seeing him before I fell asleep.

"In our lifetimes," Maggie continued, "we fulfilled our dreams, rocked our babies, told our stories, and fought our wars." The din of pomp and procession reeled around and around. "Here, my child, we are who we were. Forever."

Then Luna appeared, quelling the clamor to a whisper. "We are the ancestors," she said, her voice like a summer breeze. "We are the remembered. We are the future. Some took the high road," she looked at me. "And some took the low," she looked at Mom. "But we have all arrived here tonight to celebrate our family, to honor our talents."

"Talents?" Mom laughed. "I have no talents. I am only a mother, a sister, a friend." *You are the best Mom in the whole world,* I tried to say, but Mom shrugged. "All I ever wanted was a man to love deeply, a window from which to watch my child at play, and a best friend to share that life. And I failed."

"No, dear, you did not fail," Luna pointed to the lake-facing window that instantly became a magic movie screen. Through it, we all saw a girl—me!—playing amidst the flowers in a field of sunshine, protected by a large dog. Angus. "There. Your child."

"Bonnie!" Her face lit up; the old smile returned. "Look at her," she said to the multitude. "Isn't she's beautiful?"

"I'm here," I strained to tell her. Here. Not there, across the lake. I worried that Luna would also show everyone everything bad about me, that I wasn't beautiful, that I blew my nose into my shirt, played hooky, made fun of kids, and vaped. But she didn't. We only watched me dance. The screen cut to Anam and Nog, locked arm in arm, peering out their kitchen window.

"And there is the friend and brother with whom you shared the joy of life. You did not fail, Maura."

"But the accident ... I ... I ..."

"Ah," Luna sighed. "Yes. Some people have car accidents

and survive. Others die. You died before your prime. But you protected your little girl. She lived. You were a good mother."

"And her father?"

Luna directed us back to the window screen. It cut to Dad, Deborrah, and Benjy.

"Ben's not perfect," she said. "But no one is. And he loves your child, his child. He found a good woman to help him guide her." I suddenly saw my stepmother differently. I remembered that she sat through my recital, bought me new luggage, and made my favorite lunch for me to take on the train. Looking at her through this magic window, she seemed to be doing it to *help* me rather than to *punish* me. "You did not fail, Maura. You succeeded. You did what you were supposed to do and you were who you were meant to be."

Mom stood alone as the party danced behind and around her. The rhythm soothed the weary traveler, who now smiled the broad grin that I remembered. All doubt fell from her as did the cloak, revealing a flowing green silk dress.

"Celebrate your life, my child." Luna then tossed into the air the crystal vial I had coveted at the Keep. It arced toward me. "Celebrate your child, Maura." A tiny drop of magic potion must have leaked through the plasma and spilled onto my head, because suddenly, without thinking, I stood up. I could move! I reached for Mom. She parted the veil between us, gathering me into her softness and sprinkling me with coveted fairy kisses.

"Momma!" I dissolved into her warmth and scents, into the comfort I had sought now for too many years, into tears, into the name I whispered only to myself. I found where I belonged. "I love you, Momma! I miss you. Why did you leave me?"

"Bonnie Baby, I never left you. I am here." She pulled away just long enough to press elegant fingers to my heart. Elegant fingers that flashed her emerald ring. My ring. "Always."

"But Baylar said I'm the reason you died. And I'm going to have to fight with some kid named Tony to replace ..."

"Baylar? Tony? Oh my goodness, no." She laughed, then turned serious. "Baylar misunderstood. I died, my dear Bonnie, not because of you, but because of me. I made a huge mistake. I wasn't paying attention. It cost me my life with you. I am so sorry for your sadness. But it's not my mistake or my death that I want you to remember."

She moved her firm yet gentle hands from my heart to either side of my face. Her eyes, my eyes, matching green eyes locked on to each other.

"Listen carefully," she instructed. "You must remember not why I died, just as I had to learn why my father died. It's why he lived, why I lived. I was born to be your mother. Your birth made my life complete. Your purpose ..."

"I don't want a purpose," I interrupted. "I want you!" She kissed away the tears that streamed down my face.

"You've had a hard lesson to learn, so listen carefully. I don't have much time. In suffering, we learn more than we learn in joy."

"I don't want lessons. I don't want to suffer. I want joy. I want you."

"You have me, always, baby. You are always with me. Always."

Momma drew me into her breast, wrapping her arms warmly around me like Anam did. And then she released me just long enough to stroke my temples, smooth my brow, and search my eyes.

"I fulfilled my purpose, Bonnie. And what a wonderful purpose. You are the best of your dad and me. Beautiful, smart ..."

"But I don't look like Dad, and I don't look like you. I don't belong!"

"You belong to me. It doesn't matter what your outsides

look like." She gestured to the crowd. "You belong to us." We held each other in silence for an eternity. She kissed my fingers. We both looked at the thumb I chewed and watched it heal.

Luna reappeared to hold Mom and me together. "Bonnie, you are the reason Knobby summoned us all here tonight. You reminded him that although the clan has changed—people have changed—it is the same as it ever was. You spent so much time focusing on what you looked like that you didn't see that you've accomplished what no one else has. You memorized the ancestors, the old stories, and the songs."

Wrapped in love, I nodded. Nog had taught me well. "And you have the Sight." The crowd that ringed us now hummed with *oohhhs* and *aahhhs*. Again, they sounded like the ghosts they were.

"And you, Maura," Luna said as she wrapped Momma in her arms, "you have embraced your purpose here tonight. You are free to cross over."

"Come on," Mom entreated, laughing the laugh I remembered. "Let's dance. With me, with Knobby and Nana, with your aunts and uncles, kith, and kin. Come dance, for soon I must go. But when I do, I will still be with you."

I took her hand and followed her intricate steps in a circle dance that surged and ebbed as it inched around the silvery room. *Tap tap creeaakkkkk. Tap tap creeaakkkkk.* Soon, I was prancing and swaying like everyone else.

"Look, Mom," I pointed to Angus, who paraded along with us until we circled past Knobby. The dog stopped, halting the procession, and stretched out his front paws in a bow toward the old man. Moving a step to the right, Angus cued Mom's turn.

Looking like a queen, Mom held the skirt of her dress wide and dipped into a curtsy before Knobby, much as Nana had done when this all started. The hem skimmed her knees. The fitted sleeves fluttered like wings. And when she tucked her chin into a deep V-shaped neckline, I noticed the scooped back that was gathered into a simple bow. She was beautiful.

Then it was my turn.

Although I knew how to curtsy—I'd learned how in dance class—for some reason, at the last moment I bowed instead. When I bent at the waist, Knobby raised his shillelagh—the stick that Angus had found, the stick that led me here, the stick that seemed to have turned into a magic wand. Ever so gently, he lowered it upon my right shoulder, then my left. Then he held it horizontally with open palms, exactly as Porter had handed it to him.

Instinctively, I stretched out my hands, palms facing upward. In the fading moonlight, he passed it to me. As my fingers curled around it, energy pulsed through me like electronic music, only there was no sound. Without thinking, I held it upward with my right hand, jabbed my left forward, and scissor-kicked my feet in a dance I seemed to have known forever.

"*Sláinte!*" Knobby bellowed and tossed his head, shaking loose the bat on his shoulder. I winced in horror when it landed on mine. It was surprisingly gentle, though, like a bird. Before I could react, it spoke directly into my mind—not with a voice or even a sound. But I distinctly heard words in my head.

In this realm where there is no death—where past, present, and future are one—you now have freedom to live.

That's what Porter had said!

I didn't have time to comprehend the message, because Knobby took my hand and thundered to the masses, "Behold Bonnie the Warrior."

The hall exploded in applause. For me?

"Below," he continued, "she imbibed the spirits of wine. Now above, she is a spirit divine. Protect her, Angus." The dog bowed his head. To me, he said, "Protect your family."

Before I could ask how, he stood at attention, dropped my hand, and took Nana's. "Oh, Bonnie, bonnie banks," he boomed, "take the high, high road! *Céad míle fáilte!*"

With that, he and Nana disappeared into moon dust.

"Bonnie the Warrior," Momma said, curtsying to me as I held the shillelagh or magic wand or whatever it was. Then she gestured to the gathered masses. "You will lead us on the high road into the future."

Warrior? No way. My only weapons were imaginary ones from the ironsmith at the Mill Shops—things to slay Baylar, or smash my grudges to smithereens. Leader? I couldn't lead my way out of a paper bag. High road? As opposed to what? The low road where I saw Momma the stranger? And the future? I was a kid who only wanted to go home, and just like everything else in my life, I didn't have a choice. Momma knew exactly what I was thinking.

"Leading the clan is something that will take ages to figure out," she whispered so that only I could hear. "Just as Knobby has done." Like Knobby? Swell. Erin got a normal life; Jenny, California; Sara, dancing. Me? Eons as an alabaster shadow drinking no beer and smoking a dead pipe. Momma reached in and caressed my worries.

"He realized that while our clan has always been led by a man, now we'll be led by a woman—a beautiful young woman. Be yourself, that's all. It doesn't matter what you look like. Or how long it takes. Knobby saw that you are what this family of love needs, what it is capable of. Find the good in all. Release your grudges."

With that, my plain clothes were transformed into a green dress of Luna silk and silver threads. The crowd pulsed with the rhythmic *tap tap creeaakkkkk*. Knobby and Nana danced in its midst. With Mom, Angus, and my wand as partners, I whisked in Luna, Maggie, Kelty, Dobbin, Tory, all the aunts and uncles, and the children I had wanted to play with.

Skip and weave, grasp and change, dip and twist. They knew me and accepted me with warm hands and bowed heads. And whenever the panic of being with myriad strangers overwhelmed me, there was Momma. She never missed that crucial step where the circle was yet unbroken. We whirled in a tornado of past, present, and future. We changed, yet stayed the same. We danced, and danced, and danced, until in a hush, the room went dark. Except for a single candle. In the darkness, we heard a soft voice. Momma's voice.

Could somebody please turn out the light so I can go to sleep?

We all stopped. I had forgotten about the story of strange-talking people. Assuming the role of the innkeeper's son, Kelty quickly licked her thumb and forefinger, pinched the wick, and extinguished the flame.

Good night.

23

Dawn

Mo stirred before I did, initiating a series of stretches that synchronized themselves with brushed-aside shreds of music, dancing, and Mom.

Momma.

The dream lingered in that zone between awake and asleep as I, too, stretched, inch by inch. Something—a doorbell, a church bell, a *tap tap creeaakkkkk*—nudged me away from silver apples and strawberry moons. Pale daylight pried open my eyes.

Something was wrong. Very, very wrong. This wasn't my room and I wasn't in bed. Through the window, I caught sight of the barn, but I'd never seen it from this perspective. But maybe I had. It was at night. Last night? From the attic?

The attic! Oh no. I was in the attic. I jolted awake, spilling the cats from my lap. In disdain, they meowed across the floor toward the stairs. "Shhh," I pleaded. But being cats, they protested themselves into emptiness.

Emptiness. I shook and re-shook my head. Not so last night, when the room pulsed with masses and music. But it was empty like this to begin with, wasn't it? My gut twisted and re-twisted in confusion. How did I get here? The door! If it was open, would Anam and Nog close it and lock me in? Or if they discovered me, would I tell them that Angus made me do it? But he did, didn't he? No, that was preposterous. I had spent the whole day chasing him, and then he led me to the attic? They wouldn't believe that—I didn't believe that. But isn't that what happened? And where was Angus?

Never mind Angus, I needed to pee. Go downstairs, I told myself, but I couldn't move. Not because a magic spell had turned me to stone, but because I couldn't grasp what had happened. It was a dream, I told myself. No, it wasn't, I argued. What are dreams, anyway? Nog called them weird ties to the Otherworld. Dream or not, last night was definitely some weird tie to Kelty, Luna, Knobby, and Momma.

I would have to tell Nog. No, I couldn't tell Nog. Not yet, anyway. First things first. I had to get downstairs, and I had to be quick and quiet. The expanse from where I sat to the stairway may have been only two leaps for a cat, but it was a vast gulf for a trapped girl. Think like a cat, I told myself.

Uncurling arms and legs that still ached from what— Dancing? Rowing? Sleeping all scrunched up? I commanded feet to floor and thrust my rigid body upright. Teetering at first, I caught my balance by grabbing the arm of my chair. Wasn't it a throne? Where was my stick? With no time to figure that out, I centered myself and took a deep breath like Anam had taught me.

With feline agility, I followed the cats' path across the parquet floor that no longer shimmered in fairy light. Almost there, I paused to brush away a cobweb from my forehead. My fingers sensed something missing. My glasses! I had left them on the chair. Holding my breath, I silently retraced my steps, consuming precious seconds. When I made it back to the top of the stairs, I took one last look at what was simply an empty attic. Last night's world was now closed and the real world was within reach, just steps below. Tiptoe, I prodded myself, just tiptoe. Quickly.

Hugging my back to the wall, I extended one toe downward. *Tap.* My mouth grimaced, my eyes popped, and my heart jumped. I retracted my foot, held my breath, and stepped again. *Tap.* I froze. After a few seconds, I took a relaxation breath and exhaled slowly. Then I tried again. *Tap. Crrreeeeaaakkk,* the house responded. *Tap tap crrreeeeaaakkk. Tap tap crrreeeeaakk.*

I had become a noise in the attic! If Anam and Nog heard me, what would they say? I listened, but heard nothing. Tiptoeing can be such a noisy venture, so I scampered. Nothing. Down and almost free, I inched open the door across from Anam and Nog's bedroom and imperceptibly squeezed through it—most likely as the animals had done. Seeing no one, I propped it closed and dashed to the bathroom. Almost there. Almost safe. Shut the door ...

"Bonnie." My heart sank. Anam's voice, however, came from downstairs. I was safe. "Hurry. You need breakfast before you leave."

"Yeah, Anam. I'll be down in a few." It was just past six o'clock. We all had plenty of time. I ran enough water to feign a morning ritual, when, in fact, all I could do was stare in the mirror and try to understand what happened. Vapor swirled before clinging to the silvered glass. The only thing I knew for sure was that I talked with Mom, danced with her, and basked in her love. And that all those people who were so strangely familiar, yet so distant, said things I didn't understand, yet made absolute sense. I was a warrior? A matriarch? How could that be? I didn't know how to fight and I was only 12.

Through the foggy mirror, I eyed my eyes, as I did when I was on the train. They were Mom's eyes. I was five when she died.

I knew her as a sensory collage—bits of auburn locks that I grabbed in handfuls; the scent of a bedtime story; giggles chased around the yard; kisses like strawberry jelly; and the souvenirs in my treasure box. I could touch her when I opened it, especially the crayon-colored baby card she had drawn and decorated with pressed flowers the week before I was born. There was a smiling moon on the front with the carefully penned letters, "Welcome, Baby." On the inside, she wrote, "May your life be Bonnie."

And the photos: Mom as a little girl under the Christmas tree with Nog; playing with Anam; dancing with Dad on their wedding day; proudly pregnant with me; us at the beach, with matching hats, where the sun was so bright our eyes squinted shut. I had memorized the images, even the blurred and silly ones. Especially the blurred and silly ones. Life unedited.

Vapor threatened the memories. I watched as Dad-like hair and Mom-like eyes dissolved into the mist that was me. I traced a lopsided heart around my reflection. It didn't matter what I looked like, or who I looked like. Etching it into my memory, I watched the heart and our images dissolve.

I took a few extra minutes getting dressed. It was opening day, there would be guests—and James. A new green blouse and high-rise skinny jeans showed off my neatly developing waist. I added a beaded necklace, brushed my hair into a chic ponytail, and smacked on some cherry lip balm. I looked in the mirror and saw a beautiful girl—sort of like the waitress at the Avalon, sort of like Dad, sort of like Mom. The girl in the mirror glanced down at my hands. Something was missing. I dug into the jewelry box and slipped on Mom's emerald ring. My emerald ring. Mom would be with me all day. Every day. The young woman in the mirror and I smiled at each other.

I ran down the stairs and into the kitchen. Slipping behind my aunt, I gave her a hug. When she turned around, I hardly recognized her.

"Wow, Anam." An apron wrapped around a simple shirt-waist dress showed off her trim figure. Her hair was coiled in a bun and she wore simple makeup. "You look totally epic!"

"So do you. I guess we're both ready for the big day."

"Yeah, but first, Anam, I have to tell you about last night. I saw Mom."

No longer distracted by methodical slicings of berries and arranging a breakfast bar, my aunt gestured me toward the nook, where a basket of freshly baked muffins and fruit salad awaited. She poured herself some coffee and me some milk, then scooched in close.

"Was she as beautiful as ever?"

"Oh yes. Her hair was long, very long. She wore her emerald ring." Anam's eyes fluttered to my left hand. Her eyes widened. She reached for my hand.

That simple gesture triggered an electric shock that opened the time warp to Elsewhere. My belly tugged, spine shivered, face slacked, fingers tingled, and lips puckered. Anam and I had slipped into that place where—and I know this sounds strange—our two bodies, two minds, and two hearts, shared one hole. Same hole, different names. Hers was called Maura; mine, Momma. Without either of us sharing a word or a glance, I knew I'd been here before, reliving some private moment.

"I saw you," Anam stammered, "in this kitchen, when you were born." Her face was pale and her hands trembly. What was weird was that I saw it, too. The house *tap tapped,* and the hearth *hiss hissed.* The saga hung over us, much as the pot over the fire. I covered her hand with my own, oddly feeling as if it were my turn to protect her.

"You know I was there when you were born, Bonnie." I had heard this story many times. Anam was there because Dad—of course—was out of town. Anam worked her mouth from side to side, like Luna and Nog telling the story of the weary traveler. Words returned. "It was like a spirit I seemed to have known forever erupted into the world in a moment of wonder. And before you let out your first wail—and what a wail it was!—we made eye contact."

We gazed into each other's eyes for what seemed like an hour, but was really a few seconds. "I didn't even remember it until …" Vapors hydrated the air. I waited for syllables. Finally, one word emerged. "Now."

It was that déjà vu thing. I squeezed her hand.

She drew me into herself in that Momma-like embrace and I melted into her for a few minutes. I finally understood the meaning of *anam cara*. Reexamining my ring, she encouraged me to continue my dream story.

"It was a big party. Momma wore a green silk dress and your red cloak," I said, pointing to the garment that hung apart from the other outdoor gear.

"Green dress?" Anam interrupted. I nodded. "Red cloak?" I nodded. Shaking her head, she released my hands so that she could clasp hers in front of her heart. She spoke with her eyes closed. "Remember the night you came? When I said I saw you here?"

How could I forget?

"When your mother came to tell me she was pregnant, she was wearing her favorite green silk dress. What did it look like?"

"Long sleeves, short flouncy skirt—just below her knees. V-shaped neckline. The back …"

"Had a bow."

I nodded slowly.

"That was her favorite dress. How did you know? There's no reason I ever would have told you that. She wore it that day. We sat in my kitchen, not this one, of course, but in a way, it was. Coffee was in the air." She waved one hand about. "We were eating store-bought muffins, not these. So, it was the same, but different. Your mom said, and I can hear her as if she were here now, 'My life is complete.'"

Before I could tell Anam that's what Mom had said last night, she continued.

"And you said *my* red cloak? That was your mom's. Nog brought it back from Ireland for her before he and I started dating. Your dad gave it to me after she died." How did I not know that? In a magical shimmer, she took my hands between her berry-stained ones and I knew that she was simultaneously holding Mom's hands in the city and mine in the country, 13 years apart. She saw me—all at once—as Maura, Maura's baby, and Maura's grown-up girl. I know, because I saw it, too.

"Tell me more, Bonnie. I need to know more."

"There were all these people. And a stick. A large wooden stick. And Knob ..." I caught myself. I couldn't tell Anam about Knobby. Not now, anyway. First, I needed to talk to Nog. "And knotty. It was a knotty branch. An old man gave it to me." Angus then trotted into the kitchen with my stick. I just stared, then I held my hands out, palms up. He dropped it into my hands. "Like this!"

"Seems like you taught an old dog a new trick," my uncle said, emerging from the shadows of his portal. "I heard you say you had a dream about your mother."

"Yes! There were all these people eating, singing, and dancing." He nodded, helping himself to coffee, all the while watching me.

"Sounds to me like you were at a *céilí*."

"Or you had too much wine," Anam said. "That or you were envisioning all the guests we're expecting!" She brushed breadcrumbs into her coffee cup and headed to the sink. Cookie, however, was nowhere to be seen. Nor was Mamie, or Seamus, or Gramp. Had they left me? Were they still in the attic?

"I'll be right back," Anam said, picking up a platter of muffins and fruit, already back to business. She headed into the dining room to set up the breakfast bar, leaving Nog and me alone.

"Tell me more," he said. "Who else was there, Bon? Besides your mom?"

"Grandma Maggie and Luna. Kelty sang songs and told stories. And lots of people I didn't know, but they all knew each other." I paused and looked Nog in the eye. "Your father was there. Grandpa John." Nog nodded and smiled slowly.

"Who else?"

"An old, old man." Nog lifted his heavy eyebrows in punctuated silence. "I could see everyone and hear everything, but I couldn't move. I couldn't touch or even talk to Mom because there was this film that separated us. Until Luna tossed me a magic vial and Mom separated the veil between us. And we danced. She told me it doesn't matter that I look different. It's being connected to the family that matters. But here's the best part. She told me it's not why she died, but why she lived that mattered. Just like your Grandpa John lived to be her—and your—father, she lived to be my mother."

Nog's eyes opened so wide that his brow disappeared into his forehead. Ever so slowly, he turned to look over his left shoulder. Even I could see the door to the attic ajar. Beside it sat Angus with his head cocked to the side, looking quite pleased with himself. As Nog rubbed his baldness with his left hand and covered his heart with his right, he murmured, "*Tír na nÓg.*"

"What's that, dear?" Anam asked as she returned from the other room. "Tear not, Nog? Are you crying?"

I smiled, remembering that I thought Nog had said the same thing not so long ago. Then I noticed there were indeed tears in Nog's eyes.

"*Tír na nÓg,*" he said, wiping them away. "The land of the forever young. There Maura is forever my little sister, scraped knees, tooth fairies, chubby cheeks, and whispered secrets of bats and boogiemen."

"And my mom," I said, thinking of my conversation with her in the attic.

"And my friend," Anam added, wiping away her own traces of tears. She kissed my forehead and squeezed me across my upper back. "Oh, my goodness! You've got some heft there. What happened to the skinny little girl with mopey shoulders who arrived here a few months ago?"

"Skinny little girls grow up to be beautiful women," Nog said. "I told you the inn would change you."

Anam glanced at the grandfather clock in the parlor, beyond the hearth. "Beautiful girls and talkative old men need to get a move on. It's almost time to head to New Grange. Let's talk about this later."

"I don't think they're new guests," Nog whispered as Anam bustled around. Water sizzled. The ceiling creaked. Rafters whispered a distant *tap-tap-tap*.

"Then who were they?" I insisted.

"The old birds in the attic." He joked, but his serious eyes were leveled on mine. He looked at the attic door and then back at me.

"Attic?" Anam heard only the last word. "No one is going up to the attic." It was that kind of declaration that Nog and I knew better than to question. Each word was a sentence. But when she glanced away, he winked, sealing our conspiracy.

"Speaking of guests, Bonnie," Anam broke the spell between Nog and me. "I almost forgot. Your dad filled out a reservation online overnight. They're coming up the first week in August. For your birthday. I booked them into the large suite in the downstairs section, so that you don't have to feel as if they're right on top of you. So that if Benjy cries ..."

"I miss Benjy!" I surprised myself as much as I did my aunt and uncle. "I can't wait to show him the wind chimes. I think he'll like them. I'm so glad they're coming." I remembered his soft cheek. I surprised myself even more when I added, "I miss Dad. I even miss Deborrah. Maybe I should bead her a necklace." Anam's eyes popped.

"Oh," she interrupted me. "Speaking of beads, Glenda stopped by early this morning on her way into the Keep. I was afraid the doorbell woke you." The doorbell? I remembered waking up in the attic to the sound of a bell. I thought it was the church carillon, but it couldn't be—that was broken. It must have been the doorbell. But before I could figure that out, Anam handed me a small box. "Glenda said when she saw you in town yesterday, she realized how much you've grown up since you got here." I carefully lifted the lid to find the magic blue crystal vial cradled in tissue paper—the same one that Luna tossed to me last night, the one that Kelty told me was not mine—yet. I gulped for words, but nothing came out. Anam placed a hand on my shoulder. "She said something told her it belonged to you."

I clasped it to my chest, much the way I often did with Mom's ring—my ring—and like Anam did with her hands when she was being emotional. There was too much to absorb. Noting that it dangled from a sturdy silver chain, I fastened the amulet around my neck.

"Come on, Bonnie," Nog said. "Guests to fetch in the station wagon. You can tell me all about your dream on the way. Take a muffin for the road. Anam, make sure you've got Angus. He needs to be on the porch when guests arrive."

My aunt lovingly draped her arms around the dog's shaggy neck to hold him back. But he didn't look as if he were going anywhere.

As we headed out the door, Nog loosely pumped my ponytail then gave me a strange look. "Where are your glasses?"

For the second time that morning, I had forgotten them.

"You know what, Nog? I can see without them."

"Ah, you've got the Sight, eh?"

Before I could answer, he took my left hand in his, caressing the ring. My thumb was no longer chewed up. My fingers looked as elegant as Mom's. "Now that you've seen the entire family, can you see its future?"

"What? Um, yes. Actually, Nog, I need to tell you something." I closed the door behind us. "I've been seeing the family since I got here. I could see Knobby on his porch and a whole bunch of ghosts—17 of them to be exact—who followed me everywhere. Until this morning. Now they've disappeared." I held my breath.

He took me by the shoulders. "I think they accomplished their goal, my princess. They led you on your *immram*. To find the meaning of life. It's a hard lesson."

"Yes, but Mom said in suffering we learn more than we learn in joy." That stab of suffering returned. I dropped my head.

"Your mom was a wise woman." He lifted my chin. "She passed that on to you. Now, tell me, what is Knobby like? And Nana?"

"Knobby was exactly as you described him. And Nana had the most beautiful smile."

"And Kelty and Dobbin?"

"Wait. How do you know who was there?" Silliness melted into confusion. I tossed my hair and twitched my hip into my uncle's side. "It was *my* dream."

"Yes, but it's *my* belfry." He opened the station wagon's door with a flourish. "Speaking of bells, did you hear the carillon this morning?" The bell. I thought it was the doorbell. I nodded slowly. "Lovely sound, isn't it? I guess the new pastor got it fixed." He paused and winked. "Or perhaps Knobby found a successor and passed over to the Otherworld. We'll have to stop by and see if the eagle has flown away."

Before I could respond, he pointed skyward. "Look, a kestrel, the smallest of the falcon family. Not quite an eagle, but it does represent seeing the bigger picture, the survival of self and family. Good omen for this grand morning. Bodes well for the future, don't you think?"

I swallowed hard. "The future's a mystery," I managed to say as I climbed into the passenger's seat. I checked the back for the welter. They were gone.

"Did I ever tell you why the bats ..."

"You know what, Nog?" I placed my hand on his arm as he slid into the driver's seat. I wanted to tell him everything, especially the bat's message that I had the freedom to live in the realm where there is no death. But now was not the time. Instead, I simply said, "A bat told me that you have to stop telling that story."

Speechless, Nog focused his eyes elsewhere for a few seconds. Then he pressed the engine into action, and started down the azalea-glazed road. I started to sing, *"By yon bonnie, bonnie banks ..."* He joined in with, *"an' by yon bonnie, bonnie braes."*

And when the sun shone bright on the Old Mill, I left my grudges to be ground to dust.

Glossary

Anam cara [aun-im KAHR-ah]: A Celtic term, meaning *soul friend*

Banshee [BAN-shee]: A female spirit who announces death by crying and wailing

Céad míle fáilte [kayd mi-lə FULT-chə]: A blessing that means *a hundred thousand welcomes*

Céilí [KAY-li]: A big party, a celebration of family and friends with lots of food, music, and storytelling

Clíona [KLEE-uh-nuh]: Patron goddess of County Cork, Ireland, who may appear as a fairy, witch, mermaid, and banshee; legend says that she left the Otherworld, but was washed back with a ninth wave

Déjà vu [day-ZHA VU]: The feeling that you have lived through the present situation before; some experts say it is having a dream while awake, that the brain is matching a current experience with a stored one, or that it is a form of extrasensory perception (ESP)

Enbar [EN-bär]: An old Irish word for imagination; also, the name of a magic horse that can transport riders to *Tír na nÓg* as long as their feet don't touch the ground

Epona [uh-POW-nuh]: Celtic goddess of horses

Immram ['ɪm rəm]: An old Irish word for a mystical journey to the Otherworld

Indentured servitude: The practice of paying off a ticket to the United States during the Colonial Period by agreeing to work without pay; while not slavery, indentured servants were sold, loaned, or inherited for the duration of their contract period

Kelpie [KEL-pee]: An evil shapeshifter that appears as a tame horse but will drown riders and then eat them

Máel Dúin [MAHL-dwin]: The main character of an Old Irish tale, who goes on a sea voyage (*immram*) to avenge his father's death, but instead finds the meaning of life

Otherworld: Also known as *Tír na nÓg*, the land of eternal youth, beauty, health, abundance, and joy

Pandora: A Greek goddess

Pandora's Box: A box of treasures that Pandora was told never to open; but she did, releasing all the problems in the world

Shillelagh [shuh-LAY-lee]: A walking stick, weapon, or magical symbol of power

Sláinte [SLAHN-chə]: To your health

Thaumatrope [THAA-muh-truhp]: An animation device also known as a wonder turner; made from attaching a disk with a picture on each side to string; when the string is twirled between the fingers, the two pictures appear as one

Tír na nÓg [tir nə NOG]: The Otherworld; the land of eternal youth

Welter: A jumbled mess

Ys [EEss]: A legendary city that sank into the sea, turning the king's daughter into a mermaid; when it emerges again, church bells will ring

topics for Discussion

Bonnie's *Immram*

1. What is an *immram*?

2. What was Bonnie's *immram*? What was she looking for?
   Did she find it?

3. Did Bonnie change? Physically? Emotionally?

4. Can you find some examples of how she changed?

Family Histories

1. Where is your family from? How did they get to this country?

2. Do you know of any famous ancestors, matriarchs, or
   patriarchs?

3. Chart your family tree through genealogical records.

4. Document your family's oral history, which is information
   that people have handed down by telling stories rather
   than writing them. Record interviews with family members who participated in significant events, like wars and
   immigrations.

5. Do you have a family story or a legend? Perhaps there is a
   story involving journeys to find meaning to life, or a
   religious story of a journey?

6. What does your name mean? Is there a story behind it?

7. Does your family have a coat of arms? What pictures are
   on it? What words are on it? What do they mean?

Ghosts

1. Do you have a favorite ghost movie?

2. Do you know any good ghost stories?

3. Who is your favorite ghost in this book? Draw a picture or write a story about this ghost.

Afterlife

1. Do you or your family have a belief in an afterlife?

2. What is it called?

3. Can you describe it?

Labyrinths

1. Mazes are puzzles that have one correct path from beginning to end. Scientists use rats in mazes to study problem solving. Corn mazes are giant puzzles that you walk through. Research how mazes teach us about human behavior, or explore a corn maze and tell a story about it.

2. Labyrinths have only one route and contain no wrong turns. They are walking meditations that represent a spiritual journey through life. Many churches and spiritual organizations maintain labyrinths. Find a labyrinth near you, walk it, and report on it.

3. What is the Greek story about a labyrinth?

4. Create a maze puzzle and have friends solve it.

Plant Lore

1. Some plants like hazel and blackthorn have medicinal properties. Others are used for aromatherapy. Research some plants to see what they are used for.

2. Write a story about a plant that has magical qualities.

Bullying

1. What is your school or community doing to address bullying?

2. Have you or someone you know been bullied? What happened? How did you react?

Grudges

1. What is a grudge?

2. Do you now, or did you ever, hold a grudge against someone?

3. If you've read a book or watched a movie about a grudge, write a report on it.

History and Furniture

1. Do you have a favorite chair or another piece of furniture? What style is it?

2. Does your family have an heirloom desk or other piece of furniture? Is it an antique?

3. What style is it?

4. Write a report about a favorite piece of furniture

Famines

1. Research a famine.

2. What did it have to do with climate, agriculture, wars, and politics?

Slavery and Indentured Servitude

1. Research slavery in a country other than the United States, for example ancient Egypt, the Roman Empire, during the Stone Age, or between African countries.

2. Research indentured servitude.

3. Write a story about someone who was a slave or an indentured servant.

acknowledgments

This book would not have been possible without Bob Markle, my husband, friend, and proofreader extraordinaire. He knows more than anyone that for over 20 years, this story got me up in the morning and kept me up at night.

I've heard it said that readers who tell you what you want to hear will make you feel good, but honest readers will make you successful. I have been blessed with a cadre of honest readers.

My first brush with that candor came from members of the Thomas Jefferson Library Writers' Group in Fairfax, Virginia. I can't adequately thank Kacy Cooney, who read almost as many iterations of *Ghost Girl* as I wrote. She consistently encouraged me to focus on the story, its characters, and my audience, and not on my preoccupation with words. Karen Hammond, Jonathan Corsini, and other members provided valuable feedback that polished my storytelling skills. My colleagues at the Pelican Pens in Fort Myers, Florida, helped fine-tune my voice. Finally, the positive critiques from judges in the Florida Writers Association 2021 Royal Palm Literary Awards gave me the oomph I needed to bring *Ghost Girl* to life.

Many friends—too many to mention for fear of omitting someone—have encouraged me throughout the years. A few stand out.

Andie Goodwin and Peggy McCarthy finessed *Ghost Girl* with professional vision and thoughtful edits. Blessings to my beta readers, who honed the book's readability for young readers: Mary Ellen Banks; Reggie Bok; Jeannie Branch; Isabel Lindblad and her dad, Matt Lindblad; Martha Lindblad; Patty Elliott; Jan Fischer; Olivia Markle and her dad, Seth Markle; Alec Mathison and his stepmother Jessica Mathison; Audrey Powell; Celia Rubinstein and her dad, Jeremy Rubinstein; Erin McKeon; and Vincent Parker Verillo and his "Grand," Bob Walsh.

The editorial and art staffs at Atmosphere Press, especially Colleen Alys, seamlessly wove all that feedback into this finished piece. I sincerely appreciate their insights and patience.

I tip my hat fondly to William E. Green III, who forged a masterful map of Tory Island from a simple sketch.

And to Ann and Charles Balas, I leave a special turndown mint. Based on their decades as innkeepers at the Anchor Inn in Nantucket, Ann provided a comprehensive checklist to ready Companion Moon for its inaugural season as a bed and breakfast.

Ghost Girl was born over 20 years ago when my then-four-year-old niece asked me, "Why did Mommy die?" I wanted to tell her that death gives meaning to life, but explaining that concept to a child seemed impossible—until I read *The Celtic Book of the Dead* by Caitlín Matthews. In it, I found appropriate motifs—the *immram*[1]; islands of refuge, like the Crystal Keep; and monsters, like fiery pigs—that conveyed the Celtic Otherworld in a tween-friendly manner. I am grateful for Ms. Matthews's inspiration and permission to use her poem, "Immram Chant." I also thank George Gibson, who

---

[1] *immram* ['ɪm rəm], from Old Irish: a mystical journey

introduced me to her catalog of lore and wisdom, and with whom I shared many hours bringing Celtic mythology to life.

Acknowledgments would not be complete without a nod to Andrew Lang, the 19th-century Scottish poet who wrote "Loch Lomond," and to the unknown bugler and lyricist behind "Taps."

Finally, I am grateful to have grown up in an endless *céili*.[2] On any given day or night, friends and relatives would gather in someone's kitchen. Although money was scarce, food and drink appeared endlessly. Songs broke out, stories emerged, laughter prevailed. My clan, whose colorful names and idiosyncrasies shaped Bonnie's welter of Invisibles, accompanied me in my *immram*, as well, directing me to fathom the meaning of my own life. Someday, I'll be one of the ancestors. As such, I hope to guide succeeding generations in their quests.

---

[2] *céili* [KAY-li], from Old Irish: a celebration of family and friends with food, music, and storytelling

aBOUT aTMOSPHERE PRESS

Atmosphere Press is an independent, full-service publisher for excellent books in all genres and for all audiences. Learn more about what we do at atmospherepress.com.

We encourage you to check out some of Atmosphere's latest releases, which are available at Amazon.com and via order from your local bookstore:

Dancing with David, a novel by Siegfried Johnson

The Friendship Quilts, a novel by June Calender

My Significant Nobody, a novel by Stevie D. Parker

Nine Days, a novel by Judy Lannon

Shining New Testament: The Cloning of Jay Christ, a novel by Cliff Williamson

Shadows of Robyst, a novel by K. E. Maroudas

Home Within a Landscape, a novel by Alexey L. Kovalev

Motherhood, a novel by Siamak Vakili

Death, The Pharmacist, a novel by D. Ike Horst

Mystery of the Lost Years, a novel by Bobby J. Bixler

Bone Deep Bonds, a novel by B. G. Arnold

Terriers in the Jungle, a novel by Georja Umano

Into the Emerald Dream, a novel by Autumn Allen

His Name Was Ellis, a novel by Joseph Libonati

The Cup, a novel by D. P. Hardwick

The Empathy Academy, a novel by Dustin Grinnell

Tholocco's Wake, a novel by W. W. VanOverbeke

Dying to Live, a novel by Barbara Macpherson Reyelts

Looking for Lawson, a novel by Mark Kirby

Surrogate Colony, a novel by Boshra Rasti

aBOUT The aUThOR

Patti M. Walsh
Author, Photographer, and Adventure Seeker

A storyteller since her first fib, and an explorer since her first runaway, Patti M. Walsh is an award-winning author who writes short stories, novels, and memoirs. In addition to extensive experience teaching, counseling, and coauthoring an animation curriculum, she has been recognized for business and technical writing.

Subscribe to her blog, *What the Cats Are Reading;* sign up for her newsletter, *Come to Think of It*; and learn more at www.PattiMWalsh.com.

If you enjoyed *Ghost Girl*, tell others with a brief review on Amazon.